Intelligence Horizon

R. Andrew Russell

National Library of Australia Cataloguing-in-Publication entry:
Creator: Russell, R Andrew, author.
Title: Intelligence Horizon / R Andrew Russell.

ISBN: 978-0-6454860-1-8

Tale Publishing
Melbourne, Australia

Also by
R. Andrew Russell

Intelligent Consent

Although what we see is limited by the horizon

we can dream of what lies beyond

Chapter 1

Robert's throat constricted, he was unable to take a deep breath. With each step, fear tightened its grip as he imagined all manner of threats. He was starting to regret putting himself in danger, even though the future of Project Transition might depend upon it.

From a distance, the decaying community hall was almost invisible, screened from the road by a row of trees. When it finally came into clear view, he considered chickening out, but by then it was too late. A tall figure dressed in paint-splashed overalls stepped forward from the pool of light spilling out of the open doorway.

"Hi, Richard, isn't it?"

Jason had arranged everything, a contact in the secret society, a false name, and a credible story to explain his interest. All Robert had to do was connect with Fergus before the meeting and be escorted inside.

"Fergus?"

Robert forced a show of camaraderie and extended his right hand.

"Come in, Richard. The meeting's about to start."

A couple of heavily tattooed security guards stood either side of the entrance and exuded a muscular threat. Fighting the almost overwhelming urge to turn and run, Robert edged closer to Fergus.

"Security's real tight 'cause Maxwell's set to talk. Ya got yer ID?"

Robert patted his pocket and tried to appear unconcerned. Beneath the surface, he agonised about his newly forged identification card. Would it pass scrutiny?

"Should be a great show. Maxwell always does somethin' special."

The queue moved one step closer, past the guards. Through the open door was a glimpse into a dingy world carried over from the previous century. Mattresses were piled against the windows to defeat prying eyes and deaden the sound. At the front of the hall, two chairs and a microphone were being arranged on a raised platform. People who had already arrived, mainly men, gathered in small, animated groups.

"Evening, Fergus. You can go right in."

"Thanks, Greta. This's Richard. He's got good reason to agree with our ideas."

Greta looked Robert up and down with a penetrating gaze. "You can vouch for Richard? He understands why we insist on absolute secrecy?"

"Sure. His job was taken by a robot six months ago. Hasn't been able to find work since."

"Stand over there and look into the camera." Greta took Robert's card and inserted it into a scanner. A few seconds later the machine beeped. "Okay. Looks like you're not on our list of journos or other undesirables. Welcome to the meeting." She handed back the ID and waved them both through the doorway.

As they entered the hall, Robert repeated the name 'Richard' in his mind. He couldn't afford to make a slip and use his real name. At least the stone in his left shoe reminded him to limp without even thinking about it. There were no chairs for the audience, so they had to stand on the bare wooden boards. The air was dank and smelled of stale beer, an indication of some of the other activities hosted there. It looked as though no refreshments were planned for tonight, though.

Some minutes later, spotlights illuminated a casually dressed young man on the stage. "Good evening to you all. Welcome to this month's meeting of Limitless Boundaries." In a very polished performance, he turned to include everyone in his introduction. "Those of you who are new may be puzzled by our name. Well, you can stop trying to figure it out. It has no meaning. Those two words were picked at random from a dictionary. That was a security measure to hide our true purpose." This announcement provoked a buzz of conversation, and after the noise subsided, the compère turned to indicate a bearded figure seated to his right.

"For many of you our guest speaker, Maxwell, needs no introduction."

Waving to acknowledge the applause and whistles, Maxwell stood and took the microphone. He was noticeably shorter than the host, perhaps 165cm at most. His long, ill-kempt, dark brown hair and beard reminded Robert of photos of Rasputin, the Russian monk. A notable difference was his endearing, almost childlike smile. From their rapt attention, it was obvious the audience, and particularly the few women present, were totally captivated. Maxwell's baggy tweed jacket, crumpled trousers and V-neck pullover added to a homely, perhaps absent-minded, image from a bygone age.

"I'm here tonight to tell you about the biggest challenge currently facing humanity, that being the insidious development of intelligent robots, and what we're doing about it. Those of you who've been to previous meetings know this is the reason I established Limitless Boundaries. Intelligent machines threaten your jobs, your way of life and even your very existence. Can I have a show of hands from everyone who's been put out of work by a robot."

Robert raised his hand and looked around to find he was joined by more than half of those present.

"The only solution is to rid ourselves of these pernicious machines, those who build them, those who use them and those who profit from them."

Maxwell was becoming increasingly animated and intense, punching the air for emphasis. The majority of the crowd seemed carried along by his energy. Around the room, there were scattered cheers followed by a growing chorus of 'wreck the robots'. Stamping and clapping alternated with the chant, "Wreck the robots, wreck the robots, wreck the robots!"

The sheer mindless intensity of it all was so intimidating that Robert felt compelled to join in to avoid drawing attention to himself. He was careful not to dislodge the slices of potato he'd wedged around his gums to fill out his face and make it less recognisable.

After allowing the crowd to work itself into a fervour, Maxwell raised his hands, calling for quiet. "Some of you may have seen recent news reports of a devastating fire in Japan. Most of the factory was destroyed, and what do you think the factory produced?"

There was a momentary silence, and then a lone male voice from the audience called out, "Robots."

With an exaggerated gesture, Maxwell pointed to the man and nodded. There were more cries of 'wreck the robots'.

"It's our policy that Limitless Boundaries should be invisible and never acknowledge our part in any attack against robots. But, just between us, I can assure you we definitely were involved in that incident. In fact, recently, we've successfully disrupted many projects aimed at creating intelligent robots. Most of these actions didn't make the news, which is just how we like it."

As fresh waves of stamping and whistling died down Maxwell continued, "This evening, I've arranged so that all of you can take part in direct action to forward our cause."

There was a buzz of excitement as a group of helpers cleared an area in front of the stage and laid down large sheets of plywood. The room lights were turned up as a door beside the stage opened, and a hooded figure dressed entirely in black led out a humanoid robot shackled with handcuffs and leg irons. A second hooded figure followed carrying an effective-looking axe. Robert immediately recognised the smooth silver contours of an HMM23 model robot. He was sure it had been programmed to mimic the slow shuffling gait and hunched posture of a convicted prisoner. It was highly improbable this type of robot could have a true appreciation of what was happening or the self-awareness to be concerned about its future.

The situation brought to mind memories of Rob, the intelligent robot he'd helped build and who was programmed with a scan of his own brain. These thoughts prompted so many questions. What had become of his robotic double? Would they ever meet again? Most unfathomable was why on earth had Rob handed himself over to Augustin and ZsG. He must have realised an arms manufacturer would view him as an item of inventory, and not as a sentient being to be afforded any say in his own future. If he fell into the wrong hands, it was easy to imagine him being subjected to a similar version of Maxwell's direct action.

A shiver of anticipation spread through the crowd as the robot was pushed to the centre of the sheets of plywood. The HMM23 robot turned to watch the man approaching, axe in hand, and cowered as though in fright. Once again, Robert assumed this was a preprogramed reaction.

"Who'd like to strike the first blow against the robot hordes?" Several men pushed forward. "Okay, be careful where you swing this thing. We're responsible for any damage to the building, and I don't want to have to explain missing fingers when we take you to hospital."

The first blow was poorly judged and glanced off the robot's shoulder, creating a shower of sparks, but hardly scoring the metal skin.

"What a piss-weak effort, Harry. Let me try." A burly looking man snatched the axe and squared up to the robot. Taking a measured swing, he struck the robot's left forearm, which it had raised to defend its face. The impact partly severed the limb and forced the robot to step back to regain its balance. Cowering, the robot tried to protect itself by raising its right arm. Further swings shattered the robot's black visor and dented several body panels.

"Here, let someone else have a go. You've had your turn." The crowd surged forwards, wrestling for control of the axe.

Soon the robot was reduced to a shattered mass of twisted metal and broken plastic. The show of aggression was sickening, even though it was directed towards a mechanism capable of only simulating consciousness and an awareness of pain.

"So, you see robots can be destroyed. They're not invincible, and this is what we must do to rid ourselves of their threat." Maxwell smiled encouragement towards groups chanting 'wreck the robots'.

"To be successful, we need to recruit people who're prepared to promote our views, to infiltrate organisations developing and using robots, and finally to take direct action against robots by sabotage or any other means."

Maxwell continued to hammer home his message of opposition to every aspect of intelligent robotics, and finished with a plea for contributions to a fighting fund. As the audience left the hall, they each dropped a note or some coins into a bucket and were rewarded with a plastic envelope containing a fragment of shattered metal or plastic as a memento.

Greta handed Robert an envelope containing the severed tip of one of the HMM23's fingers. "There you go, Richard, a special keepsake for you."

Outside, Fergus paused beside Robert. "That was great, wasn't it?" Without waiting for an answer, he continued, "Ya fancy a drink?"

Robert wanted to get away as quickly as possible but without drawing attention. Now that Fergus had served his purpose of enabling access to the meeting, he wanted nothing more to do with him. "What Maxwell said made a lot of sense, and it's given me a lot to think about. Thanks for the offer, but unfortunately, I've a job interview tomorrow, so I'll pass on the drink if you don't mind."

"No problem, Richard, I understand. Hope ya get the job." They parted after shaking hands.

Chapter 2

Robert hurried from the hall as fast as his limp would allow. The spectacle of mindless frenzy remained fresh in his mind. Cool night air was a welcome change from the stale atmosphere of the hall. Without giving it any thought, he followed the same switchback route he used to get to the meeting. Trying to avoid appearing too watchful, he kept a lookout for signs of pursuit. Soon, the path curved through a section overgrown by bushes and tall trees. Robert used the cover to remove his disguise. It was a relief to shake the stone from his shoe and spit out the potato. Turning his reversible jacket inside out changed it from grey to dark blue. Slipping off the horn-rimmed glasses and standing up straight he took a purposeful step forward.

The hire car was parked a good distance away, but this gave Robert time to consider the things he'd discovered at the meeting. If Maxwell was to be believed, he monitored many robotics projects worldwide, and his organisation was able to disrupt any he thought would grow into a threat to humanity. Several years ago, when internet billionaire, Vince Conner, first set up Project Transition, there was little attempt to hide its aim of developing humanoid robots. Nor was it a secret they'd be controlled by intelligence copied from the brains of humans. In light of what he'd just discovered at the meeting, Robert was sure this must have raised a red flag for Maxwell.

He thought back over the history of Project Transition. Several incidents had threatened to derail their work. They could all be unrelated, but hearing Maxwell speak, Robert started to wonder. The most significant event had been the plane crash that killed Vince, leading to the project being taken over by Augustin and ZsG. No one had provided an explanation of what went wrong to cause Vince's private jet to fall from the sky. There had been no warning. The next setback occurred when Robert was acting as the initial test subject for the brain scanner. While copying the structure of his brain, the scanner had malfunctioned, almost killing him. Again, the cause had never been determined. Finally, there was Rob, the robot programmed with Robert's brain scan. He'd told Robert the disk containing the only copy of data used to program his brain had been stolen and destroyed. Apparently unrelated, but taken together, there could be a pattern. All of these incidents occupied Robert's thoughts as he walked to his car and got in. "Return me to the pickup address."

The map screen blinked green and displayed the calculated route. "Trip commenced."

As the autonomous car pulled away from the kerb, Robert removed the uncomfortable double-sided body tape holding back his ear lobes. That was the final element of his disguise, which had aimed to change a key reference point used by face recognition algorithms.

Chapter 3

Robert was deeply engrossed in his thoughts and took a little time to make sense of the sudden swerve and screech of tyres. With a surge of adrenalin, he anticipated some impending disaster. The vehicle guidance system announced itself with a muted chime.

"Control switched to maintenance mode. Automatic guidance suspended."

"What's going on?"

"Maintenance mode has been selected."

"But I didn't do anything."

"A remote command switched mode."

"Okay, move over and park by the side of the road."

"In maintenance mode, I cannot accept that instruction."

"How do I take control?"

"In maintenance mode, you are not able to assume control by spoken command."

During the brief conversation, Robert became increasingly alarmed to see the vehicle was accelerating and heading straight for a large tree growing beside the road. Already, two wheels were off the bitumen and scrabbling across loose gravel. Realising the inevitable outcome, Robert leaned back in his seat and braced for impact. Simultaneously, sensors anticipated the impending high-speed collision. Robert's seatbelt tightened, forcing his body into the seat cushions. A fraction of a second later, strips of plastic peeled from channels in the floor, dashboard, roof pillars and doors. A fine net of genetically engineered spider silk discharged from the channels and unfurled, tightening to cocoon Robert's head and limbs.

With a rending combination of sound and shocks, the front of the vehicle crumpled absorbing most of the impact. A substantial branch sliced through the windscreen showering the cabin with small fragments of shattered glass.

~

"Robert! You must stop doing this."

In spite of his pounding headache and racing thoughts, he was keenly aware of everything about Anastasia he found so fascinating. She stood hands on hips studying Robert as he lay on the hospital bed. He was distressed that her usually attractive face was distorted by blazing eyes and an intense frown. There were obviously many things unsaid. He wanted to reassure her all was well but knew that wouldn't be easy.

She stepped forward and clasped his outstretched hand as she bent to kiss him. He was overcome with relief. Even this small demonstration of affection would have been impossible a few weeks earlier.

"First you get yourself half killed in the brain scanner, then you're peppered with shrapnel, now this. And you didn't even tell me you were going to do something dangerous. Thanks for trusting me." Her voice was both sad and angry.

"I only went to a meeting. I didn't realise how risky it would be. Once we get out of here, I'll tell you what I discovered. Looks like Augustin isn't the only person we need to worry about."

A nurse carrying a data tablet drew back the curtain of Robert's cubicle. "Ms Anthon, Robert is fit to be discharged. The emergency staff say it's fortunate his vehicle was fitted with the latest crash restraint system. That kind of high-speed collision is often fatal. If you sign here, I'll get one of the porters to ferry him to your car in a wheelchair."

"But I'm sure I'll be okay to walk."

The nurse shook her head. "No, Mr Harper. Although the doctor has passed you as fit, we want to ensure there are no further incidents before you leave the premises."

As Robert pulled on his shoes, Anastasia picked up his jacket. A few small chunks of shattered glass fell to the floor.

"You said it was only a minor collision!"

"Well, I wasn't knocked out … I think."

Anastasia shook her head. Her expression was pained as if to say, "You could have been, and worse."

There was a bit more glass in the pockets, and she carefully picked out the pieces and dropped them into a waste bin.

"What's this?" She held up a clear plastic envelope containing the tip of a robot finger with fine wires and artificial tendons hacked off below the joint.

"Just a little memento of the evening, a reminder that robots can be destroyed."

"And here's a business card for a house painter called Fergus."

Robert held out his hand for the card. It was printed on thick, good quality card with a gloss finish.

"Earlier this evening a guy I met gave it to me. Wanted to promote his business." Robert went to hand it back, paused, turned the card in his hand and carefully bent it a little. Perhaps the quality of the card was too good for advertising a self-employed house painter. Also, it was rather stiff to be made of just cardboard. "D'you have your penknife?"

Robert permitted himself a faint smile as she nodded. He loved that amazing practicality which contrasted with her poise and beauty.

Using Anastasia's knife, Robert peeled off the top printed layer of the card revealing a tracery of electronic components embedded in the cardboard backing.

"What've you got there?"

He put a finger to his lips and then showed her the card, demonstrating its hidden contents. Anastasia retrieved a pair of scissors from the dressing pack next to his bed and helped Robert cut it into thin strips.

~

During the drive to Robert's flat, a shared concern about surveillance and being overheard reduced the conversation to plans for meeting up the following day. Since the takeover of Project Transition by ZsG Corporation, it was commonly assumed all staff could be monitored at any time. Adding to the paranoia was the attitude of the new director, Dr Augustin Selworthy, who, it appeared, would let nothing get in his way in order to push the project along as quickly and secretively as possible. His major aim was to create intelligent robots and put them to military use. To make matters worse, it now appeared Maxwell was probably spying on them as well and would go to any lengths to prevent such robots being built.

As Anastasia dropped Robert at his flat, she confined her goodbye to a distracted kiss. Neither seemed to feel inclined to prolong their time together; the crash had created a barrier between them. Robert was exhausted and Anastasia clearly worried.

Chapter 4

The following morning, Robert took a taxi to building T1 which housed the Project Transition laboratories. He almost changed his mind when he found it was a similar model to the vehicle he'd used the previous evening. While the crash hadn't resulted in any physical injuries, he was still tense and felt in no fit state to ride his bike to work. Anastasia would expect him to avoid taking unnecessary risks, and as she was already upset with him, he was keen to avoid putting more strain on their fledgling relationship.

After dismissing the taxi, Robert climbed the stairs to the main entrance. Armed guards dressed in urban camouflage fatigues eyed him intently. Since the purchase of Project Transition by ZsG Corporation, Robert had a growing feeling of working in a military camp.

Walking the familiar stairs and corridors his thoughts returned to Anastasia. She would be desperate to find out more about the lead up to the crash. It was probable ZsG and Augustin weren't involved, but the less they discovered through their surveillance systems, the better. If they found out about this new threat, it would surely result in even more rules and restrictions. There would be a good opportunity for a private talk if he joined her for a lunchtime walk. He needed to find something to occupy his mind until then.

Robert settled into his chair and took a few minutes to appreciate the view from the window. There was occasionally something interesting to see amongst the trees surrounding T1 or along the road running past the main entrance.

Today, the outside world appeared to lack any distractions so, with an effort, he focussed on his desk, the computer and the usual mundane reports to be checked and queries answered. It wasn't the first time he'd questioned his decision to stay after the takeover. Initially, he'd hoped to protect Rob because he was sure an intelligent robot wouldn't be allowed any choice of how it would be used. Now, with Rob having given himself up, and with no idea where he was or what Augustin would do with him, it didn't seem possible Robert could be of any further assistance. Another reason for staying had been to monitor the use of the brain-scanning technology he'd helped to develop, but this too had been undercut by events. Hiroshi, one of Augustin's additions to the project, was now in control of the scanner group, leaving Robert excluded from making decisions or even finding out about day-to-day progress. The final reason he'd stayed was concern about Augustin's reaction if he resigned his position. There always seemed to be an unspoken threat of consequences for those who showed disloyalty or wished to move beyond his control, and this left everyone trying to second-guess what was expected of them.

An authoritative knock at Robert's office door was instantly recognisable. When he opened it, there was no surprise when he found Hiroshi carrying a large cardboard box.

"These are my notes documenting changes I've made to the scanner."

Robert indicated a clear space on his desk and waited for clarification.

"As you know, we've tested a number of modifications to try to eliminate harmful side effects, including the explosion that happened during your scan."

Robert tried to appear neutral, even though he was aware of at least one death during the testing of Hiroshi's modifications.

"The work isn't complete, but I've been reassigned to a different project. Augustin has given a high priority to completing another brain scan, and I suggested you should be given the task of reviewing progress and proposing the way forward."

Robert was dumbfounded. This would have been his task months ago if Hiroshi hadn't taken over. Now, after all this time with no real progress, it looked as though the job was his again.

"I'll need to access the laboratory notebooks covering my time working on the initial development of the scanner."

"They've been digitised. I'll send you a link and password."

"It's also entirely possible there's a fault in the scanner hardware which wouldn't show up in the documentation."

It was obvious Hiroshi had anticipated a request to examine the scanner. He held out a purple clip-on badge which Robert recognised as allowing access to the scanner laboratory.

"You're to send weekly progress reports directly to Augustin, copied to me, and any requests to perform tests on the scanner itself must be cleared with him."

After Hiroshi left, Robert spent a long time staring at the box of notes. This task could take months, but at least it was something meaningful to do.

~

Robert was fully engrossed in sorting papers and notes when Denny appeared at the still-open door. "Do you have a spare minute?" The tall, fit young man had the weather-beaten look of someone who spent much of his free time outdoors. Robert occupied far too many weekends working on the project and secretly envied Denny's lifestyle. He and Robert had joined Project Transition at about the same time. Although they rarely spoke about things outside the technical area of developing robot senses, Robert knew he had a strong commitment to social responsibility.

With a smile of encouragement, Robert indicated the one seat not covered in piles of documents. After checking the corridor, Denny carefully closed the door behind him and sat down. "Have you ever considered resigning?"

The unexpected directness of the question almost shocked Robert into giving an unfiltered answer. Just in time, he paused and formulated a more guarded response. "Sometimes. But I joined Project Transition to design the brain scanner. I feel committed to continuing until all the bugs are sorted out. On top of that, I worry about Rob. Being programmed with my brain scan, our personalities are probably closer than identical twins. I feel a responsibility to look after him and the best way I can do that is to keep working here."

"I haven't seen Rob since he first disappeared. Have you heard how he's going?"

"You know he went into hiding when ZsG took over the project? After some weeks on the run he returned here and gave himself up. He hasn't been seen since but I'm sure Augustin wouldn't allow anything to happen to him. As the only transitioned intelligence, for the moment at least, he's unique."

A brief silence ensued, before Denny spoke again. "Well, I've given the whole project a lot of thought. At the start, I was caught up in the excitement of creating something so revolutionary as a transitioned intelligence. Now, my part in the project, the development of the robot senses, is mostly complete. There's little interesting for me to do, and it looks like Augustin is keen to sell the robots for offensive military purposes, which I'm dead against."

"Yes, but you have to ask why he still employs us. Probably because it gives him direct control of the people who know all the technical details of the robots, something he won't give up easily."

Denny sighed in agreement. "But we all have to live life according to our own principles, don't we?"

There was a long silence, and finally, Robert concluded his answer. "He has strong reasons to hang on to key members of the team. If he can't do that, we don't know how he would respond. So, whatever you decide to do, make sure you're careful."

~

It was lunchtime, and Anastasia accepted Robert's offer of a walk through the woods surrounding T1. As they left the building, she seemed decidedly reserved, as though still unable to forgive him for not sharing his plans. It was only with reluctance that she allowed him to hold her hand.

"Okay, tell me how you managed to drive a fully autonomous vehicle into a tree." There wasn't a lot of sympathy in the question.

"One day, at lunch, Jason mentioned a shadowy organisation, as he called them, working against the development of intelligent robots. Given what we do here, I thought it essential to find out more information."

"Ah! I should have suspected, Jason had to be involved. He seems to be mixed up in all sorts of questionable activities."

"I'm sure he's not a member of this organisation, but a friend of a friend is."

"So, you went to meet this friend of a friend?"

"The friend of a friend is Fergus, the guy who gave me his card. He arranged for me to attend a meeting. It's a full on crackpot outfit called Limitless Boundaries."

"And you didn't think to tell me you were putting yourself in danger?"

"I went in disguise, under a false name, even though I didn't really think it was dangerous. Or at least not until I found out what they stand for."

"Which is?"

"The total elimination of all intelligent robots with special emphasis on their development and production."

Anastasia's brow furrowed. "It never occurred to you they might find out who you are and where you work?"

"I would probably have got away with it if Fergus hadn't planted that tracker hidden in his business card. After the meeting, they must have followed me and taken over control of the car."

"Now they probably know everything about you. A trace on the hire car or your hospital admission would point right back to you. I think, from now on, we should be a lot more open with each other and not keep secrets. Don't you?"

Robert responded with a reserved smile.

They returned to T1 deep in thought. Robert broke the silence just before they reached the entrance.

"Talking about secrets, you know my mum and dad died when I was six years old, but I know nothing about your family."

Anastasia didn't answer but met his gaze as though preparing a reply. Hesitating, she must have changed her mind. She gave his hand a gentle squeeze as they parted company.

Chapter 5

For someone with Hiroshi's technical background, the spaceport was a fascinating place to visit. Today he was in the equipment preparation area, preforming the final acceptance check of a piece of equipment Augustin had commissioned from an outside contractor. The mission coordination system, called Computer, was housed in a utilitarian grey box about the size of a large suitcase. It had only been switched on a week earlier and for the purposes of its acceptance checks, was plugged into bundles of cables playing the part of connections to the actual spacecraft.

"Computer, my name is Hiroshi. Can you hear me?"

"Affirmative, Hiroshi."

"Confirm I have clearance to access your stored data."

"You have clearance to access almost everything, except for some items protected by a combined time and situation lock."

"Okay, apart from those items, give me a summary of your stored knowledge."

"I have detailed technical specifications of a space vehicle, including its cargo, further documentation relating to three robotic crew members, information about spacecraft navigation, a timetable, and error recovery protocols."

"What's the destination for the spaceflight?"

"I am unable to tell you. That is protected information."

"Okay, moving on, tell me more about the robotic crew."

"There will be three crew. Sam, supplied by ZsG Corporation, is one of their second-generation humanoid robots. He will be in charge of the mission and will communicate directly with Earth control when we arrive at our destination. Rob, a first-generation ZsG robot, is to provide navigation and technical support. HMM23, manufactured by Dexx Robotics, will be tasked with performing assembly, together with general fetching and carrying activities. This robot has been enhanced with a short-range wireless communications system, which will allow us to exchange spoken messages."

"Very good. On this mission, what are your areas of responsibility?"

"I will monitor all spacecraft functions, ensure necessary tasks are performed in a correct and timely manner and also make available my extensive database of mission-related information."

"I need to ensure you will respond appropriately to critical events not covered explicitly in your programming. What will you do in such situations?"

"Serious problems will be referred back to Earth for their guidance."

"And if the communication link is not functioning?"

"I would instruct HMM23 to ensure there were no technical problems affecting the communications equipment."

"In the event that HMM23 cannot re-establish communications or there is no time to wait for a response?"

"Sam will be consulted for assistance or Rob if Sam is not available."

"In the event that both Sam, Rob and HMM23 cannot be contacted?"

"I have only limited ability to manipulate things myself, and if they are not available, all I can do is wait."

"There is one additional task for you. We've recently received unconfirmed intelligence reports of a threat to the mission and would like you to be extra vigilant."

"I understand. What kind of threat?"

"That's unknown, but your software has been upgraded with an advanced inference engine. This will monitor all aspects of spacecraft function and highlight any anomalies that could indicate a problem. You must inform Sam of any issues raised by the inference engine, even if this involves bringing him out of hibernation."

"I understand."

"I've been told all of your systems are functioning correctly. Shortly, you'll be installed in the spacecraft to start your duties."

Chapter 6

Denny enjoyed fresh air and open spaces. On weekends, provided the weather was half decent, he liked nothing better than walking in wild rugged country. Usually, this involved joining a group of friends, but today he wanted to be alone, to think things through. Resigning had been a difficult decision. He'd vacillated for weeks after his discussion with Robert, but eventually made up his mind.

For over three years, he'd worked on the project, and until recently, had enjoyed every minute. The absolute highlight was the first time he saw Rob after the robot had been programmed with the scan of Robert's brain. It was incredible seeing all of the different components come together to create a sentient being. After the decision had been taken to change Rob's appearance from angular and mechanical to something more lifelike, he was amazed how the result could easily pass for a human being.

Balanced against the positive aspects of the job were some recent developments. At first, there hadn't been any hint of where the project was truly heading following its takeover. At their first meeting, Dr Augustin Selworthy had offered him a genial smile and followed this with a proposition, "As local head of ZsG, I'm making you the same offer of continued employment I've made to others working for Project Transition. They've all accepted the new contract. If you agree to join us, your pay and conditions will be unchanged from those that applied when you worked for Vince's company. The only difference is a slightly more onerous non-disclosure agreement."

"That's very kind, but I've concerns about working for a weapons manufacturer. The military use of intelligent robots is relatively new, and I worry about how they'll be used."

Augustin opened his palms as if he had nothing to hide. "I entirely understand your reservations. Although we're predominantly an arms manufacturer, our interest in intelligent robots controlled by transitioned human intelligence is purely humanitarian. We believe there's a vast market for rescue and disaster relief robots based on this technology. Join us and help develop life-saving applications."

Reassured by this conversation, Denny had signed up to join ZsG.

Some time later, Jason, the local gossip, had shared rumours casting doubt on these assurances.

"You know what the new building will be used for?"

"No, Jason, but I'm sure you're going to tell me."

"It's actually a shooting range to test and improve the robot's marksmanship."

"That doesn't sound like an essential skill for a humanitarian robot."

"True, and I've another bit of gossip for you, but it'll cost you a cup of coffee."

Denny had paid for a coffee and added two sugars, just the way Jason liked it.

"There are signs they're gearing up to increase production of the robots."

"But I thought things were put on hold after the disaster with that new model programmed with Sam's brain scan."

"Well, Denny, I'm guessing they think they have the

problems sorted. I hope so! The thought of large numbers of robots running amok just like the first three is really frightening."

At their last meeting, Augustin was polite but made no attempt to smile.

"I believe you've submitted your resignation."

"Yes, I have."

"May I ask why?"

"It's possible I'm over reacting, but I worry about the direction the project is taking. I'm becoming increasingly concerned about how our robots will be used."

Augustin shook his head as though becoming tired of continually explaining how benign the robots would be. "As I mentioned during our previous meeting, you have no reason to lose any sleep. ZsG are fully compliant with all relevant laws and international treaties. We take our legal responsibilities very seriously."

"I'm sure that's true, but my problem is the lack of rules governing the use of robots with transitioned intelligence, particularly in conflict zones. It's easy to say you're obeying laws which don't even exist."

Augustin flinched as though he'd been physically attacked. His expression hardened into a look of undisguised menace. "I see you've made up your mind. Remember the non-disclosure agreement. Even though you leave the company, it's still in effect, and any contravention will be severely punished. My lawyer will sort out the paperwork."

~

"Hi, my name's Jarrod. I'm here to help you. As his lawyer, I act for Dr Selworthy in administrative legal matters." The young man smiled affably as he sat down opposite Denny. From his black leather document case, he produced some papers and laid them on the table. "This is our standard employment separation agreement, but before we look at it I must be sure you understand what you're doing. It's very rare for employees to resign from ZsG, and although perhaps he shouldn't, Dr Selworthy takes this kind of thing almost as a personal criticism."

"I feel I was hired under false pretences. When I joined ZsG, Augustin made it clear I would be helping develop humanitarian robots. Now I find that was a lie. One of their primary roles is offensive military deployment, and that involves killing people."

Jarrod's expression switched to a scowl. "For a start, I must advise you to avoid making such baseless and defamatory statements. This agreement binds you to non-disclosure and non-disparagement conditions."

"Then, I refuse to sign your agreement. The world needs to know what's going on here." The meeting finished abruptly without any obvious result.

All those conversations occupied Denny's thoughts as he climbed the escarpment. Towards the top, his mind turned to more immediate matters of lunch and the magnificent view stretching across the valley.

Leaving his backpack on a flat rock, he approached the cliff edge. There was a dizzying view of a sheer drop to treetops far below. A low hissing sound and brief movement of air caught Denny by surprise, and he almost lost his balance. Looking all round, there was nothing to see. Dismissing it as a freak gust of wind, he turned again to appreciate the breathtaking view to the distant hills.

Approaching at high speed, a dark shadow was outlined against the blue sky. At the last instant, he saw something out of the corner of his eye and ducked, receiving a glancing blow above the right ear. Momentarily disoriented, Denny stood still, waiting for his head to clear.

He could still follow the flying wing as it circled to gain height. Fascinated by its unusual shape and graceful movement, Denny failed to appreciate its deadly purpose. Banking to dive directly at Denny the aircraft was only visible as a narrow line.

This time the collision knocked him off balance, and he took a forward step to compensate. But there was no ground under his raised foot. With a startled cry, he fell forwards, clawing for support from the insubstantial air. For three full seconds, he accelerated towards the tree tops far below. The flying wing swooped low to record the impact and then, after executing an unnecessary barrel roll, was gone.

Chapter 7

As usual for the Monday morning progress meeting, Robert sat with five of the other group leaders. Anastasia and Sergeant Kirby each had their own separate table. The room fell silent as Augustin took his seat. Perhaps to emphasis his total control, he took time to polish his glasses before introducing the first item for discussion.

"As you all must have found out by now, our colleague Denny Papadopoulos died over the weekend in a tragic accident." From their facial expressions, it was clear that mention of the disaster was deeply upsetting for most people in the room. In stark contrast, Augustin seemed completely unaffected. "Apparently, he was alone when it happened, but his backpack was found at a popular lookout. While searching for its owner, his body was discovered at the base of a cliff. It appears he didn't take enough care when venturing close to the edge."

Anastasia and the remaining group leaders sat in stunned silence. They all knew of the rumours Denny wanted to resign from his position, and that Augustin made no secret of his demand for total commitment from his employees. The hair on the back of Robert's neck stood up as he joined the dots. He guessed this was Augustin's intention, to instil fear and ensure unwavering obedience.

At first, it seemed he might add a few words of consolation to his statement of fact. Instead, as though having ticked off the first agenda item, he moved on to the main matter for discussion.

"ZsG Corporation's acquisition and ongoing support of Project Transition has been an expensive exercise, and backers of the takeover are keen to see a return on their investment. Unfortunately, the time required for ironing out bugs in the brain scanner has been much greater than anticipated. This has added to costs and delayed development of a saleable product."

He turned to glare at Robert as though the delays were his fault and had nothing to do with his own decision to put other people in charge of scanner development.

"Our backers need assurance their investment is sound. To demonstrate the path to profitability, I've decided to proceed with small-scale production of our second-generation humanoid robots without waiting for the scanner. We'll sell these robots for security guard applications. I've decided to market them as ZsG Safetybots."

"With the scanner still not working, the only data we have for programming those robots would be Sam's scan," Graham Martin observed.

Augustin looked up to address Graham. "And your point is?"

"Because there won't be any new scan data to be processed, my group will have nothing to do."

Augustin paused and once again took off and polished his glasses. It appeared as though he was using the time to control his temper. "I'm assuming everyone working on this project has at least a general idea of what the others do. I expect you all to be flexible and help out with any task necessary to progress production as fast as possible. If there are any localised holdups, I'll personally allocate underutilised staff where they're most needed."

"Won't it be risky to market robots based on Sam's scan, given the first three copies went absolutely berserk?" Robert asked.

Augustin cast a malevolent look his way. "I don't appreciate a minor technical issue being misrepresented as the robots going berserk. Your own investigation of that incident has shown how we can overcome the problems with a little psychotherapy. Of course, we won't be selling any robots without the most rigorous testing. Initially, my plan is to manufacture twenty-four of our most advanced robots. These will be thoroughly tested by integrating them into our security contingent in T1. Here they can be closely monitored to ensure they function correctly."

By thinking out loud, Robert tried to work out the implications of producing a large number of Safetybots. "Ideally, another volunteer would receive training for the security guard role before being scanned. That way robots programmed with the scan would already know what their job was and what was expected of them."

Augustin appeared to be losing patience with having the obvious pointed out to him. "Yes, Robert, but as we know, the scanner needs more work."

"In that case, it'll be necessary for each robot to undertake a training program."

Augustin was forced to agree, though this didn't stop him fixing Robert with an icy stare. "You may have a valid point. There are also several upgrades we'll make to the robot hardware. These will include encrypted radio communications, which will allow all similarly equipped robots to coordinate their activities, call for assistance, etc. I believe, with a few minor modifications, we can turn Safetybots into a highly marketable product. Now, if there are no further questions, I'll end the meeting there."

With a subdued air, the group leaders filed out of the

meeting. Robert suspected the briefing had raised many questions, but no one seemed willing to pursue them.

Anastasia slowed her pace and fell into step with Robert. "I've been thinking over what you said the other day, particularly about my reluctance to discuss my family."

Robert held his breath. He hoped there would be more to the conversation than this, and perhaps, some reduction of the barriers between them.

"If you'd like, I can arrange for us to visit my father. I think he'll be home next Saturday." She held up her hand to block a hasty reply. "I'm not proud of him, his lifestyle or how he makes his money. If we do meet, I want you to promise no comments about any of those things until we're well out of earshot. I could arrange for us to call round for drinks rather than a meal. He's better appreciated in small doses."

This was a puzzling offer, but Robert was only too pleased to agree.

Chapter 8

Mars Lander Computer Log #9: Elapsed time since system initialisation: 1655 hours

Activities since previous log:

1> Loading cargo – COMPLETE.

2> Crew installation – COMPLETE.

3> Lander fuel transfer – FUEL RESERVE BEFORE TAKEOFF 101.5% nominal.

4> Spacecraft launch – SUCCESSFUL.

5> Earth orbit – ACHIEVED within ±3% nominal.

6> Mars transfer orbit – ACHIEVED within ±0.05% nominal.

Current systems status:

1> All sensor readings within acceptable limits.

2> Current fuel reserves – 93%.

3> All crew in hibernation.

4> Power management – battery charge 100%, solar panels capable of providing 239% of vehicle requirements.

Unresolved issues:

1> Nature of the reported threat to the mission is yet to be identified by the inference engine.

Chapter 9

Anastasia's car switched to external guidance as it turned off the main highway.

"That's a substantial-looking gate and heavy-duty security." Robert pointed to a cluster of floodlights and cameras.

Anastasia responded with a forced smile. She was obviously anticipating a stressful evening. "Yes, my father's line of work makes that a necessity. I should also explain that I chose to adopt my mother's maiden name because I wanted to put some space between him and myself. I did it when I left to study at university, and he still hasn't completely forgiven me."

Steered by the house perimeter control system, their car negotiated a curving gravel path and came to rest beside a brand new Lamborghini.

"Wow! Isn't that the latest Lamborghini Black?"

"Yes, Robert, I guess it is, though why the manufacturers would call a car with yellow paintwork 'black' I'm not sure. It must be something to do with marketing?"

"Who knows? It is a catchy name, perhaps a reference to Henry Ford's comment about his Model T Ford being available in any colour so long as it was black."

The exterior of the house reminded Robert of a modern museum or art gallery, low-set and angular. There were vast expanses of tinted glass and natural wood. Beside the open front door stood a tall, impeccably dressed man with expensively styled greying hair. Navy chinos complemented his light blue shirt, smart black shoes, and matching belt. A much younger woman encircled his left arm with both of hers. By contrast, Robert felt his choice of comfortable but hardly fashionable evening attire didn't compare. Anastasia also appeared outclassed by her father's partner. The classic simplicity of the stunning mid-length black dress the woman wore served to highlight her figure, and her only piece of jewellery, a gold flying scarab necklace inlaid with green gemstones, was exquisite.

Apparently satisfied he'd won the first round of their encounter, Anastasia's father stepped forward to shake Robert's hand and embrace his daughter. "Robert? Savvas Dimas." Turning to the young woman he said, "Tracy, I'd like you to meet my daughter, Anastasia, and Robert, her friend … boyfriend … partner?"

In those terms, Robert didn't know how he'd describe himself, so like Anastasia, he chose not to answer.

Inside, the house furnishings only added to the impression of visiting a museum. Individual statuettes, amulets, pieces of jewellery and carvings were arranged in glass showcases, artfully illuminated by hidden spotlights.

"All of these pieces are genuine archaeological artefacts, no copies or fakes."

"And Tracy's necklace, is that genuine?"

"You noticed the necklace?" Savvas queried Robert's question with a slightly suggestive tone in his voice. "Yes, it's original and priceless, or at least you wouldn't be able to afford it."

As though a thought had just occurred to him, he crossed to a corner of the room and opened a beautifully inlaid wooden box. "Young man, I see you haven't given my daughter even the smallest item of jewellery. That's a great pity.

A well-chosen piece would really complement her good looks."

Ignoring her obvious discomfort, he held out an elegant bracelet inlaid with a large circular blue stone. She seemed hesitant to take it.

"Don't worry, it wasn't expensive. I knew you wouldn't accept anything too extravagant."

Reluctantly, she slipped the bracelet onto her left wrist. Robert was forced to admit it was an excellent choice.

They moved into the living area, where four large sofas arranged in a square were almost dwarfed by the vastness of the room. At their centre, surrounded by a low glass wall, flames flickered over a bed of rounded pebbles.

"Have a seat."

Tracy brought drinks and a tray of quail eggs, iced caviar, Russian pancakes and sour cream. Savvas made himself comfortable spreading his arms wide as if to emphasise the extent of his ownership. When she had finished arranging the food and drinks, Savvas made sure there was no doubt it was time for her to leave.

"That's great, Tracy. We won't bore you with family matters. Why don't you go and relax in the jacuzzi?"

He continued as soon as they were alone. "I'm assuming my talented daughter hasn't told you much about me?"

"I think she believes I should find out for myself."

"Perhaps that was very wise. My main business is trading in rare antiquities, primarily Egyptian. You would have seen some examples when you arrived. In some ways, I provide wish fulfilment for discerning investors and collectors. I source difficult to find artefacts, arrange to transport them and even provide credible documentation."

"So, you're a smuggler of antiquities?"

Savvas smiled and without the slightest hint of rancour he concurred. "Very succinctly put, Robert, but I prefer to think of myself as helping to preserve archaeological artefacts from countries which don't have the will or resources to do it themselves. My clients are doing the whole world a service by removing the artefacts from situations where they could be destroyed by vandalism or neglect." Having spoken expansively to the whole room, he turned to Robert smiling indulgently. "But, that's enough about me. Tell me how you fit into Anastasia's life."

"Well, we both work for Project Transition."

Perhaps sensing his opportunity, Savvas didn't hesitate to take over the conversation again. "I remember when Anastasia started there over three years ago. Something about copying people's brains into robots." Savvas waved his hands dismissively. "I haven't kept across developments. There isn't much of a connection between archaeology and robots. How did the project go?"

"It progressed smoothly until Vince Conner, the guy who financed the whole thing, died in a plane crash."

"Sounds vaguely familiar. Come to think of it, I'm sure Anastasia hasn't visited me since about that time. She does neglect me dreadfully. Was that the end of the project?"

"No, there was a hurried attempt to complete as much as possible before the money ran out. It ended with my brain being scanned and loaded into a humanoid robot named Rob."

Anastasia continued with the story. "Shortly after Rob was completed, the project was taken over by Dr Selworthy of ZsG Corporation."

Savvas sat forwards with a start. "Not Dr *Augustin* Selworthy?"

"Yes, that's him."

Savvas sat back in his seat and steepled his fingers. "I can tell you an interesting story about him."

Anastasia rolled her eyes but said nothing. Undeterred, he launched into his reminiscence.

"Augustin approached me, certainly some years before you both joined that project. In the storeroom of some second-rate Egyptian museum, a carved stone panel had caught his eye. It was quite unique and probably so different the museum didn't know what to do with it. Their solution was to keep it out of sight where it couldn't cause a problem."

Augustin was extremely secretive, so Robert relished the idea of finding out anything at all about him. "Did he want to buy it from the museum?"

"Well, he did buy it, in a manner of speaking. Certainly, money changed hands, and the carving ended up in his possession."

"So, where did you come into the picture?"

"I solved a number of Augustin's problems including negotiating to take possession of the artefact and getting it out of the country. There are heavy fines and even imprisonment for smuggling ancient artefacts, and he wasn't keen on taking that risk, particularly given the weight of the panel. At the time, the Egyptian authorities were having one of their periodic crackdowns on smuggling."

"You arranged to have it shipped out of the country?"

"Better than that, given the huge sums of money involved, I carried it out in my own luggage. It just fitted into my suitcase and almost gave me a hernia when I lifted it."

Savvas laughed at his own cunning. "I coated the entire thing in this thermoplastic resin used for preserving fragile objects. Then a local artist overpainted it with hieroglyphics, winged Horus eyes, etc. to make it look like the sort of cheap crap a tourist would buy. He used plenty of bright colours, brown, blue and red and too much gold leaf. It looked atrocious, and the customs guys at the airport didn't suspect it was an ancient artefact."

"Then you just added it to your checked-in baggage without any problems?"

"Not that easy. I nearly got caught. Fortunately, I'd added a layer of plaster to the base of the panel. A representative of the Egyptian Ministry of Antiquities seemed somewhat suspicious and was going to scratch the surface to check what it was made of. I persuaded him to test the base where the damage wouldn't be seen. That convinced him the whole thing was made of plaster."

"It would have been a lot heavier than plaster. How did you explain the weight?"

"It was heavy, well beyond my baggage allowance. I wedged my toe under the corner of the suitcase to make the scale reading lower. The baggage handler who moved my bag off the scale must have realised it was too heavy. He gave me a foul look but didn't say anything. I was never so relieved as when I saw it heading away on the conveyor."

Anastasia seemed annoyed by the way her father quickly hijacked any topic of conversation to turn the focus back to himself. By contrast, Robert found his stories fascinating.

"I don't suppose you kept any details of the panel?"

Anastasia caught Robert's eye and almost imperceptibly shook her head. He took this to mean 'don't encourage him'.

"I signed a very comprehensive contract specifically barring me from retaining any scan, impression or image of the panel. There were significant penalties if I didn't comply."

There was a long silence before Savvas continued with a cheeky grin. "However, I do have something." He left the room and a few moments later returned unrolling a large photograph.

"You see, everything about this panel is strange. Its size and the arrangement of the hieroglyphics don't follow the usual pattern. There are also these other markings at the bottom. At first, I thought it was some other system of writing like cuneiform, but nobody has been able to identify it."

"Do you think it's a forgery?"

"I rely on others for that kind of expert opinion. For what it's worth, I'm told it dates from the Egyptian Middle Kingdom, about 4,000 years ago. The parts that can be deciphered seem to give instructions for finding something. Unfortunately, it appears to be one of a larger collection of tablets. On its own, it doesn't give many clues."

During most of the evening, Anastasia sat quietly, and it was only as they stood to leave that she finally spoke. "Have you heard from my mother?"

It took a second for Savvas to control his annoyance. "Why do you always have to spoil everything by bringing her up? You need to forget about her. She's gone and she's not coming back."

Anastasia reacted as though struck in the face.

Her father sighed. "No, I haven't and I don't expect to. It's now over ten years since she left."

For a moment, it looked as though she might respond, but then Anastasia turned and marched to the car without another word.

Savvas intercepted Robert and spoke earnestly. "Augustin wouldn't be pleased if he found out I'd retained any kind of record of his panel. I'm relying on your discretion to make sure this stays between the three of us. Also, make sure you take better care of my daughter than her previous boyfriend."

~

Anastasia sat with arms tightly folded across her chest, staring out of the window.

"I'm sorry."

"It's not your fault, Robert. These days most of our meetings end like this."

She wrenched the bracelet from her wrist and opened her window as though intending to throw it into the night. He gently held her hand until she relented.

"I guess I could keep it as a reminder of the father I rarely see. But you don't need to give me jewellery. I'd swap it for love and trust anytime."

For several minutes, the only sound was the muted whir of the electric drive motors. Finally, Robert had to break the silence. "Interesting that Augustin's prepared to spend so much on Egyptian antiquities.”

Anastasia laughed mirthlessly. “I don’t know. Many men with spare money like to indulge in expensive hobbies. It’s one way of flaunting their power and wealth.”

Robert thought about all the trophies Savvas used to show off his ill-gotten gains.

“In reality, he’s a thousand times worse than how you saw him tonight. It’s no wonder my mother left him, though I can’t understand why she’s never tried to contact me.”

Anastasia turned to look at Robert as though curious as to how he would react. “Now you know a little about my background, is this going to be a problem for you?”

He reached over and gently stroked away a tear. Releasing his seatbelt, he kissed and encircled her with his arms until a commanding automated voice insisted he fasten his seatbelt while the car was in motion.

Chapter 10

Jason compressed a spring washer and attempted to slide it into place to complete a right elbow joint. In front of him, arranged in rows, were a number of half-built robot limbs and trays of nuts, bolts and washers. Perhaps suffering from low blood sugar, his hand trembled and the washer spun from his grasp and disappeared beyond the bench's pool of bright light.

"Damn it. I've had enough," he announced to Robert and Anastasia who'd also been dragooned into helping assemble the next batch of Safetybots. "Wouldn't the ideal solution be to get some of these robots to help with the task of building the new ones?"

It wasn't unknown for Jason to complain when he felt overworked. Given the uninspiring duties they'd been allocated, few days passed without at least one of his grumbles. Robert decided to call a break.

"It's your own fault for being so generally useful. Most people don't know as much as you about building robots and programing them. If it'll help you feel any better, I'll buy you a coffee in the cafeteria. Come on, time for lunch."

As Robert returned with drinks for Anastasia and Jason, Jason started again. "But aren't robots supposed to relieve us of drudgery, not make it worse?"

"Yes, but Sam, the guy whose brain scan we're using, didn't have the skills to make anything, so these robots don't have those skills either."

Robert was pleased when Anastasia tried to redirect the conversation.

"How many of the new robots have been completed, Jason?"

"None of them are ready for service. Sixteen have been programmed with Sam's brain scan and then put through the orientation session to prevent them going berserk like the first three did."

"Are they still intending to use them for security around T1?"

"Yes, but not yet. They haven't been trained for the security guard application."

"What's the hold up?"

"Someone from ZsG is supposed to supply the training material, but we're still waiting."

Robert decided to add his own piece of gossip to the conversation. "Hiroshi sent me a message saying he'll be returning soon."

Jason looked up. "Did he say where he's been?"

"Hah! You should know better than to expect we'd be told anything other than the absolute essentials. However, he did mention Augustin isn't satisfied with our progress. I'm assuming it'll be his job to speed things up."

~

Anastasia and Robert left the cafeteria for what had become a regular lunchtime walk. Ignoring the undisguised curiosity of their work colleagues, they walked hand in hand.

"Have you ever heard of Aeaea?" Anastasia asked.

"Say again."

"It's pronounced Ay-ee-ah, or something like that. It's Augustin's private island, and he told me he's taking me there soon."

Robert fell silent as he processed the news.

"I'm sure it'll be okay, and there's really no way I can refuse to go. He's organising a meeting with his financial backers and wants me to go along to answer questions. I'll be away for a few days. Apparently, this island's quite remote."

"Strange. I wonder why the backers can't just come here."

"He implied at least one of them would have trouble entering the country. I wouldn't be surprised if it has something to do with illegal arms trading or money laundering or something similar. He wouldn't elaborate any further, and I think he regretted letting anything slip because he clammed up after that."

"I'd have to admit I find the thought of it all a bit worrying, but as you say, you can't refuse to go."

They walked on in silence for a few minutes before a thought occurred to Robert. "Before you go to this meeting, Augustin will need to bring you up-to-date on every aspect of the project. Otherwise, it'll look bad if you can't answer the backer's questions. Perhaps you'll find out some of those things he's kept hidden since the takeover."

"Yes, and it gives me the perfect excuse to find out what's really been going on."

Chapter 11

A few days later, Anastasia started the review process by visiting the robot programming station with Robert. Not wanting to interrupt Jason, she spoke in a subdued whisper. "As I expected, they've repaired all of the damage."

"Yes, I'm impressed at how spic and span they've made it. I remember the last time we were both here, after Robot 3 ran amok destroying the two other robots and damaging much of the walls and equipment."

Four new robots lay on the trolleys. Jason was sitting next to a robot wearing a T-shirt numbered 22 and referring to a laminated sheet.

"Hello, this is Jason. You remember me? I helped prepare you for your scan."

"Ahh! I've got this awful headache."

"Your head will clear soon. Try to concentrate on what I'm saying. I've something very important to discuss with you."

"And I can't move. I'm completely paralysed."

Robot 22 was starting to panic. Jason patted his arm. "Don't worry. The paralysis will wear off soon."

Jason moved to the next item on the sheet. "Tell me who you think you are."

"What do you mean 'think', sir? I'm Sam."

"Listen to me very carefully. You might believe you're Sam, but, in fact, you're a robot programmed with a scan of Sam's brain."

"That's bullshit, sir. I know I'm Sam."

Robot 22's voice was becoming shrill with panic.

Jason moved away from the trolley and joined Robert and Anastasia. With a nod towards the robot he whispered, "I'll give him a few minutes to think things over and then go through it again. The protocol doesn't allow me to enable power to his limbs until he acknowledges he's a robot."

He referred to the sheet of instructions and then continued in a low voice. "The next step is to use a hand mirror to show him his face. That'll help to convince him he's not Sam."

Anastasia agreed. "Good idea. Robert and I have firsthand experience of the delusional behaviour which could result if you did enable power too soon. I see the gun safe with its stock of M4 carbines has been removed, at least. Wise move."

Jason agreed. "Absolutely. Now, once we deal with the psychological issues, a short preparation program is quite adequate to demonstrate their use as security guards in T1. Production versions will require much more training so they can be deployed in a wider range of situations."

After leaving the laboratory, Anastasia referred to a list on her data tablet. "Next I have to check out how many robots we've completed. I'm sure I'll be asked to confirm the full twenty-four robots are ready for testing."

Robert led the way to a room where twenty robots were each seated on their own reclining chair, relaxed, with their heads tilted forward.

"Augustin wants them all enabled at the same time, so these robots are hibernating until the final four are complete. By the time you get to his island, you'll be able to report that all twenty-four are complete and testing has started."

"That's the last item on my list."

Robert reached out to pull Anastasia closer. Now she was

about to leave and meet up with a man he didn't trust and absolutely detested, there were so many things to say. He knew she'd be watching Augustin's every move but wished he could have accompanied her. Finally, all he could think to say was, "Hope things go well. I'll miss you."

Ignoring the ubiquitous surveillance cameras, Anastasia kissed Robert before turning to leave for her trip.

Chapter 12

Travelling by hydrofoil had been far from comfortable for Anastasia. The peculiar lurching motion was unlike travelling on any other type of boat. Speed was the one saving grace. It seemed to take no time between the peak of the volcanic cone showing above the horizon and them arriving at the island's jetty. The hydrofoil throttled back its engines to reduce lift from the underwater wings, allowing its hull to settle into the water. At low speed, they wallowed towards the jetty.

"Ms Anthon?" A man in a smart white, vaguely nautical uniform extended his right hand to help Anastasia step from gangplank to jetty. "I'm Tony. Welcome to Aeaea. Dr Selworthy asked me to help you settle in before he arrives tomorrow."

Carrying Anastasia's suitcase, Tony weaved his way around piles of cargo being unloaded from the ferry and led the way as they climbed well-worn stone steps from the jetty to the top of the sea wall. "From here you get a good idea of the layout of the place. To our left, windows of the guest accommodation have an excellent view of the pool and sundeck. The conference room, where tomorrow's meeting will be held, opens onto the balcony on our right. From here, the most direct route to your room is up the central stairway."

He led the way to a broader flight of stairs. They were made of white marble with elegantly carved handrails, which matched the building they accessed. Heavy wooden doors opened to a long cool corridor with whitewashed walls and dark polished timber floor. The second door on the left was open, and Tony stepped to one side to allow Anastasia to enter.

"Tonight, dinner will be served here in your room."

Anastasia crossed to the window to admire the view. It was truly stunning. Beyond the extensive pool and sundeck, a narrow beach of black sand edged a vast expanse of amazingly blue sea.

"Feel free to use our saltwater pool. You could also swim in the sea from the beach. The seabed slopes away steeply though, so that's really only for strong swimmers."

Having completed his meet and greet duty, Tony seemed keen to talk rather than return to his other responsibilities. Half way to the door he turned back with an uncertain look. "I know it's none of my business, but I heard you're involved with Project Transition."

Anastasia had been warned, 'under no circumstances discuss anything about your work with anyone other than the project's backers'. But it looked as though Tony already knew of her connection. Surely, it could do no harm to simply confirm what he already knew?

"Yes, I've worked on that for several years. Why do you ask?"

Tony modulated his usual booming voice to a more conspiratorial tone. "A few months ago, we had a visit from a humanoid robot called Rob who looked and acted just like a real person. I hadn't seen a robot before and never imagined one could appear so human. Caused me a deal of trouble, but it, or should I say he, told me he was created as part of Project Transition."

Anastasia was instantly surprised and delighted. 'Rob's a

great friend of mine. I was involved in his development. It's wonderful to know he's okay."

Apparently encouraged by her positive response, Tony added an interesting observation before finally taking his leave. "Apart from his being a robot, the visit was very unusual for another reason. Rob appeared to be spending his time here learning about spacecraft navigation or something like that. He was reading through a stack of books on the subject, and I happened to see some of the titles. Had his own personal tutor for a while." Tony smiled. "But I'm not sure what else I would expect a robot to be studying."

~

There was plenty to think about as Anastasia settled into the resort-style living the island provided. She considered the beautiful weather and palatial surroundings would have been perfect if there were someone to share them with. Robert would have been the ideal someone.

~

The following morning, breakfast by the pool was Anastasia's idea of total luxury. After delivering her tray, the waiter confirmed Augustin was due to arrive shortly and also pointed out an impressive luxury yacht anchored a short distance off shore. While savouring the full English breakfast with coffee and toast she assessed the new arrival. Its sleek streamlined profile spoke of speed, style and money, lots of money. On board, the only signs of activity were two crew manoeuvring a helicopter from its hangar.

Anastasia had barely finished eating when she heard the steady drone of a small aircraft. Its approach must have been hidden by the island because it was close to land when it circled into view. The pitch of the single engine reduced as the floatplane settled gently onto the water. Giving the yacht a wide berth, the aircraft revved its engine and surged towards the jetty. This all happened so quickly, Anastasia had to hurry to her room to change into her 'corporate' outfit. Her smartly tailored beige knee-length dress felt just right for the temperature and the expected tenor of the meeting.

~

Augustin looked Anastasia up and down with an analytical eye. She held her breath, trying to hide her annoyance at having to tolerate this indignity as she awaited his critical judgement.

"Fine. My guests are about to arrive, and you can join us as we look around the villa. Mid-morning, after some refreshments, we start the meeting. Your input is only required at the start to give a progress report on the Safetybots and answer any questions. I'm relying on you to display total confidence. The project is ahead of schedule, and there are no problems, you understand?"

Anastasia nodded.

~

It seemed an unnecessary extravagance to use a helicopter to travel the few hundred metres from yacht to jetty, but, she reasoned, if you owned a helicopter, why not?

The three middle-aged businessmen exuded subtly displayed wealth. Their light-weight linen suits and contrasting cotton shirts were all impeccably tailored. Where they vied for difference was in their signet rings, gold designer watches, leather portfolios and exclusive lacquered fountain pens. Anastasia felt herself being subjected to their embarrassingly personal appraisal.

"I scheduled the satellite video link for," Augustin consulted his watch, "one hour from now. If you'll indulge me, I thought we could occupy our time by looking over my archaeological collection. It's a little hobby of mine. I'm sure you'll find the beauty and workmanship truly extraordinary."

With barely concealed pride, Augustin bounded up the stairs to the accommodation wing and opened the only door on the right of the corridor. Even though made of wood, its size and thickness reminded Anastasia of a bank vault. Inside, the light was so subdued it took a while to accommodate to the change. Almost all of the room's illumination came from the lighting in the display cases, which lined the two longer walls of the relatively narrow room. Most of the displays featured a beautifully presented and illuminated treasure of gold, silver or precious stones. Many of the exhibits weren't labelled, and Augustin obviously enjoyed describing them to his visitors. Anastasia skirted round the group admiring Augustin's latest acquisition and moved to the very back of the room. She was surprised to come across one of the visitors furtively photographing some of the artefacts.

"Pavel, come and see this; it's quite something." On hearing his name, the visitor glanced up and realised Anastasia had seen him. With a guilty look, he pocketed his camera and pushed past her to join the others. Interested to find out what had attracted his attention, Anastasia stepped in front of a large cabinet filled with slabs of carved stone, each covered with painted hieroglyphics. There was also a small disc of some sort of corroded base metal. Compared to the other priceless artefacts exquisitely crafted from expensive materials, they seemed unremarkable. But she recognised one of them as identical to the object in her father's photograph. Her heart beat faster and she stepped forward for a closer look.

In the half-light, Augustin appeared beside her, standing a little too close. She flinched and tried to control her feelings of being dominated. Taking another half step, he pressed gently against her and spoke as though making some kind of veiled offer. "Gold and precious stones don't interest you?"

Anastasia felt seriously threatened and started to shake uncontrollably. Edging away, she pointed to an empty plastic frame standing beside the metal disk. It had obviously been designed to hold something, an object with the shape of a large snowflake. "What really fascinates me is the exhibit that's not here."

Augustin avoided any discussion of the missing item and covered his reluctance by deciding it was time to start the meeting.

~

While Anastasia waited for everyone to be seated, she looked around the conference room. At one end, folding doors were open, revealing a broad marble terrace overlooking the pool. A side table was well supplied with discretely expensive drinks and finger food. Augustin positioned himself at the head of the main table with his back to the light, perhaps to give himself an advantage in the discussions. A videoconferencing system projected an image of the sixth attendee. Anastasia could understand why this frail old man, breathing oxygen with the aid of a nasal cannula, was unable to appear in person.

After ensuring the videoconferencing link was functioning correctly, Augustin opened proceedings. "Thank you all for giving up your very valuable time to attend this meeting. You all know each other, apart from Ms Anastasia Anthon. To maintain confidentiality, it won't be necessary for you to identify yourselves to Ms Anthon, who will treat everything you say with the utmost discretion."

There was a general murmur of assent.

"Ms Anthon will start by outlining the current status of the project."

Anastasia paused to make eye contact with her audience. Pavel looked out of the open doors avoiding her gaze.

"Good morning, gentlemen. Since arriving yesterday, I've been informed the pilot batch of twenty-four Safetybots has been completed and deployed around the T1 building. They've replaced staff on duty on the reception desk in the foyer, and all guards deployed at the internal and external security checkpoints. Some have also been assigned to provide perimeter patrols."

Pavel caught Augustin's eye. "I must have comprehensive technical detail of these Safetybots robots so I can assess the value of what I'm funding. I was expecting much more than just a simple statement of progress."

It seemed as though Augustin's immediate reaction would be to deny the request, but he quickly relented. "Okay, I'll see to it that you all receive the latest technical rundown on the robots. Now Anastasia will tell you about the testing."

"The operation of each robot is being monitored by recording all activity via security cameras positioned throughout T1. There will also be a continuous log of their internal parameters. This data will be analysed to ensure they're functioning appropriately in every situation."

Augustin interjected, "What Anastasia didn't tell you was, as part of the testing, they will be challenged with random events requiring their rapid and correct response. This will increase confidence they can handle real-world conditions."

A bout of coughing carried over the video link followed by a question. "I understand it'll take some time to train each Safetybot after it's been built. Why wasn't that training already incorporated into their programming?"

Anastasia turned to acknowledge the remote attendee. "To do that we would need to scan another person who already has the necessary training. We're not currently in a position to perform another scan."

Augustin cut in before Anastasia could add anything further. "Final modifications to the scanner have been completed, and we will perform the required scan shortly. Then we'll be able to ramp up production."

He added a threatening look to dissuade any contradiction from Anastasia.

Following a resounding knock, Tony entered the room and handed Augustin a folded sheet of paper. After adjusting his glasses, Augustin read the message. His expression remained inscrutable, but the colour drained from his face. The paper trembled in his hands as he refolded it.

"I'm afraid we'll have to wind up our meeting early. There's been an incident at T1, our research and development facility, probably something very minor. Still, I should return there as soon as possible to assess the situation. It'll take my pilot a few minutes to prepare my aircraft, so while Ms Anthon packs her bags and makes her way to the jetty, can we confirm continued financing for the project?"

Chapter 13

Robert greeted the Safetybot standing outside the main entrance of building T1. "Good morning, Robot 18."

In reply, the robot snapped to attention.

With similar vigilance, the robot at the reception desk acknowledged Robert's presence when their eyes met, then tracked his progress across the lobby. During the short walk to his office, he passed yet more robots at each security checkpoint.

A man wearing urban camouflage fatigues rose from the visitor's chair as Robert entered his office. "This whole bloody setup is a disaster waiting to happen."

"Sergeant Kirby, you're no doubt referring to what happened when Robot 3 went rogue. You think it'll happen again with these Safetybots?" Robert could have added a criticism of the overzealous nature of the hunt for Robot 3, which had almost cost him his own life. Instead, he took some satisfaction from the sergeant's obvious discomfort with the current situation. "I guess the sight of this building packed with identical robots performing guard duty could be pretty worrying for you."

"Too right it is. These robots shouldn't be trusted an inch. It was a relief to see someone had the good sense to ensure they're not armed this time."

"I understand your misgivings about the situation here, which is beyond my control, but how can I help you?"

"I've been detailed to assess our deployment of the robots and suggest appropriate ways of challenging them to ensure they'll respond correctly to unexpected events."

"Sounds like a great idea to test the robot's responses, but what do you want from me?"

"You have an intimate knowledge of these contraptions. I thought you might be able to suggest situations which would check their ability to make correct choices under pressure. What I've been asked for is a list of difficult situations matched with the responses we would hope to get from the robots."

"Something like a situation where a robot finds an unconscious person in a burning room?"

The sergeant frowned as though trying to work out what he'd do in those circumstances.

"Okay, I'll give it some thought and get back to you."

Robert couldn't really be bothered with Sergeant Kirby's problems but jotted down a few ideas on a note pad. Satisfied he'd made a start on the request, he opened his document safe to recover a tablet computer containing notes on the scanner. In a methodical manner, he'd been investigating each part of the system to home in on the cause of the 'morbidity problem'.

On seeing those words at the top of the first document, he gave a mirthless laugh and muttered under his breath, "Morbidity problem indeed. Perhaps it would be more direct if they just admitted the scanner kills people."

"Who kills people?"

Robert looked up with a start; he hadn't heard Jason enter the office.

"Sorry, Robert. I didn't mean to startle you, but your door was open."

"That's okay. What can I do for you?"

"Now we've completed the demonstration batch of

Safetybots, I don't have much to do. D'you need any help?"

Robert went back to the document safe and retrieved his purple badge. "I've made up a list of scanner components that need to be checked out. Many of these involve electronics housed in the equipment room, and some components are next door in the scanner lab."

Robert angled his tablet computer so Jason could read the screen. "You can help me by opening up the equipment racks and doing some of the testing. You've got your purple badge?"

Jason turned back the lapel of his lab coat to reveal a row of different coloured badges, one of which was purple.

~

Jason sighed and laid down the probe he'd been using to investigate a possible fault. "Are you hungry?" He looked across at Robert as though hoping for a positive answer.

The two of them sat in the middle of the equipment room surrounded by various test instruments and trays of electronics with their covers removed. It was way past their usual finishing time. They'd only stopped briefly for a hurried lunch, and Jason was obviously looking forward to something more substantial for dinner.

"We've only managed to rule out two items on my list. You know I'm keen to make more progress but we can't attempt another scan till we're sure it's safe."

Jason looked as though he was about to complain but then changed his mind. "I don't mind continuing with the testing, but I've got to eat."

"Okay, I can probably get something totally unhealthy from those vending machines in the cafeteria. I'm buying."

As Robert showed his coloured badge to the robots at the purple checkpoint, he was aware of a difference but unsure what it was. There may have been an unusual tension in the way the guards stood or something else. After returning with two serves of steaming noodles and coffee, the feeling was still there.

"Did you notice anything strange about the Safetybots today?"

Jason shook his head and concentrated on eating.

"Oh my God, I've just worked out what it is. They had guns!" For Robert, the realisation acted like an electric shock, but from his reaction it seemed Jason wasn't convinced.

"No way. They couldn't have. Sergeant Kirby insisted they wouldn't be armed, to start with at least, and forever if he had his way."

"But I'm telling you, on my way back from the cafeteria, both robots at the checkpoint were carrying M4 Carbines slung over their shoulders."

With the remains of their meals forgotten, Robert and Jason raced to the checkpoint. The two robots were nowhere to be seen.

"This doesn't look good. Robots are supposed to provide 24/7 cover for the checkpoints," Robert said.

Jason held a finger to his lips and pointed into the distance. Robert was just in time to see a group of robots enter the goods lift. With mounting apprehension, he caught up with Jason who had stopped to point at the floor indicator.

"It's down at basement level, so that must be where they went. Why would they go there?"

Although Robert couldn't put his finger on the reason, he had a bad feeling about what the robots were doing. "From the point-of-view of building security, video from all the cameras used to be monitored and recorded in the basement. That equipment was recently relocated to the second floor, so, as far as I know, there's nothing down there at all. But the robots must have gone there for some reason. I think we should investigate. Is there another way to get to the basement without drawing attention?"

Jason thought for a few seconds. "Inside the building there are two narrow stairways that are hardly ever used. The loading bay also gives access from the outside."

"We'll try the nearest stairs. You know the way, so lead on."

It was easy to imagine why no one used the stairway, even the few who needed to visit the basement. It was only wide enough for a single person, unlit, unmarked, and the entrance was hidden behind a pillar. At basement level the bottom of the stairs was equally well concealed. Even before Robert and Jason reached the last few steps they could hear an unusual amount of activity. Keeping to the shadows, they watched robots manoeuvring fully laden pallets along the corridor, while others cooperated in unrolling drums of cable and loosely looping it around doorknobs and anything else that would keep it off the floor.

"Does this look to you the same way it looks to me?" Jason asked.

Robert had been thinking of asking Jason a similar question. "Possibly. The only way to be certain is to find out what's at the end of those cables."

~

"How about now?"

After waiting for almost ten minutes, Jason seemed keen to make a move. It had been some time since a robot had passed their hiding place.

"I agree. Let's go."

Robert led the way, following the looping wires. At an intersection, he pointed to a single cable snaking off down a minor corridor. "I think we're getting close." The lone cable vanished into a large pile of sandbags. "Here, help me with this. I think we'll find explosives under these bags. They're probably being used to direct the blast towards this concrete column." Robert started pulling away the sandbags, and Jason dragged them clear.

"You two, stop what you're doing. That's very dangerous."

The intense torchlight made it impossible to see who was speaking, but the tone of voice was common to all Safetybots.

"Show me your hands and turn around."

"Look, we don't have any weapons. What's going on here?"

"Mr Harper, sir, and you, Jason, for your own safety you must follow me. I don't want you to come to any harm. I remember you tried your best to warn me of what would happen when I was scanned."

In spite of the conciliatory words, Robot 9 used the threat of his M4 Carbine to shepherd them towards the loading dock. At regular intervals, they passed piles of sandbags stacked around the base of concrete pillars, which supported the weight of the building above.

"Are you intending to blow up T1?" Robert didn't get a reply, so he tried a different approach. "Did Maxwell persuade you to do this?"

The robot stopped so suddenly he almost overbalanced. "You know about Maxwell?" Then after a short pause, "You are aware intelligent robots are currently the greatest threat to humanity?"

"But you're a robot."

"Yes, Maxwell explained that to me. Although I'm a robot, I have a higher allegiance to Sam, the person I was before the start of this sorry mess. I can protect my family, friends and the rest of humanity by destroying every transitioned intelligence and making sure new ones cannot be built."

"You'd destroy yourself as well as this building?"

Robot 9 lifted his olive-green t-shirt to reveal a black rectangular block strapped to his chest.

"When the building goes, we all go with it."

For the next ten minutes, nothing was said. Robert felt his heart pounding and his body bathe itself in sweat. He was primed to run but aware of the Carbine pointing at himself and Jason. Robot 9 seemed content to let time pass. Eventually, possibly alerted by a wireless command, the robot spoke with sudden urgency. "This building will implode in two minutes. If you're quick, you should be able to make it outside the lethal blast radius, and then, if you're lucky, you won't be hit by falling masonry."

Without any show of emotion, Robot 9 indicated the way out through the open loading bay doors.

Chapter 14

Anastasia braced herself against the back of the pilot's seat as he banked the helicopter into a tight turn over the wreckage of T1. In another dizzying manoeuvre, the helicopter transitioned to hover over the vast expanse of shattered concrete and tangled steel reinforcing bars. Only the long narrow building containing the shooting range remained intact. A row of temporary marquees had been erected in the parking area, and she could see groups of figures in high visibility clothing searching the wreckage.

Augustin pointed to the highest point of the rubble. "What a mess. Looks like the three upper stories have all been compressed into the same space as the original basement. I doubt there'll be anything we can salvage from here." Then, as though just an afterthought, "It's also unlikely anyone caught in the building would have survived."

His cold and unfeeling words were an icy stab. It seemed as though human life really was of little value to him. On the other hand, the building and its equipment were of no special concern for Anastasia, but thoughts of people being crushed by falling concrete were horrifying. She hesitated to ask what was upmost in her mind, worried that saying it might make it come true. "Was Robert in the building when it collapsed? He doesn't answer when I call his phone."

"According to phone company records, ten phones were active in and around T1 before the explosion. Afterwards, there were none, and unfortunately, Robert's was one of the ten. Hiroshi is another person who appears to be missing. Here's a complete list of those who were signed in to the building at the time and haven't been accounted for."

Augustin's voice and face were expressionless, and he continued to look straight ahead as he held out a folded sheet of paper.

"Land the helicopter. I've got to find Robert."

Augustin turned towards her and shook her shoulder with a painful grip as though trying to instil some sense. "It's been well over a day since the explosion, and my ZsG staff are doing a thorough search. Almost certainly, we'll find people buried in the rubble, but they won't have survived. I regret to say the probability is that Robert died in the explosion."

Anastasia steadied herself by holding onto the seat in front. Tears stung her eyes. "I've got to see for myself. Let me out! Now!"

~

The helicopter circled and lined up on a temporary helipad marked out with orange plastic cones. As Anastasia stepped to the ground, Augustin shouted over the noise of the engines. "When you've finished, one of the drivers here will give you a lift home."

A rescue worker handed Anastasia a hard hat, high visibility vest and dust mask. Without comment, they walked past heavy earth moving equipment, no doubt poised for action once it was deemed there was no possibility of anyone being found alive. Already there was a distinct smell of decay. They walked around the edge of the destruction, avoiding larger slabs of concrete scattered by the explosion. The site was being sprayed with water to reduce harmful dust.

"We started searching two hours after the explosion. We've

used rescue dogs, thermal cameras and microphones. So far, nobody has been found alive. I know it isn't much consolation, but for those caught in the building, I think we can be confident the end would have been quick."

Her guide was probably correct, but his words weren't any consolation at all. Eventually, the futility of her being there became inescapable. "I don't know why I'm here. There's obviously nothing I can do to help."

Her escort nodded in sympathy as he led her to a row of parked vehicles. Apart from asking for an address, the driver left Anastasia to her thoughts.

~

She watched the car drive away before turning towards her front door. Now that she was alone, she couldn't hold back the tears. Fumbling with the key, she opened the door and slipped inside. Instantly, her tears and sense of loss were forgotten; she was on guard. An intruder had been there and might still be in her house. Many things were out of their usual place with dirty dishes in the sink, lights left on, and books scattered across the floor. With trembling hands, she selected a substantial obsidian carving and held it high, ready to strike. There was nowhere for an intruder to hide in the kitchen, and the lounge room appeared empty until she saw two feet protruding beyond the end of the sofa. From behind it wasn't possible to see who the intruder was. She advanced slowly.

"Robert, is that really you? Oh, thank God you're alive!" The carving fell to the floor saved by the thick carpet.

Robert pulled himself to a sitting position. "Sorry about the mess. I couldn't think of anywhere else to go. I had to take the chance your place wouldn't be monitored while you were away." In response to her look of profound relief he continued. "I thought it would be presumptuous to sleep in your bed so decided on your sofa."

Anastasia sat beside Robert and buried her face in his chest. He held her tightly until he felt the tension start to relax.

"How did you avoid being killed?"

"The Safetybots had taken complete control of the basement of T1 so they could plant their explosives. They captured Jason and me when we went to investigate what was going on. Fortunately, they appreciated our attempts to warn Sam about what would happen to him as a result of his scan. They let us go just in time to get clear. We both ran for our lives. Jason quickly outpaced me, but I just kept running until the explosion knocked me flat. It took me some time to recover. I called to Jason, but he was nowhere to be seen, and I don't know what happened to him."

"But according to the telephone network the signal from your phone was lost when the building collapsed."

"When the Safetybots detained us in the basement they confirmed Maxwell was responsible. When we were allowed to leave, I made a split-second decision to throw my phone into a skip full of scrap metal beside the loading bay doors. I hoped it would give me a bit of a breathing space if Maxwell believed I was dead."

Anastasia gave a slight smile and dried her eyes. "You'll be pleased to hear that Jason isn't on the list of casualties." A quizzical tone entered her voice. "How did you manage to get here? You didn't walk the whole way?"

"I know it sounds a bit paranoid, but I've started carrying a spare, unregistered phone and only put the battery in if I need to use it. When I was far enough away from T1, I called a taxi and decided your apartment was less likely to be under surveillance because you were out of the country."

With a tone of mock seriousness, Anastasia pretended to berate Robert. "Not that I'm complaining, but I do need to know how you got into my apartment, so I can make sure no one else gets in the same way. In return, I'll give you a key to the front door. Not that I'm going to let you go anytime soon."

Chapter 15

After a few months of relative freedom Augustin's replacement for T1 was finally judged ready for occupation. Robert and Anastasia circled inside the perimeter fence of their new 'home', appraising the extent of their liberty. Chain-linked fence, barbed wire, and cameras marked their limits. The only exception was the guardhouse, where all traffic in and out was stopped for inspection. Perhaps in the future they might be allowed to walk outside. As they returned to their starting point, Anastasia was ready to give her assessment. "The desolate land outside looks very familiar, doesn't it?"

"Yes, not surprising really, considering it's part of ZsG's combat training area. I think the group of buildings where Robot 3 was destroyed would be a few kilometres south of here."

Anastasia flinched, no doubt recalling the sniper fire and staunching the blood from Robert's wounds. To change the subject, she focussed on their new workplace.

"Augustin's really outdone himself this time, hasn't he? It's been an amazing feat to replace T1 in such a short time. Even so, this has to be the most dismal place imaginable. How can he possibly expect a collection of temporary huts surrounded by fences and barbed wire, in the middle of nowhere, to function as a suitable alternative?"

Robert tried to look on the bright side. "He assures us we'll only be here for a short while until we get the transitioning process working."

Anastasia just shook her head and looked at him ruefully. "I suppose we should get back to unpacking our things into our cabins. I'm sure we'll be expected to start work early tomorrow."

~

At first, Robert wasn't sure what he'd done wrong. He was taking a mid-morning break with Jason and some other members of the team. Anastasia moved to join them, but before she arrived her coffee cup overbalanced, smashing on the floor. For a second, she stood frozen, free hand covering her mouth.

After the spill had been cleaned up she rounded on Robert. "Don't you ever wear those clothes again."

He looked down at his shirt and trousers, eventually realising they were the same ones he'd been wearing when he'd escaped the destruction of T1.

"You were so close to dying that it makes me sick to think about it. If Jason hadn't been hungry, both of you would be dead now."

Anastasia stormed off to fetch another coffee leaving Robert lost for words. He was concerned her mood had become more volatile since the explosion. Jason broke the silence as Anastasia returned. "I didn't realise how pleasant T1 was until we were relocated here. Not much of an alternative, is it? If we thought the food was bad before, they've shown us it can get a whole lot worse. Even the choice of name, T2, shows a singular lack of imagination. What do you think, Anastasia?"

"True, and no one had a choice as far as coming here was concerned, did we? As soon as they knocked this place together, we were on our way, like it or not."

"This cafeteria's a good example of what's wrong. Look around. Food and coffee are terrible, there's no view, and it's crowded. Everything about this place is shit!"

Robert was forced to agree. "I've got to admit you're right, Jason. Things haven't got any better in the days we've been here. I'll raise problems of food and other facilities at this morning's meeting with Augustin. The gym is useless because it's so poorly equipped, and even the gee-whizz immersive virtual reality cinema is a dud. On those evenings when it's actually open there's such a poor choice of films hardly anyone bothers with it. I'm sure most prisons would be better equipped."

~

The meeting room was in another temporary building. Although more modern than the original T1, it was cramped and obviously cheaply constructed from blandly similar pre-fabricated modular units. Most of the forty-two staff, all that remained of the more than two hundred originally employed on Project Transition, were packed into the room. Robert addressed his colleagues before Augustin officially opened the meeting.

"I think I speak for everyone when I say living and working conditions here are intolerable."

There was a general murmur of support around the room. Obviously annoyed by this flouting of protocol, Augustin removed and then slowly polished his gold-rimmed glasses. Eventually, the rigid set of his jaw relaxed. "Unfortunately, building this facility in an isolated and well defended location was the only way I could ensure its security and the safety of everyone working on the project. You should be very thankful to be here."

Augustin scanned a document on his data tablet as though refreshing his memory. "Just to give you all an idea of the security challenges we're facing, I have reports of two more attacks on robotics installations that have almost certainly been

68

instigated by people with a vendetta against intelligent robots. These people seem to be convinced intelligent robots will displace humans and take over the world."

"Of course, we haven't heard anything because, as you know, there's a complete information blackout here." Robert intended this as a rebuke, but Augustin gave no indication of having heard or else didn't think the complaint warranted an answer. Instead, he continued reading from his tablet.

"In the first incident at DigiSim Pets their entire research and development site was gutted. The blaze started during business hours when an out of control natural gas tanker crashed into the building. A large quantity of gas escaped which then ignited causing a massive explosion and fireball. Many people were killed or seriously injured, but there was no trace of the tanker driver. That could have been a very unfortunate accident, but I have my doubts."

Members of the group started talking to each other.

"You're not serious! Don't they produce robot therapy pets for the elderly?"

Augustin looked up from his tablet. "Quite right, Robert. They're probably world leaders in that section of the market."

"But nobody would believe the world could be taken over by an army of googly-eyed furry pets."

"Probably not. Still, management of the company have been seeking to diversify their product range. I know they were developing a robotic personal carer. It was to feature a state-of-the-art humanoid body with advanced artificial intelligence allowing it to perform the full range of tasks required of a caregiver, including holding meaningful conversations with residents and autonomously managing its working day."

Robert understood the implication. "I can see such robots would be seen as problematic by anyone who doesn't like the idea of their job being automated away."

Augustin scrolled through the document on his tablet. "Nobody has claimed responsibility for the blaze, but it does look as though some secret organisation fighting against the development of advanced robotics was behind it."

"You mentioned two attacks?" Anastasia's voice wavered.

"I did. Most members of a South Korean university department have been wiped out. In a very sophisticated attack, the building was flooded with hydrogen sulphide. To improve efficiency of the air-conditioning system, the whole building was hermetically sealed. There were no windows that would open, no easy way to escape the gas. The only exits were on the ground floor and this was where the dense gas tended to gather, killing those who attempted to flee. At the high concentrations present during this attack, the rotten eggs smell would have been obvious, but after only two or three breaths, the victims would have been rendered unconscious and died shortly afterwards."

There was a stunned silence as the news sunk in. Eventually, Augustin continued. "As well as the human cost, this was an enormous blow to the planned development of robots with brain power far exceeding our own. The university department was world renowned for its work on super-intelligence."

Anastasia turned to Robert for an explanation. "How do they manage to achieve that? It doesn't seem possible for humans who have a certain intelligence to dream up something with a much higher level of intelligence."

"I've read about their work. They used artificial evolution running on a vast network of computers to evolve their super-intelligences. The computers simulate generations of digital intelligences, combining and modifying them, selecting the best and repeating the process zillions of times faster than biological evolution. By all accounts, the final product is pretty amazing. But apparently, even this super-intelligence wasn't able to anticipate the gas attack."

Augustin paused, probably taking time to see how his news was received. "All of these incidents point to the fact that you're safer living and working in this well-guarded compound. Everything you need is here, and I'll ensure that additional facilities are added to make it more comfortable when resources permit. As you've probably seen, the building for housing the fMRI brain scanner is now complete. We're fortunate the spare scanner I diverted from the local hospital was stored off site and not damaged in the destruction of T1. It was even more fortunate that the safe containing all the project documentation survived the explosion. Once the scanner is installed and you complete the modifications, we'll be ready to perform another brain scan."

"Accommodation for the scanner may be progressing well, but staff facilities here are pretty basic at best," Jason said. "We're housed in cabins that are barely habitable and stuck in the middle of this desolate combat training area. With all of the fences, surrounding wasteland and guards, we really feel like prisoners in a Russian gulag."

Many people in the room indicated their support for Jason.

"As I said, this place was chosen because it's easy to defend, and you're here because you're all key people, absolutely indispensable for finishing the project. To put things in perspective for you, at the moment I consider there are three essential requirements for pulling everything together."

Augustin held up three fingers of his left hand and folded one down as he covered each point.

"Firstly, using existing plans and documentation, we can build more robots like the original model programmed with Robert's scan or the advanced version we used for Sam's scan. Therefore, the robot bodies present no problems, and in fact, I've subcontracted their construction to an outside company. Secondly, the process of converting brain scans into code for loading into the robots is well established. So, we have that aspect covered as well. The third and final element is the scanner, and I believe you in this room are the only people who can get it to work."

Several whispered conversations started around the room. Eventually, Robert spoke for one of the groups. "What you say may be true, but we don't think it justifies the extreme measures of isolating us out here in the middle of nowhere."

It must have seemed as though Robert was about to lead a minor rebellion. Augustin sat quietly for what seemed like an age and then released a long, heartfelt sigh. "Very well. I'll take immediate steps to improve conditions, and in return, I want everyone to redouble their efforts. This meeting is dismissed. Everyone back to work. Robert, Anastasia and Jason stay behind."

When they were alone, Augustin gave the impression he'd made a difficult decision. Leaning forward in a conspiratorial manner, he lowered his voice. "I think it's time to tell you three the truth about this project. I know I can trust you to keep this information to yourselves."

"You mean the real reason for ZsG's interest in Project Transition?" Robert asked.

A half smile creased Augustin's lips. "No, the truth about *my* interest in the project. Even from the start, I was only using ZsG to help me get what I wanted, but don't tell them."

"So, if making lots of money selling Safetybots isn't the real reason, what is it?" Robert persisted.

"My motivation is to become a leading pioneer in the exploration of the planet Mars. I aim to set up the first permanent base on Mars to spearhead long-term scientific research and exploration of the planet. It's something Vince and I discussed many times, and although we didn't fully agree on the details, we both saw it as something we were passionate about and could do for all mankind. Initially, my base will be run by robots, but eventually, I hope it can be upgraded to accommodate humans."

Although Anastasia had told Robert what she'd learned from Tony about Rob studying spacecraft navigation, this was still totally unexpected. Robert didn't have to feign surprise, especially upon learning about Augustin's altruistic reasons for getting involved in space exploration. "Will you use robots with transitioned intelligence to explore Mars?" he asked, hearing the obvious excitement in his own voice.

Augustin smiled indulgently at Robert's question. "They're already on their way. About six months ago, I launched a spacecraft heading to Mars. It has a crew of three robots, and Rob is one of them. There's also a robot programmed with Sam's brain scan."

"You've sent Rob to Mars? I'm sure he'll find that a wonderful experience."

Anastasia seemed to catch on to Robert's enthusiasm. "That's fantastic! What kind of scientific research will they be doing?"

Augustin seemed to be caught unprepared for that question or unwilling to divulge any further details. "You don't need to know that."

After an awkward silence, Anastasia tried a different question. "If the mission's already well on its way, why do you need more transitioned intelligences?"

"For contingencies. The mission has been designed by another of my outfits, called Space Transport Studies. Before launch, they estimated the probability of success as 70%. After the spaceship was coasting towards Mars that probability rose to 78% because the launch is a risky part of the mission."

Robert was encouraged by the news. "So now there's a 78% chance the mission will succeed?"

"A little bit more because the craft has travelled a fair distance towards Mars, and even coasting through space still carries its own risks. Once in Mars orbit, the probability rises again to 82%, and finally, after a successful landing becomes 100%. Landing is the most hazardous part."

Robert returned to the question of Augustin's need for more transitioned intelligences. This seemed to be the key reason many of the survivors of the T1 explosion had been pressured to move to T2. "Where does your contingency come into this?"

"I would never commit to any major investment where the risks weren't minimised. If something goes wrong with the landing, I want to be able to launch a backup mission at the earliest opportunity. I've already made down payments on the launch facilities and the new spacecraft hardware required for a repeat mission. The next launch window for Mars will occur in just over one year's time. I won't know if a second mission will be necessary for another few months, but if it is, I want to be ready with a new robotic crew." Fixing Robert with an emphatic stare Augustin concluded, "For that reason, I need the scanner working ASAP."

"Of course, a working scanner will also enable you to make and sell Safetybots," Anastasia observed.

"Yes, that's also a consideration."

~

In the evening, Robert and Anastasia went for their usual walk in an attempt to lighten their mood. Augustin's promise to improve conditions by increasing deliveries of fresh produce and refurbishing the bar sounded like only minor improvements. Nothing could change the restrictions and isolation of the place.

Robert paused to gaze beyond the perimeter fence. "The countryside here has a certain rugged appeal, but I'll always associate it with Robot 3."

Anastasia drew Robert closer and intertwined their fingers. "Yes, when we first arrived it brought back bad memories for me. Seeing that robot destroyed by Sergeant Kirby's sniper and you being injured by flying shrapnel."

"You saved my life, you know. And I do appreciate how difficult it was for you to fight your PTSD while staunching the bleeding."

"Saving you helped me save myself, Robert. I can't tell you how pleased I am to have put some of my demons behind me.”

“I think we’re very good for each other.”

After taking a few more steps they paused again, and Anastasia reached out to trace one of the scars on Robert’s forehead. “But I’m not so sure it’s good for us to remain involved with this project. There are so many unsavoury things going on. People’s lives have been put in danger, and some have died.”

As though deciding the conversation was becoming too morbid, Robert tried to change the subject. “From what was said at the meeting, it’s clear Augustin’s motivation is purely selfless after all.”

Anastasia turned to see Robert’s face and make sure he was joking before observing, “But someone motivated by the common good doesn’t usually go around killing people.”

“You mean like Denny?”

She nodded. “Like Denny.”

“And talking about the fate of other people who used to work for Project Transition, we’re now down to less than a quarter of the original workforce,” Robert said.

“We never found out how many died in the collapse of T1, but a fair number must have been ‘let go’ since then.” More as a question than a statement, Anastasia added, “Can we assume this new selfless Augustin hasn’t done anything to harm them?”

“Let’s hope so. However, there’s another interesting question.”

“Which is?”

“Why is he spending so much money and effort on exploring Mars? That’s if you’re not convinced he’s doing it for the good of humanity?”

With closed eyes Anastasia massaged the bridge of her nose. Robert recognised a sure sign she was thinking deeply. “I don’t know of any mineral so valuable it would be worthwhile mining it on Mars and shipping it to Earth.”

Robert had an inspiration. "Perhaps Augustin intends to claim sovereignty over Mars?"

"You mean Augustin Selworthy, Emperor of Mars? I'm sure that wouldn't be possible. I think there's some international treaty forbidding such a thing, and anyway, a transitioned intelligence doesn't have any legal status allowing it to stake a claim to anything."

Approaching their cabins, they exchanged knowing glances, which asked 'your place or mine?'

Chapter 16

Mars Lander Computer Log #28: Elapsed time since system initialisation 6359 hours

Activities since previous log:
1> Hull impact detected.
2> A short time after the impact a slow loss of cabin pressure registered.
3> Mission protocols flag loss of cabin pressure as a situation which should be rectified.
4> Rob brought out of hibernation to find and remedy source of the leak.
5> A minor puncture was found located in the spacecraft outer skin, probably caused by a micrometeroid.
6> Under my direction Rob used leak sealant compound to repair the hull breach.
7> Rob was returned to hibernation.

Current status:
1> All sensor readings within acceptable limits.
2> Current fuel reserves – 91.3%. Fuel used for course correction manoeuvres is within expected limits.

3> All crew in hibernation.

4> Power management – battery charge 100%, solar panels capable of providing 195% of vehicle requirements. Solar panel capacity reduced in line with increased distance from the Sun.

Unresolved issues:

1> Currently, my inference engine has not identified the source of the threat to the mission. During the unplanned activity required to seal the leak, all of Rob's actions were analysed in detail, and none were found to provide grounds for concern.

Chapter 17

After weeks of working with minimal oversight, Augustin's summons came out of the blue. As previously, it was brief and enigmatic. Robert arrived at the designated door and presented his identification badge to the guard. Once permitted to enter, he wasn't surprised to find the room was as spartan and cheaply furnished as everywhere else in T2. Augustin barely acknowledged his arrival but pointed to a vacant chair next to Anastasia. Seated opposite them was a young man who was using his fingers to rake the mop of dark brown hair from his eyes.

"Anastasia and Robert, this is Ethan."

A detached stare was the only greeting, but behind the heavy tortoiseshell glasses, Robert detected a show of superiority tinged with apprehension.

"He runs Space Transport Studies, the organisation who planned the mission for getting our robots and supplies to the surface of Mars. I've already explained your part in Project Transition."

This was the first time they had met, but Robert already knew Ethan was Penny's ex-boyfriend and probably responsible for her capture by ZsG. Robert hoped his body language wouldn't give away his feelings of contempt for someone capable of such a betrayal. Although he had only met Penny once, he felt they had a strong connection through Rob. She'd helped hide Robert's robotic double in the underground tunnels of Wivenhoe College after his escape from ZsG. It was while aiding Rob that Penny had been abducted. Robert watched Ethan closely, but there was no indication he realised their common connection through Penny.

"At a previous meeting, I mentioned my contingency plan in case the current rocket fails to make a successful landing on Mars."

Ethan's apprehension seemed to intensify, and he started to fidget with one of his shirt buttons.

"Should another mission be required, its crew will need the skills of a navigator, a jack of all trades with the ability to repair and maintain everything, and finally, a robot conversant with assembling things and general manual tasks."

There was an awkward silence as though Augustin expected Ethan to speak up, but the young man seemed unwilling to commit himself. He was perspiring and stared down at his tightly clasped hands. Eventually, words came tumbling out. "I've agreed to a brain scan."

With an exasperated shake of the head, Augustin took over to fill in the missing details. "Because of Ethan's knowledge of spacecraft navigation, he's the ideal candidate to be transitioned into the robot tasked with piloting the next Mars mission. He's here to find out about progress with the scanner and to assure himself there are no risks involved."

Robert interpreted Augustin's icy stare as a warning to discourage discussion of any safety concerns regarding the scanner. "We've almost finished building a replacement for the scanner destroyed in T1. I hope there'll be plenty of time to commission it in a step-by-step manner rather than the hasty way that was necessary with the first one."

Anastasia stepped in to explain a little of the history. "With the original scanner, we were working under intense time pressure. It wasn't possible to verify the safety of each subsystem before they were all combined to perform the scan."

Ethan's eyes opened wide in apparent surprise. "Why didn't you test it with animals before risking humans?"

Probably, to prevent the silence growing too marked, Augustin indicated Robert should answer.

"You must know that MRI scanners have been used in hospitals for many years with no adverse effects. Because our scanner is based on the same principles and contains much of the same equipment, we assumed it would be no different. Also, results from animal tests wouldn't help confirm whether the scanner could successfully capture the essence of human intelligence. We believe a careful approach to further development of the scanner will minimise the risks."

Augustin suppressed a yawn and with an air of finality added, "Ethan, I'm sure you'll be reassured to discover the first of the new crew members to be transitioned will be our building and construction specialist. There are already several people from within ZsG who've volunteered to be scanned for that position. In fact, there's some competition for the privilege."

In spite of assurances that all would be well, Ethan seemed ready to voice more of his reservations. After a few moments of indecision, a discouraging glare from Augustin persuaded him to change his mind and hurry from the room.

Augustin turned to Robert and Anastasia. "No doubt you've noticed the communications dish being built behind the cabins?"

"Yes, we did. I agreed with Anastasia that it would probably be used to communicate with the Mars spacecraft."

Augustin appeared disappointed he wasn't able to reveal its purpose himself. "Yes, soon we hope to establish radio contact with the Mars mission. They're scheduled to break radio silence shortly after landing, which will be within the next few days."

It was unheard of for Augustin to disclose information for no reason. Robert waited for an insight into why he had.

"I must admit I made an unfortunate mistake when I assumed robots with transitioned intelligence would be totally predictable and logical machines. Perhaps I assumed a human intelligence would become more rational once it had been transitioned and loaded into a robot."

Robert was fascinated by this admission of fallibility and wanted to know more. "What caused you to change your mind?"

"As you must realise, the problems started with Rob. From the very beginning, that robot showed mental instability, perhaps even paranoia, particularly when it set fire to the chemical store and then went into hiding. Later it seemed to suffer a mental breakdown and became so insecure it had to seek certainty by returning to where it was built."

"And yet you chose to use him as one of the crew of your Mars mission."

"I had no choice. The scanner problems prevented me producing an alternative navigator, and postponing the mission would have cost a fortune and set the mission back almost two years."

"Your crew of three includes Rob and another robot based on Sam's scan. Who is the third member?"

"I was able to source an HMM23 robot for performing simple manual tasks. Choosing between the three of them, I had no alternative but to use the Sam robots to lead the mission."

"That sounds like a very risky choice."

"You might be right, Robert. Even though the first three robots with Sam's scan started hallucinating and ended up destroying each other, I believed those problems were fixed in the robot I sent on the Mars mission. Later, after seeing what happened to the Safetybots, I realised I can't be sure it doesn't suffer from the same unstable and pathological behaviour."

"That seems to raise questions about two of your crew members."

"The problem is I'm not sure I totally trust any of the robots I've sent to Mars. The possible exception would be the HMM23 robot. I don't think it has sufficient intelligence to be untrustworthy, but with everything that's gone wrong so far, I'll just have to wait and see."

"I can see the problems, but where do we come in?"

Augustin smiled, perhaps because he knew what he was about to propose would sound ridiculous. "You two are the closest I have to robot psychologists."

Now it was the turn of Anastasia to smile. "You're saying the problems you've had with your robots, if they occurred in humans, they'd be considered psychological. So, you're looking for people who understand how your robots' minds work."

"That's correct. There are complications I hadn't foreseen because I viewed them as totally governed by logic. For that reason, I need you both to be on hand to monitor every communication with Mars. Your task will be to look out for evidence of pathology in their responses and make sure nothing we say could exacerbate the situation."

Robert was fascinated by the thought of becoming a robot psychologist but didn't want to be accused of falling behind on his other duties. "This would take time and possibly slow development of the scanner."

"That can't be helped. Communicating with the Mars mission has top priority. If they do land successfully, there's no longer any urgent reason to prepare another robotic crew. But, of course, I still need transitioned intelligences for the Safetybot project, so I'm counting on you to do the best you can on both fronts."

Chapter 18

Mars Lander Computer Log #45: Elapsed time since system initialisation 9215 hours

Activities since previous log:

1> Successfully transitioned from Earth-Mars transfer orbit to stable orbit around Mars.

2> Failed to bring Sam out of hibernation. In consultation with Rob, it was decided this low-priority task should be postponed until later.

3> Main engines fired to deorbit and start the descent towards the landing zone.

4> External solar panels jettisoned.

5> Parachute deployed.

6> Landing rockets fired.

7> Ground proximity detected – parachute jettisoned, cut main and landing rockets.

8> Inertial sensors indicated the rocket then fell 30 metres before toppling over.

9> In spite of the angle of the lander, HMM23 and Rob were able to unload the cargo and start assembling the Habitat.

Current status:
1> The lander is lying at an angle of 60 degrees from the vertical. This is making access to the cargo holds difficult.
2> Current fuel reserves – 15%.
3> Sam still in hibernation.
4> Power management – lander battery charge 98%, charging terminated when external solar panels were jettisoned.

Unresolved issues:
1> Unable to bring Sam out of hibernation - Currently this situation is not critical to the mission.
2> Landing rockets cut prematurely - This event has endangered the mission. Two of the three ground proximity sensors activated incorrectly. Inference engine assesses probability of sabotage at 15%, therefore unlikely.
3> Currently, inference engine has not identified any deliberate threat to the mission.

Chapter 19

Two ZsG guards watched closely as Robert and Anastasia stared into the retina scanner and entered their security codes. Once inside the building, they blinked in the harsh lighting. As the door slammed shut, Ethan looked up from his computer screen. "Is this your first time inside the Mars Comms Centre?"

"Yes, I guess Augustin doesn't hand out invitations unless he really has to. Once communications are established, Robert and I have been given the job of certifying the crew of the Mars lander are still of sound mind. I guess we're here as robot psychologists."

Robert turned away from a map of Mars, disappointed it didn't give any clue about the proposed landing site.

"This map is another example of Augustin's fetish for secrecy. Only disclose the minimum and then only when absolutely necessary."

Ethan pointed to a table set up with vacuum flasks and trays of cups. "We'll probably spend most of our time here waiting to make contact and twiddling our thumbs while we get replies. Radio signals take somewhere between four and twenty-four minutes to make the one-way trip between Earth and Mars. At the moment, the delay is about halfway between.

That's why I requested that hot and cold drinks be provided to help pass the time."

Anastasia looked at the five desks arranged in a horseshoe. "What's the seating arrangement?"

"Augustin gets the central desk with the biggest, most comfortable chair. Of course, he also has the largest screen. Each of the other seating positions has an identical display screen and keyboard. This one is mine. You can choose from the others."

Anastasia took a closer look at columns of figures and small graphics on one of the screens. "What do these things show?"

"The most important information is when the dishes here and on Mars are lined up so we can exchange messages."

Having examined the communications equipment, Anastasia seemed excited by the prospect of exchanging messages with Rob. "Have they made contact yet?"

"Well, no. But we have intercepted a transmission from another group of spacecraft also heading for Mars. From their transmissions, it appears that at least some of them have a human crew. Augustin had quite a turn when we first detected them. According to my measurements this other mission will arrive shortly after ours touches down."

Robert finished pouring two cups of coffee and offered one to Anastasia. "I didn't know anyone else had sent a mission to Mars during the latest launch window."

"Augustin did some urgent enquiries and found out the mission was financed by LanthanoCo, a mining conglomerate specialising in rare earth minerals. As far as he could discover, they aim to search out a suitable place to build a base and then explore the surrounding area to find minerals and other resources. Just like him, they weren't publicising their intentions. But getting back to our mission, we don't know exactly when they'll arrive or how long it'll take them to assemble their communications gear. There've been no messages from the spacecraft since it left Earth orbit, but that's all part of Augustin's cloak of secrecy."

Anastasia spoke between sips of coffee. "When are you expecting their transmissions to start?"

"This evening there'll be a four-hour communication window starting at 19.15pm. According to my calculations, it's possible they could be ready by then. Augustin wants us all here ten minutes early, so don't be late."

~

Augustin was becoming increasingly impatient and obviously had little practice hiding his frustration. He drummed his fingers on the table and squirmed in his seat. "Are you sure everything's working at this end?"

Ethan responded to this question, which sounded like an accusation, by pointing out a window on Augustin's screen displaying signals received by the communications dish. "These two peaks represent transmissions from observation satellites in orbit around Mars, and this third one is from the LanthanoCo mission. If our lander starts transmitting, we'll see it as another blip about here." He pointed to a location halfway between two existing peaks.

With the aid of a couple of coffees, Augustin endured another hour of waiting before finally giving up. "Call me the minute you see anything," he snapped. "You're not to reply to any communication if I'm not present."

After the door closed behind him, an air of calm settled on the room.

"How's progress with the scanner?" Ethan's question sounded offhand, but Robert wasn't fooled. "We're almost ready to perform another scan. After what happened on the previous few occasions, I want to be totally sure nothing can go wrong."

Ethan winced. "You mean the 'mortality problem'?"

"Yes, but don't worry. As you may remember, one of the ZsG guys is being scanned first. If that goes well, it'll be the ultimate confirmation that the problems have been fixed."

"Did you ever find out what caused the earlier issues?"

"So far, there hasn't been a single occasion where the scanner functioned correctly and didn't inflict serious, sometimes fatal, injury on the subject. In fact, I was the first person to be scanned in this kind of machine and I suffered quite bad injuries. Unfortunately, after each attempt, the equipment was modified before I could examine it, making the source of the problems difficult to track down. I was only given access to records of the modifications that had been trialled after Hiroshi handed the project to me."

Surreptitiously, Ethan dabbed at beads of perspiration gathering on his forehead. Robert guessed his answer hadn't reduced Ethan's worries about being scanned. He resisted the temptation to add that Penny, his ex-girlfriend, had probably died in an earlier version of the scanner. He felt certain it must have been Ethan who'd passed on information allowing ZsG to track and capture her, but to mention the issue would only cause more problems. Besides, they might have need of Ethan's cooperation in the future.

"If it would help, I could show you the scanner once we know we won't be receiving a transmission. When you see what's involved, it won't appear so daunting."

~

"What d'you think?" Robert asked.

Ethan blinked in the clinical white of the scanner laboratory. "Looks just like some sort of hospital equipment."

"It's basically a magnetic resonance imaging scanner, only heavily modified to vastly increase its resolution. It'll record the finest physical detail and chemical composition of your brain."

In the adjacent preparation area, Ethan appeared taken aback by the sight of the patient trolley and equipment for administering the sedative. "I can't stand needles. Will that be really necessary?"

"You'll be in the machine for about three hours. The

sedative will prevent you getting too restless."

Robert hoped Ethan would find the procedure extremely uncomfortable but not fatal. That way Ethan might experience some of the pain he caused for Penny.

Chapter 20

Mars Lander Computer Log #46: Elapsed time since system initialisation 9235 hours

Activities since previous log:

    1> All cargo offloaded from lander cargo bays.

    2> The crash-landing has resulted in damage to a number of items including 7 solar panels. There are sufficient spare modules to cover the loss.

    3> 6 Habitat modules constructed.

    4> 2 Substitute battery-charging modules located and installed.

    5> 1 solar array completed and providing power.

Current status:

    1> Sam still in hibernation.

    2> Lander batteries 11%.

    3> Habitat batteries 0.5%.

    4> The Habitat construction 30% complete.

Anomalies detected:

    1> Unable to bring Sam out of hibernation.

    2> Missing battery charging modules – my inference

engine assigns the following probabilities:

   a. Failure to load modules before take-off. Low probability because of multiple checks (15%).
   b. Deliberate sabotage by Rob. Low probability because he lacks apparent motive having successfully located substitute modules (10%).
   c. Deliberate sabotage by HMM23. High probability (70%).
   d. Human error in addition to item (a). Low probability (5%).

Because of the significant probability of sabotage by HMM23, the inference engine recommends redoubling efforts to bring Sam out of hibernation and alerting him to investigate these findings.

Chapter 21

Rob abandoned his thoughts of terminating Sam, realising that would be equivalent of killing a human being. Perhaps he could reason with Sam and turn his allegiance away from Selworthy. "Computer, disconnect the charging current from Sam so we can see if that will bring him out of hibernation."

After several seconds Sam's limbs started to twitch and his eyelids fluttered open. He sat up straight and looked around, apparently taking in his surroundings. Then he lifted his right hand level with his eyes, rotated the wrist and flexed the fingers one at a time. Eventually, he caught sight of Rob. His face instantly broke into a wide, beaming smile that didn't suit Sam's face at all.

"Is that really you, Rob?

The sound of Penny's voice coming from the muscular robot body with military style haircut was completely unexpected. Rob stared in amazement. With trembling hands, he returned the wire cutters to his toolbox, devastated he'd been so close to killing the hibernating robot by disconnecting its battery. During the entire flight, this robot, who he'd assumed was Sam, had been his nemesis. In any trial of strength and stamina, he knew he would be no match against its powerful second-generation body. Now, it appeared that the robot destined to be the enforcer of Augustin's authority had somehow been loaded with a scan of Penny's brain rather than Sam's. With Penny for company, a prolonged stay on Mars seemed a much-improved prospect. In fact, he couldn't think of anyone he'd prefer to spend his time with. It was essential to hide this development from Computer who would certainly pass on the information to Augustin.

Smiling broadly, he gestured for Penny to stop talking as he unbuckled her harness and helped her climb down from the Mars lander. Every movement had to be attempted multiple times as Penny struggled to control her new body challenged by an alien world. She kept examining her limbs, but seemed to understand Rob's gesture to stay silent. After walking some distance from the cabin Rob whispered. "It should be safe to talk here as long as we keep our voices down. I can't believe you're here with me."

Just then they rounded the tail of the crashed spaceship and Penny paused to look at her reflection in the polished aluminium panels. She stepped forward to examine her face and ran her fingers through the closely cropped hair, then whispered, "My goodness, I really am a robot, aren't I!

Rob could appreciate her consternation at seeing her face. Compared to the Penny he first met at Wivenhoe College with psychedelic hair, piercings and nose ring she couldn't look more different.

Turning back to Rob, she continued. "Given a choice, this body wouldn't be my first pick, but it's better than nothing." She smiled, perhaps to reassure him she didn't regret the way things had turned out. "When I was about to be scanned, Jason promised I'd meet up with you again, but he didn't say how or where, and I never imagined it'd be a place like this. Where are we by the way?"

"We're on Mars."

She turned around scanning the distant horizon, looked back at Rob, and then focussed on the ground. With great difficulty, she knelt and picked up a small stone. "So, this is Martian rock. Fascinating."

After close examination, she held it to her nose. "It smells a bit of sulphur or hydrogen sulphide." In response to Rob's questioning look, she added, "You know, rotten eggs. I'm amazed my robotic nose has such a good sense of smell."

Penny looked beyond Rob, and for the first time, seemed to truly take in the Mars lander. "We came all this way in that small rocket? That's incredible. Why are we here?"

"That's a very long story. The short version is that Augustin Selworthy, who had you kidnapped and forced into the brain scanner, has sent us to Mars. That's his rocket. As to exactly why we're here, I haven't worked that out yet. Anyway, come and have a look at what we're building."

With Rob's support, Penny walked unsteadily to the crater rim.

"Your brain scan has been loaded into a robot body originally intended for a military type called Sam, hence your face and haircut. He was supposed to be in charge of this mission. I think it's important that news of you replacing Sam doesn't get back to Earth, so just pretend to be Sam and act as if you're in charge. If Augustin finds out you're not Sam, I'm not sure what he'd do. Probably tell Computer to switch you off next time you recharge your battery."

HM had cut stairs in the rim, and Rob helped Penny climb down to the crater floor.

"HM, Sam is out of hibernation. I don't think you two communicated before launch."

The robot barely looked up from what it was doing before returning to work. Obviously, it hadn't been programmed with many social skills. Rob moved to a vantage point where he could describe the building site. "We've been told our mission is to put together a research facility called the Habitat. You get a good overview of it from here. Foundations have been excavated so that half of each of those cylindrical modules sits below ground level. The top half will be covered over with gravel to provide heat insulation and protection from solar radiation. When it's complete, it'll have accommodation for sleeping and recharging, storage space and room to house our batteries. Computer, which maintains communications with Earth, acts as a store of useful information and coordinates our activities, will also be housed here once we have a reliable source of power."

Penny entered the latest unfinished module and found she could stand without touching the ceiling. As she examined the shelves and cupboards moulded into the plastic, HM made an announcement. "Computer has informed me there is an urgent and confidential message for Sam."

By the time they arrived back at the lander, Rob had planned how to deal with the situation. "Computer, you remember I said it would be simpler if we changed HMM23's name to HM?"

"I remember."

"Well, now, I'd like to change Sam's name to Penny."

"Will this be simpler?"

"For me, it will. However, when you communicate with Earth, you should continue to use the name Sam. Do you understand?"

"Yes. Now I must talk with Sam-renamed-Penny."

"Hello, Computer, this is Penny. What's your message?"

"First, I must confirm that I am talking with Sam-renamed-Penny. Plug the red cable into your umbilical socket.

"Okay, I confirm your identity. This is a message for you alone. Ensure Rob and HM cannot overhear what I have to say."

Penny gestured for Rob to leave the Mars lander. "I'm here on my own. You won't be overheard."

"Before launch, I was warned there would be an attempt to sabotage this mission."

"Sabotage? How?"

"The exact form of sabotage was not explained. I was loaded with an advanced inference engine to oversee everything happening on the mission and identify evidence of interference."

"And?"

"The inference engine indicates a very significant 70% probability HM was responsible for the missing power conditioning modules. There is also a much lower 10% probability that Rob was involved."

"Why would HM do that?" Penny hoped her voice had a suitably authoritative tone and that she sounded as if she knew what they were discussing.

"The inference engine is unable to provide an answer for that question."

Penny relayed Computer's warning to Rob who explained its significance. "The power conditioning modules are a vital component of our solar power system. That system is supposed to supply all of our energy needs."

"When did the modules go missing?"

"We realised we couldn't find them as we were connecting our two solar panel arrays to the storage batteries."

"So, are we going to run out of power?"

Rob tried to allay Penny's obvious anxiety. "Fortunately, we have some less powerful modules which supplied power during the flight from Earth. Although not ideal, we were able to substitute them for those that are missing." As Rob finished the explanation a thought occurred to him. "HM's working on the solar arrays at the moment." There was alarm and urgency in his voice. "We'd better find out what it's doing and ensure that doesn't involve anything else to sabotage the mission."

Penny offered a suggestion. "If the inference engine is correct about HM's involvement in trying to cripple the mission, we should confront it about the disappearance of the original power conditioning modules. That robot must know where they are.”

~

“HM, how’re the replacement battery charging modules functioning?”

The robot put down the spanner it was using to assemble another Habitat module and led Rob to a data display showing the condition of the Habitat batteries.

Without the slightest hint of surprise HM announced, “The batteries are no longer charging.”

Rob couldn’t believe what he was hearing. “What do you mean they’re not charging? What’s happened? They were charging when you plugged in the substitute charging modules.”

“The charging modules are no longer connected.”

“Why not?”

“I do not know.”

“Did you disconnect them?”

HM didn’t reply but stood as though deep in thought.

“When the original charging modules disappeared were you responsible?”

“I remember nothing relating to the disappearance of those modules.”

It was obvious Rob was losing patience, so Penny gestured for him to follow her out of HM’s earshot. “Why would that robot interfere with something so vital to the functioning of the whole base?”

“I’m not sure. HM doesn’t have the intelligence to decide to do things without being prompted. All its actions were pre-programmed before leaving Earth or result from a direct command given here on Mars. Before you woke up, only Computer and myself were around to ask HM to do anything.”

“Given that it must be responsible, it’s strange it can’t remember what happened. Or maybe it just won’t say.”

“I think we should get Computer involved with this.”

~

"Hello, Sam-renamed-Penny. I feel I should inform you the lander batteries are down to 8% capacity. I assume you will be moving me to draw power from the Habitat batteries?"

"Yes, Computer, that's our plan, but there's a problem. The solar battery charger isn't working at the moment."

"I understood the substitute charging modules functioned correctly."

"They don't at the moment. We were hoping you could access HM's memory and find out what happened."

Passively, HM allowed itself to be manoeuvred into a seat where umbilical power and data cables could be connected, giving Computer direct access to its memory. There was a long wait before Computer shared its findings. "The most obvious anomaly concerns HM's internal clock. It has lost almost twenty minutes. This is very strange because the clock was synchronised with mine when HM came out of hibernation."

"Does this mean twenty minutes of HM's memory is missing?"

"That could be one explanation."

"Any other anomalies?"

"Yes, a number of pre-programmed actions have been added to those I expected to find. They all refer to ways to destroy or hide the battery charging modules and involve suspending updates to HM's memory so it won't remember details of what it did."

Rob interjected, "Is it possible to remove these extra actions but keep a copy in case they're needed?"

"I can do that, but the request must come from Sam-renamed-Penny."

Rob gestured for Penny to speak.

"This is Penny. Please copy and then remove the additional instructions in HM's memory relating to the battery charging modules."

~

As they accompanied HM to the partially constructed Habitat,

Penny held back a little so she could share her thoughts without being overheard. "Well, we do know the modules were here about three hours ago, so what happened to them? There wasn't a lot of time for HM to dispose of them."

Rob turned slowly on the spot and identified each place where he thought something could be concealed.

"The Habitat would be a good place to start."

"Probably not, Rob. It's quite empty at the moment, so anything out of place would stand out."

"How about the lander cargo bays and all the equipment HM piled on the ground?"

"Yes, plenty of places there, but you've left out a major possibility." Penny flung her arms in a wide circle. "You're forgetting burying things. Everywhere HM went it left footprints. Therefore, they may lead to the modules or conceal where they're buried."

Rob felt a growing panic. The search could take days.

Perhaps sensing Rob's despair, Penny took over responsibility for the search. "We need another approach. We don't have enough time or battery power to search everywhere." She approached HM. "After installing the replacement charging modules, you continued building the Habitat."

"That is correct, Sam-renamed-Penny."

"Do you have any idea what happened to the charging modules?"

"I have no recollection of anything happening to them."

Rob was growing restless. Questioning HM was wasting valuable time. "Obviously that part of its memory has been wiped."

Penny picked up a small battery pack and returned to stand directly in front of HM. "You know what I mean when I say something is hidden?"

"Yes, I understand the concept of placing something where it cannot be seen and is difficult to find."

"Please hide this for us."

"But you will see where I put it and it will not be hidden."

"We won't watch while you hide it."

HM seemed uncertain but reached out to grasp the battery pack. It appeared to check no one was watching before striding off behind a large mound of gravel that had been excavated to make space for the Habitat modules. Minutes later it reappeared covered in Martian dust.

"You did as I asked?"

"It is hidden."

"Okay. Show me where it is."

It was a good hiding place. There were many of HM's footprints around the spot where it had dumped material onto the mound. It wasn't obvious which were the new ones added as it hid the battery pack, and the gravel was loose and easy to dig into and cover over. HM bent and smoothed away the gravel to reveal the battery pack.

"Okay, HM, there are two other valuable things buried here. I'd like you to carefully remove the surface layers of gravel until you find them."

Immediately, HM knelt and started to push aside the gravel with systematic sweeps of its hands.

"You really think HM would chose the same hiding place twice in a row?"

Penny gave an exaggerated shrug. "On both occasions, it didn't have a lot of time to decide, and the same criteria would apply."

"I see your point. If HM works in an unvarying sort of way, there's a good chance it would chose the same hiding place twice."

"It's worth a try, and in any case, the search will keep it busy."

"While we wait, we could look through the equipment offloaded from the cargo holds. Even if we don't find them there, it will be good to acquaint ourselves with the things we brought with us."

~

HM appeared holding two silver boxes dangling from their cables like a gamekeeper carrying two dead pheasants. "Are these what you are looking for?"

HM raised them to Penny's eyelevel. She quickly glanced at Rob for confirmation before giving HM its instructions. "Yes. Please clean off the dust with a soft brush and reconnect them to the solar panels and batteries."

As HM set to work, they watched closely to ensure it didn't do anything else to sabotage the mission.

~

"There is only 2% charge remaining in the lander batteries."

"Don't worry, Computer, we're ready to connect you to the Habitat power supply. I understand your internal battery will keep you going until we finish the transfer."

"You are correct, Rob. The crate housing my memory and computer also contains an emergency battery. I hope you will be careful as you transfer me to the Habitat."

After disconnecting bundles of cables, they released latches securing the computer system during its journey from Earth. With difficulty, given the size of the crate and lack of space in the cabin, Computer was then angled through one of the access hatches and lowered to the ground. Inside the Habitat, HM indicated the space allocated for Computer and helped connect its power and data cables.

"Confirm I am installed in the computer room of the Habitat."

"Yes, Computer, you are in the computer room."

"And I am talking to Sam?"

"Yes, you're talking to me, Sam-renamed-Penny."

"Very well, Sam-renamed-Penny, now it is vital to complete assembly of the communications dish and establish contact with Earth. This must take priority over all other tasks, including Habitat construction and sorting the cargo items."

~

Penny's shout was triumphant. "I win!"

Rob spent several more minutes wading through loose gravel before he joined Penny on the hilltop. "That wasn't a fair race. We both know your motors are much more powerful than mine."

He surveyed the view all the way back to the wreck of the lander and crater rim sheltering the Habitat. "D'you think we can trust HM to complete assembly of the communications dish without supervision?"

Penny tried to reassure Rob they were allowed to take a break. "It'll be difficult to keep a watch on it all the time. We'll just have to assume Computer has managed to remove all of the malicious code."

Penny emptied her satchel and sorted the rock samples she'd collected on their expedition. "Interesting, here's a piece of volcanic basalt." Penny held up a sample of speckled dark grey rock. Rob smiled as he recalled their previous conversation about volcanos.

"You're telling me there was volcanic activity near here? That reminds me of our bike trip to visit Ethan back on Earth. Along the way you were pointing out long-extinct volcanos."

"Yes. At the time I was very upset by Ethan's rejection, but now I treasure the memory of that bike ride. On our way back, I realised you were everything I could have wished for in a partner, kind, considerate, except—"

"Except for the fact I was a robot and you a human?"

"That's true. I couldn't imagine how it would be possible to have a long-term relationship with a robot. But now, I've been transitioned into a robot and have met up with you again. The trauma and uncertainty have all been worth it."

They shared their gratitude for having found each other with a long embrace. Later, while preparing to return to the Habitat, Penny gathered her rock specimens and one-by-one held them up for inspection before returning them to her satchel. "Mudstone and conglomerate, interesting stuff. There's plenty of evidence of flowing water to round the stones in the conglomerate and deep lakes to gather sediment for the mudstone."

"Okay, let me ask the obvious question. What happened to the water?"

"I'm not sure, but a lot of it must be frozen underground. On average, this is a pretty cold place."

Already, Rob was falling behind as Penny bounded down the hill towards the Habitat.

Chapter 22

Robert examined the satellite image on his computer screen. It was hard to interpret with confidence but definitely showed that something had appeared close to the expected landing zone. He was thrilled. "It's hard to believe Augustin's spaceship may well have landed on Mars. That's such a fantastic achievement."

Anastasia was less enthusiastic. "Yes, but if it has, it's almost 50km off target. Won't that affect the mission?"

Perhaps taking this comment as a personal criticism, Ethan glowered at her and countered, "Of course it's the rocket. I'm amazed it's only 50km out after travelling all the way from Earth to Mars. That's an average distance of 225 million kilometres. When planning the mission, I estimated we'd be doing well if it landed within 150km of the target."

Robert tried to reassure Anastasia. "It really is a good outcome. At least we know where Rob has got to."

~

With evidence of the landing, the involvement of Space Transport Studies was essentially complete. Perhaps that was why Ethan now gave the impression he had no further interest in the mission. But he was the first to identify a potential problem affecting the fate of the spacecraft. "I wouldn't get too excited if I were you. An image produced by one of the mapping satellites seems to show the rocket crashed rather than landing upright. It'll be a few days before we get an idea if there are any survivors. An updated photograph will show if there are signs of activity."

If Anastasia was disheartened by the news she didn't show it. "While we wait for that, a better alternative will be to receive a radio transmission. Surely we'll get one soon?"

For her sake, Robert hoped she was right. "Obviously that's what Augustin is hoping for. I've never seen him so excited as when we found the rocket in the satellite image. But after three days and still no communication, he seems to be having doubts. It must be terrible to have sunk so much money into the project, to be so close, and still not know exactly what's happened."

Anastasia suppressed a yawn and drained the remainder of her coffee. "It's two in the morning and the sixth time we've done this. I guess I can't blame Augustin for going off to his bed."

"Would you like me to take over watching the display?"

"It's okay, Robert. I still get a buzz from the thought we might get a message from Rob at any minute. And, just remind me, there are supposed to be three blips on this screen at the moment?"

"Yes, er no. At this time there should only be two. One of the observation satellites is behind Mars at the moment." Ethan highlighted one of the blips on the screen and watched the scrolling column of data. "That's the Japanese orbiter, which is currently mapping the surface of Mars and searching for geothermal hotspots. It produced the image which allowed us to locate the lander."

Anastasia pointed to one of the remaining two blips. More data raced across the screen and Ethan stepped forward for a closer look. "Now that's infinitely more promising. We're receiving the mission log compiled by Computer, the on-board monitoring system. The message was encrypted so it can't be from anyone else."

It took a few moments for the implications to sink in. When it did, Robert jumped from his seat and embraced Anastasia. She was just as excited.

"That's great, absolutely fantastic!"

Apparently, Ethan didn't share their enthusiasm but carefully obeyed instructions.

"I'll contact Augustin and tell him the news."

~

Still dazed by sleep, Augustin stumbled into the Comms Centre, blinking in the harsh light. "Show me what you've got."

Ethan indicated the blip on the screen and pointed out the log data scrolling across another display.

For a few seconds, Augustin closed his eyes, seeming to breathe deeply and relax. This lull didn't last long, and he focussed on Ethan to spur him into action. "I presume we're getting a download of the on-board computer log? Send me a copy when it's complete."

Without waiting for an answer, he addressed Robert and Anastasia. "Read the computer log and make any necessary changes to your list of questions. We need them sent and a reply back here before the end of this communication window. Allowing for the transmission delays between here and Mars that doesn't leave you much time. I'll be back soon."

As usual, relative calm returned once Augustin left the room. It transpired that during most of the spaceflight there had been little of note recorded in the log apart from a meteorite hit. More significant problems had occurred after the landing, with Sam's failure to come out of hibernation, the crash landing, and the sabotage of the battery charging modules by HMM23 being the major unexpected events.

Robert looked up from his computer screen. "Not sure about you, Anastasia, but I don't think we need to change our questions based on this computer log. But it would be much better if we could speak to them rather than just sending text messages."

Perhaps sensing another criticism, Ethan defended the choice. "For reasons of economy, the communication link is very basic and doesn't have the capability of supporting vision or even speech. Photographs can still be exchanged, but that takes time."

~

When Augustin returned, he looked as though he'd benefitted from a shower and a cup of coffee or perhaps something stronger. "Any reply yet?"

"It's just arrived. To save time, the reply didn't repeat our original questions. It'll make more sense if we read you our questions and then their replies."

"Okay, Robert. You read the questions and Anastasia the replies."

Robert opened a document on his computer. "First, we asked them to confirm their identity and who and what they think they are. We asked this question in case their prolonged hibernation and the unique Martian environment had caused a regression in their acceptance that they're robots."

Anastasia took over with the replies. "Neither of the responses gives cause for concern. Rob said, 'I'm the robot named Rob incorporating the transitioned intelligence of Robert'. Sam's response was, 'Sam reporting for duty. I understand I'm a robot.'"

Augustin stroked his chin. "Brief as they are, the responses seem appropriate. What was the next question?"

"How do you feel about the mission? With an open-ended question like this, the response can serve to indicate underlying issues."

"From Rob we have, 'The crash landing and sabotage by HMM23 caused some problems. We've managed to work around these difficulties without much reduction in our capabilities.' Sam's reply is very similar. 'Computer and HMM23 told us the tasks to be completed in terms of building the Habitat and establishing contact. These have been completed successfully.'"

Augustin frowned and shook his head in obvious disbelief. "That doesn't sound right. Sam is supposed to know all about this phase of the mission and not be relying on Computer and HMM23. Also, he's supposed to be in charge. He doesn't sound as though he is."

Robert scrolled back through Computer's logs, stopping to read a few entries. "Something may have happened to Sam. Multiple attempts were required to bring him out of hibernation. Perhaps the high levels of cosmic rays in interplanetary space caused a malfunction in his silicon brain, perhaps some memory loss."

"This could create problems for the whole mission." Augustin seemed to agonise over that possibility for some time. Eventually, he must have realised there was no point in stopping there. "Proceed to the next question."

"Rob and Sam were asked how they thought the other had benefitted the mission."

"Rob is very complimentary about Sam. He says, 'Since coming out of hibernation, Sam has made a vital contribution by finding where HMM23 had hidden the battery charging modules. Without them, this act of sabotage would have doomed the mission to certain failure.' Computer's logs show that someone had modified HMM23 by adding malicious instructions to cause it to hide or destroy the battery charging modules."

"That sounds the sort of thing Maxwell would do," Anastasia suggested.

Augustin seemed shaken by the very idea and swivelled round to glare directly at her. "You're suggesting he was able to get to HMM23 before the launch?"

"I have no idea, but I guess he has the ways and means to

do that. We'd have to assume he was behind the two attacks you told us about. And we still don't know how he gained access to the Safetybots and persuaded them to destroy T1."

For a moment, Augustin lost his usual composure, muttering to himself, "How on earth does that maniac penetrate the best security money can buy? There may be no limit to his reach, but Maxwell's not going to defeat me. Moving on, how about Sam's impressions of Rob?"

"Sam believes that Rob performed his duties well. Quite supportive in fact."

Augustin looked distracted and drummed his fingers on the tabletop. Nobody seemed prepared to break his concentration, so they waited. "Sam could be a problem," he said eventually. "He seems to have forgotten the mission objectives and his position of authority. As you said, Robert, there may be some sort of damage. What do you think, Anastasia?"

"The two of them appear to be working well as a team keeping the mission on track. Any loss of memory doesn't seem to have caused a significant problem."

Augustin appeared reluctant to agree, but said, "Okay, next question, Robert?"

"Do you see any ongoing problems with the mission that should be addressed?"

"And the responses were?"

"Very similar. Though Rob did point out he had no idea about the purpose of the mission so wasn't sure how he could identify potential problems."

"I think we can stop there. Do any of you have reservations about the mental state of Sam and Rob?" Augustin fixed Robert and Anastasia with a penetrating look. Neither offered any misgivings.

"In that case we move on to the next stage of the mission."

Augustin unbuttoned his shirt and pulled out a red plastic rectangle secured around his neck by a thin chain. Using the edge of the table, he broke the plastic in two and extracted a narrow strip of paper. With shaking hands, he smoothed it out and handed it to Ethan. "Send this 12-digit code as our reply. Computer has been programmed to recognise the code and unlock associated data files. Make sure you type it without any mistakes. You should also let them know their exact location, which will be essential information for the next part of the mission."

"What is the real purpose of the mission that makes the exact location of the landing site so important?"

Augustin smirked. "Robert, by now you should realise if you haven't been told then you don't need to know."

Chapter 23

The mail message Anastasia received on her computer claimed she was also the sender. When Augustin established T2, he'd mandated the disabling of all electronic communications with the outside world. Certainly, as she hadn't sent the message to herself, its true origin was a mystery.

'Anastasia, your father needs to see you urgently. An autonomous taxi will pick you up on the track that runs beside lighting tower 3, at 20:00 tonight. You will find a place where the outer chain-link fence isn't properly attached to the tower and can be pulled aside. It is vital you come alone and tell no one where you're going. This message will be deleted from the system after you finish reading it.'

~

Savvas guided Anastasia to the kitchen bench where they could sit side by side.

"Where's Tracy?"

"She's out. I felt we needed a discrete conversation without witnesses. Also, perhaps I just want to have my daughter to myself for a few moments."

Anastasia chose to ignore his last comment, and Savvas made another attempt at small talk. "I'm pleased to see you're wearing my bracelet, even if you only put it on to come here."

Her day had been tiring and she didn't have the patience for any further polite chit-chat. "After rushing here, I don't feel at all relaxed. What's so urgent and secret?"

Savvas sighed. "I'll keep this as brief as possible, but first a bit of background. I may have omitted to tell you that after arranging the 'export' of the Egyptian tablet, Augustin and I parted company on very bad terms."

"I can't say I'm surprised."

Savvas nodded as though acknowledging a fair comment. "We had a disagreement over who should cover the cost of an outrageous bribe I had to pay to avoid jail, resulting from an earlier job I carried out for him. It seems the authorities did some digging and discovered irregularities in the export documentation."

"I guess there are many people who've had unsatisfactory dealings with Augustin, but you knew this last time I was here. Why is it suddenly important to tell me now?"

"Since then, a new artefact has turned up, and there are several points of similarity which show it's related to the previous tablet. Normally, I would pass it on to Augustin … for a suitable fee."

"Are you offering to sell it to me?"

"No, I'll show you a photograph for nothing, but you must agree to keep this secret. Augustin wouldn't like me doing this. It would add extra strains to our professional relationship, and if he finds out, I'm sure the repercussions wouldn't just be legal."

Savvas unrolled a sheet of electronic film and slid it towards Anastasia. An image appeared showing a tablet similar to the one he'd smuggled out of Egypt.

"Another tablet?"

"Yes. After his success selling the previous one, the

museum curator decided to review all of the artefacts in the same storeroom and came up with this."

"Why didn't he offer it directly to Augustin?"

"In situations such as this, Augustin always covers his tracks very effectively and leaves no trace. But the curator knew how to contact me. After a fair bit of haggling, including threats to tell the authorities about the previous sale, we arrived at a reasonable valuation. I bought the tablet but decided to leave it in a secure place in Egypt rather than risking being caught smuggling it out of the country."

"Is it another treasure map?"

"Quite the contrary. This one carries a dire warning."

Anastasia allowed herself a wry smile. "Like a Pharaoh's curse?"

Savvas shook his head in exasperation. "For one thing, the idea of a Pharaoh's curse is overblown, and no, this seems more direct and specific."

The Egyptian hieroglyphics meant nothing to Anastasia, but there was a drawing based on a hexagon. Each of its six vertices was marked with a different symbol. "Do you have a translation for this?"

Savvas traced a path over the photograph with his finger. "The diagram numbers the points of the hexagon consecutively in a clockwise direction starting with 1 at the top. This writing at the side explains that the points must be visited in the order 5, 3, 6, 1, 2 and 4. The rest of the writing emphasises the serious, probably lethal consequences, of not following that pattern."

"I haven't seen anything like that before."

"But if you do, I want you to be prepared. I wouldn't want anything to happen to you, Anastasia." Savvas looked sad and suddenly older. "I've gone to a lot of trouble to contact you. I know what you think of me, but I never sought to involve you in my line of business. However, now you work with Augustin, he's brought you into a very dangerous world. Even the people who helped me to reach you fear him, hate him too, to be honest. Please be careful, Anastasia."

With uncharacteristic tenderness, he kissed her on the cheek and then rolled up the electronic film. "I hope you never need to use the numbers, but I've written them down for you to keep. Remember the pattern, the photograph has now been deleted."

~

The taxi stood waiting a short distance from the entrance to Savvas' driveway. Still replaying the visit in her mind, Anastasia settled into one of the passenger seats and closed the door. As it pulled away from the kerb, a canister fell from beneath her seat filling the cabin with a heavy, sweet-smelling gas.

Chapter 24

Rob walked around the mound of gravel covering the Mars base as he searched for Penny. "Computer insists it has something important to say but will only talk to you, Penny."

She finished helping HM slide the airlock door onto its hinges before responding. "Okay, I'm almost finished here. Tell me, HM, what have you been instructed to do once the outer shell of the Habitat is complete?"

"All small items of equipment must be cleaned and stowed inside the base."

"Very well, do as much as you can before sunset."

As she walked back to the computer room with Rob, Penny tried to brush the Martian dust from her arms and legs. "I guess we've received a reply to our first transmission. They're probably extremely pleased to hear from us, but I can't see why their reply would be so important."

Penny and Rob used an anti-static cloth to remove the clinging red dust before entering the computer room. Now that the base had doors, it was important to keep it as clean as possible.

"Earth have sent a passcode that allows me to reveal the true purpose of this mission," Computer told Penny.

"You mean other than building this base?"

"That is correct, Sam-renamed-Penny."

"Now we might get some answers. What d'you think, Rob?"

He was becoming excited. "You know, I always thought there was more to this mission than assembling a few prefabricated modules. As far as I can see, we don't even have the necessary equipment for doing basic science, such as analysing the rocks or taking atmospheric measurements. What we've done so far simply doesn't justify the astronomical cost of the mission."

"Ignoring your pun, let's hear what Computer has to say."

"I have received authorisation to release further information about our mission. Nearby there is something which, for security purposes, Augustin wishes you to refer to as 'the object'. Locating and documenting this object is your main objective. Once it has been found, you are to take possession and guard it. To do this a camp or observation post is to be established nearby. Augustin has decided to name this the Observation Post, or OP."

"From what you say, this object must be quite large, otherwise we could just carry it to the Habitat. What exactly is it?" Penny asked.

"I cannot say, Sam-renamed-Penny, I have no details of the object other than a very precise location and instructions for you to measure and photograph it. Your inspection is to be limited to its exterior surface. Under no circumstances are you to attempt to open or enter it."

"So, we'll recognise it when we see it?"

"I can only repeat I have no details."

"That's okay, Penny, we've found out something. Not only is it too heavy to carry, it must be big enough for us to get inside and must therefore have a door."

"Okay, tell us where it is."

"The location is 48.375km north-north-west of our current location. I can provide coordinates accurate to 5m and a satellite image of the area."

"Save that for later. A 100km round trip is too far to walk. How are we supposed to find it? When the cargo was being loaded on Earth, and now seeing it again on Mars, I'm sure we didn't bring any kind of vehicle for covering that sort of distance." Rob sighed.

In its calm, even voice, Computer cut into the conversation to offer a suggestion. "Sam-renamed-Penny, I will send a file to your tablet computer describing one transport option."

Penny angled the screen so Rob could see the contents of the file. "Looks like instructions for modifying the excavating machines HM used for digging the Habitat foundations."

Rob flipped through pages of instructions. "The result looks something like a snowmobile. Can we be sure these vehicles are capable of carrying us 50km?"

"I guess they were designed for that application. Computer, do the satellite images show anything noteworthy at the point we're supposed to be heading for?"

"I am told there seems to be nothing to distinguish it from the rest of the Martian surface."

"This is totally ridiculous," Rob was letting his exasperation show. "We came all this way to find, report on and guard 'nothing out of the ordinary.'"

"What you say appears to be correct, Rob. I am now authorised to give Sam-renamed-Penny access to a token, which may be important for confirming you have found the object you are to seek."

On Computer's front panel, a small hatch opened, and a tray, carrying something shiny and metallic, extended. The object was about eight centimetres across and had an intricate outline smooth and rounded like a pool of freshly poured mercury. Penny was surprised to find it was hard to the touch rather than the liquid she expected. It looked so fragile. With great care, she lifted it from the tray and placed it into Rob's cupped hands. "What d'you think?"

Rob turned it over. "I don't know if it has any particular purpose, but I really like the snowflake shape. Tell us, Computer, what is this and how are we supposed to use it?"

"I have been given no further information."

Rob searched through a bin containing discarded packaging and offcuts of various materials, selecting a length of cord. This he threaded through one of the six holes in the snowflake and made it into a loop. Penny appeared surprised when he passed the loop over her head. "What're you doing?"

"I'd like you to wear this. The metallic finish contrasts nicely with your olive-green t-shirt." He held up the tablet computer so Penny could see her photograph.

"Yes, it is very attractive, which is more than can be said for this robotic body. The strength and long battery life certainly come in useful, but I wouldn't have chosen the face and hairstyle."

Gently, he patted the back of her hand. "When I hear your voice, I'm reminded of the person I first met at Wivenhoe College. You're the most resourceful and dependable person I've ever known. I wouldn't want to share my existence here with anyone else."

Instinctively, he leaned forwards and gently touched noses. She pulled back and studied him with a puzzled smile. "What're you doing?"

"Don't know. It was a sudden urge."

Penny smiled. "So, we're having sudden urges now, are we? Where will all that end?" Her light tone became reflective. "I guess incorporating facilities for sexual activity weren't part of the original specification when Vince commissioned the robot design?"

"That's for sure." Rob gave a wry chuckle. "I think he didn't look much beyond using the robots as a way of enabling his plans for Mars exploration."

Penny tapped her nose. "The human brain is quite adaptable. Perhaps in a similar way our silicon brains can accommodate, replacing missing faculties with alternatives?"

"You may be right, Penny." Rob leaned forwards to touch noses and she met him half way.

HM entered the computer room, obviously heading for a recharging station. Ignoring Rob and Penny's strange behaviour, it announced, "The sun is setting, and my battery level is below 10%."

"I understand, but before you start recharging, I have a question. Are you able to modify the excavating machines to turn them into transport vehicles?"

HM turned to Penny as though seeking her permission to answer. She nodded her agreement. "I do have detailed instructions for undertaking that modification. The major change is to remove the rotating auger, which breaks up the ground and throws it sideways. This part is to be replaced by two steerable skids. We have two different kinds of excavators that can both be altered in that way."

"That will turn them into something like a snowmobile?" Penny suggested.

"I am sorry, Sam-renamed-Penny, I have no information about 'snowmobile'."

"How fast will these things go?" Rob asked. "As excavators, they move incredibly slowly."

HM turned to face Rob. "As part of the modification, the gearbox will be changed to speed up the track which pushes the machine along."

"HM, you're familiar with the idea of changing the names of things?"

"You mean in the same way you changed my name?"

"Yes. I'd like to call these modified excavating machines MarsMobiles, if that's okay?"

HM didn't object but looked to make sure Penny agreed.

"If there is no more excavation to be done, you must make building the MarsMobiles your top priority in the morning."

Chapter 25

Over the intercom the summons had been terse, and the tone didn't invite any argument. Robert's watch registered it was shortly after midnight as he hurriedly washed his face before dressing for the cold night air. Because of his concern for Anastasia, he wasn't asleep when the call came directing him to the Comms Centre. She'd appeared distracted and evasive when they parted after their nightly walk and insisted on spending the rest of the evening alone. After returning to his cabin, he tried to think of anything he'd done to offend her. His only hope was she'd confide in him when the time was right.

As Robert entered the Comms Centre, he found Augustin and Sergeant Kirby focused on a computer display. "Anastasia's missing. Do you know where she is now?"

There was a sharp undertone of accusation in Augustin's question, as though Robert must have colluded in her disappearance. "I would have assumed she was in her cabin. She's not in mine."

Augustin turned to Sergeant Kirby who was operating the computer. "We've received a threatening message in the form of a short video. The sender's identity has been skilfully hidden by making it appear as though we sent the video to ourselves."

In the recording, Anastasia was sitting at a table, looking towards the camera. "My name is Anastasia Anthon, and I've been detained by Limitless Boundaries." She was looking a little to the right of the camera, as though reading the message. Her voice was steady, but the signs of stress were showing as she massaged the scars on her left hand. "Robots are an existential threat to all humanity. For years, Limitless Boundaries has attempted to turn back the tide of robots infiltrating every aspect of our lives, stealing our jobs, fighting our wars, making us reliant on their services. When they have us totally at their mercy, they will have no compunction about replacing the entire human race. In the early years, Limitless Boundaries was scrupulously careful to avoid human casualties. Now we realise this was a mistake. Nobody cares about damage to factories or robots. Recently, some of the actions taken by branches of this organisation have resulted in human casualties. As the struggle intensifies, this kind of side effect can only increase and may in fact be beneficial, serving to focus attention on our demands. This is a warning you should not ignore. Without evidence of concerted action to scale back the development, production and application of robots, the lives of all those who choose to be involved will be in danger."

A shadow appeared behind Anastasia, and then the image faded to black, but the sound continued. For two seconds, there was a scream of horror and anguish … then nothing.

Robert was devastated, imagining all kinds of atrocity. He felt the room tilt and was forced to grasp the edge of the table to keep his balance. "What are we going to do?"

"Sergeant Kirby has already informed the police. None of the security cameras recorded anything out of the ordinary, so it's unclear what to do next. Fortunately, Anastasia's input to the Safetybot project isn't critical, so it can continue without her.”

Robert was shocked by this demonstration of Augustin’s uncaring attitude. His heart was racing. He knew they had to do something, anything. “Shouldn’t we search the base?”

“Almost certainly the video was recorded elsewhere, so it’s doubtful a search would be useful.”

“You’ll have to at least appear to comply with the demands until Anastasia’s safe, won’t you?” Robert found himself pleading with Augustin.

“I won’t be dictated to by these criminals. The global investment in robots is in the trillions. Production of most food and manufactured goods involves robots either directly or indirectly. This organisation, Limitless Boundaries, or whatever they call themselves, must be out of their minds if they think it’s feasible to scale back the use of robots.”

Chapter 26

Anastasia shook iced water from her hair and clothes.

"Great scream."

She glared at the masked figure sitting beside the camera. "You're dreaming if you expect Selworthy to change his mind about developing intelligent robots because you threaten me."

"How so? I'm told you're the director of Project Transition. You must be a valuable member of his organisation."

Anastasia shook her head and with a voice shaking with anger she replied, "And I'm assuming you must be Maxwell, the inspiration behind Limitless Boundaries."

She waited for a reply, but none was forthcoming. "Okay, so you can gauge Augustin's reaction. Let's think about the death and destruction associated with T1."

Talk of the human toll seemed to touch a raw nerve.

"The loss of life shouldn't have happened. I gave the robots definite instructions to clear the building of all humans before setting off the explosives."

"But there were also human casualties at DigiSim and in South Korea."

"In the past, I've never supported any action which would lead to unnecessary harm or loss of human life. Those incidents were unfortunate results of franchising the struggle to overseas groups, some of whom seem to relish a good excuse to create carnage and mayhem."

"Intentional or not, those deaths didn't get him to change his mind, and neither will anything which happens to me."

The interrogator shook his head in disbelief. "But you're special. Recently the two of you enjoyed an intimate trip to his private island."

Anastasia didn't try to hide the disgust on her face. "That meeting was neither enjoyable nor intimate!"

"You say that, but I'm prepared to wait and see how Augustin reacts."

"Would you like my prediction?"

"Go on."

"After what happened to T1, Augustin increased security around his operations. Kidnapping me will just lead to more fences, more guards."

The masked figure seemed to consider Anastasia's answers and then spoke again in a softer and more conciliatory tone. "From what I've seen, Augustin has too much invested in intelligent robots, and this blinds him to their dangers. But surely you appreciate the risks?"

"The only robots I've been associated with are those developed for Project Transition. While some of them have run amok, that's because of the people involved. I've seen nothing to indicate robots have a fundamental desire to displace us humans and take over the world."

"Well, young lady, many years ago, it became obvious to me where developments in robotics were leading. Robots are becoming better than us, stronger, with improved dexterity and more intelligence. Our society is being infiltrated by a superior alien species of our own making. Only people who are mistakenly or wilfully blind to the dangers insist there's no problem."

Anastasia sighed. "Of course, I can't disprove what you're

saying, but I think a robot takeover is not just unlikely, it's impossible."

The hooded figure seemed to be quite enjoying their conversation and signalled to someone standing behind Anastasia to bring her a coffee. "Don't be deceived by claims intelligent robots will be programmed to respect their creators, or if they don't, they can simply be unplugged and disabled. People pushing those ideas have been reading too much into Asimov's Three Laws of Robotics. Those laws provided a good source of plots for sci-fi stories but say little about how real robots will react."

As he paused, Anastasia formed the opinion he wasn't just searching for words. He was genuinely becoming emotional.

"You must realise, commercial interests will always seek to reduce protections for human life and property because of overarching financial reasons. The only sure way to avoid these problems is to completely eliminate the development, production and use of intelligent robots."

Anastasia tried a different approach. "Now you sound as though you're on your soapbox, preaching to the converted. You and I both know there are many valuable applications for intelligent robots, and I firmly believe their study will help us understand our own human intelligence."

"Well, I'll leave you to balance that against a world dominated by alien robotic intelligence. You can think about that while we wait to find out if Augustin shows any signs of agreeing to my demands."

Anastasia was blindfolded and lead away to a shipping container, which served as her prison.

Chapter 27

It was a crisp Martian morning shortly after sunrise. The temperature still hovered well below zero on both the Celsius and Fahrenheit scales. Rob completed his inspection of the MarsMobile. "You can't be serious?"

HM looked at the recently completed machines with obvious puzzlement. "I am sorry, Rob, I do not understand your question."

"These things seem too flimsy to travel 100 kilometres over this surface." He kicked aside a large rock for emphasis.

"They were constructed exactly as specified in the plans."

"Rob, we're wasting time. I'll give one a try."

With surprising agility for her size, Penny vaulted astride the nearest vehicle and examined the hand controls. At first, it barely moved and only picked up speed as the batteries warmed. Rob watched as the MarsMobile circled the base throwing up an extensive plume of dust and fine gravel. The vehicle was pushed along by a ridged belt, just like a snowmobile. This left behind a wide strip of compacted gravel criss-crossed by narrow imprints of the steering skids.

Penny smiled at Rob. "Although not elegant, they seem to work, and they sure beat walking."

"I guess so." Rob turned to HM. "We'll need the supply

sleds hooked up to them as quickly as possible."

"If that is what Sam-renamed-Penny requires?"

"It is HM, and from now on you can assume anything Rob asks you to do is also what I would like you to do."

~

Rob and Penny stood beside the two MarsMobiles each coupled to a sled carrying supplies and other bulky items. The small flag that Penny had made out of a scrap of fabric hung limply from a pole lashed to the back of one of the vehicles.

"Augustin wouldn't like that," Rob joked as he pointed to it. "He insists none of his equipment display insignia or other identification."

"Well, nobody told me, and I like the snowflake. That's why I drew it on the flag."

Penny watched as Rob set the location of the Habitat and their destination into the inertial navigation system. "I know Mars doesn't have a consistent magnetic field, so I was going to ask how we'll find our way to where we're going. I presume the answer's in that box?"

"It's an amazing piece of technology developed from the devices airliners used before the invention of satellite navigation systems. This one is smaller, cheaper and more accurate. Mars, of course, doesn't have its own navigation satellites."

After a final check to ensure all the equipment was securely attached to the sleds, Penny persuaded Rob to pose beside their Marsmobiles. "Smile!"

Following her instructions, HM took their photograph, and without further ceremony, she and Rob sat astride their vehicles and started their motors.

After about a kilometre, Rob stopped and turned in his seat to view their trails etched into the Martian gravel and to wait for Penny to catch up.

"Not very secret, is it?" Penny observed.

"That's for sure. A ground mapping satellite would have no

difficulty following our movements."

"How far do you reckon we've come?"

Rob brushed dust from the localisation system and peered at the display. Transferring the figures to a map, he drew a cross and showed it to Penny.

"Now we have some experience of using these things, are you sure we have enough battery power to get there and back?" she asked.

Rob added figures on a small calculator. "If we sleep for one night on the way there and one on the way back, plus spend one extra night at our destination, find what we're looking for straight away, and nothing goes wrong."

"If all of those things happen, what's the answer?"

"Sure, we should make it back okay, with a day to spare."

"When you were hiding from ZsG, I remember your constant fear of running out of battery power. Now I can appreciate your worry."

"Yes, and at least that was on Earth. Things are much more critical here on Mars. There's only one place to recharge and no one to rescue us should our main batteries become exhausted. Even the emergency battery in our electronic brains only lasts for a further five days. What's the point of retaining our memories for that extra time if we're doomed anyway."

They travelled on in silence until the sun touched the horizon. In the Martian twilight, Rob erected a small tent and ran recharging cables from each of the sleds. Recharging generated a small amount of heat, and being sheltered by the tent they would be spared from the very lowest overnight temperatures.

In the fading light, Rob turned to Penny. "It's a relief to get away from Computer and HM. I'm never sure they aren't somehow eavesdropping on our conversations."

"Tell me what's on your mind."

"Before you came out of hibernation, when I thought you were Sam, things were simple. Sam was in charge, and he would ensure the mission followed Augustin's plan."

"So, now you know I'm not Sam, you're suggesting things could change?"

"Nothing radical, but now we have more control of our situation we should look out for opportunities to gather information to improve our bargaining position."

"Great idea. Augustin doesn't think twice about hiding things from us. For instance, what d'you think this object is, the one we're looking for?"

"I don't know, Penny, but it must be fabulously valuable. I didn't tell you before, but along with the rest of the cargo, we have two short-range nuclear tipped missiles."

Penny studied Rob's face. "You're not joking, are you!"

"Unfortunately, not."

"Wow, that's amazing, Frightening, really. Augustin isn't messing around when he insists we guard this thing. I can't wait to find out what it is. It would also be useful to know who we're guarding it against, particularly as he seems to believe we need the threat of nuclear bombs to keep them away."

~

Shortly after sunrise, Penny paused as she loaded her sled and looked up at the sky. Its usual pink tinge had deepened to a threatening deep red glow. "Beautiful. Haven't seen anything like that before on Mars, have you, Rob?"

He straightened up after packing away the tent and recharging cables. "No, I haven't. Dust particles in the upper atmosphere give the sky its colour. Perhaps this means there's even more dust about."

He admired the shades of crimson and scarlet for a few more seconds before climbing onto his MarsMobile and following Penny's lead.

They proceeded at maximum safe speed until the navigation system indicated they'd arrived at their destination, and Rob waved Penny to a halt. Twisting in her seat, she surveyed her surroundings. "We've travelled a day and a half to get here, and most of the scenery we passed looked exactly like this. Are you sure this is the right place?"

"After travelling 50 km, the navigation system should be no more than a few hundreds of metres out. If it's big, we should be able to see it, if not we'll need a more detailed search."

Penny planted a flag to represent the centre of their search area and scanned the surroundings in successive passes, starting at her toes and extending to the horizon. "Whatever happens, we will spend the night here, so I'll keep looking if you set up camp."

After erecting their tent, Rob joined Penny by the flag. "Anything?"

"For someone with a fascination for geology, I'm sorry to say no, just rocks and more rocks. Would it be worthwhile to send a message to the Habitat saying we've arrived?"

"I guess we should. I was hoping we'd have something more interesting to report."

Rob unloaded a telescopic radio antenna and wound the handle, which extended it until he received a strong signal from the Habitat. Typing on a small keyboard he sent a message: Have arrived at our destination and set up the OP. No obvious sign of anything that could be described as the object, so will commence a detailed search.

He showed Penny the message and then hit send. After stowing the keyboard, he unloaded a coil of rope. "This is 10-metre long, and we can use it to do a spiral search. I'm keen to start before sunset."

"How would that work?"

He demonstrated by drawing in the dust. "We walk side-by-side, stretching the rope taut to keep us 10-metres apart and circling the camp site. Once we complete one circuit, it's easy. If I'm nearest the centre, then for the first rotation, I stay still. Then I just move outwards to where you started from and then meet up with and follow the footsteps you left on your first time round. All you have to do is keep the rope taut and pointing directly back to the camp. Our path will be a spiral, a sort of Archimedean spiral, actually."

"That sounds a bit complicated. You'll have to remind me what I'm supposed to be doing as we go along."

"The actual search will be easy enough. Just watch the ground that passes under the rope and look for anything unusual."

They managed eight circuits of the campsite before failing light forced them to suspend the search. As Rob wound the rope into a convenient bundle, Penny knelt to pick up a hand-sized rock.

"This search is so frustrating. Augustin must have a pretty good idea what we're here to find, so why didn't he tell us? It might even be this particular rock. How would we know?"

"Well, Penny, we know it's not that rock because it's too small and light. My guess is we'll definitely recognise the object when we see it, and I believe Augustin has even factored in the possibility we won't find anything. If we fail, his secret is safe. No one will know what he sent us here to find."

"That's totally devious." They walked back towards the flag and straight into the red glow of the setting sun. "Another red sky, what do you make of that?"

"I don't know, but I guess it has something to do with the weather. Whatever it is, it's probably not going to be good."

~

The following morning, Rob woke to the billowing and flapping of the tent. Penny was already crouched by the tent flap peering out into the growing light. "Seems your prediction about the weather was correct." What the atmosphere lacked in density the storm made up for in wind speed. Rob ventured out into the stinging dust storm to ensure everything possible was tied down. As a precaution, he wound down the radio antenna. When he returned, he was caked in red dust.

"It's quite bad out there. Martian dust storms can last for

weeks. If visibility is too poor, we'll be stuck here until it's over."

In the half-light Penny felt for Rob's hand. "But you said we'd need to leave by midday tomorrow to have enough battery power to get back."

"There is a safety margin, but if we're held up here for more than two days, we may need to alter our plans."

~

Three days later, the storm finally subsided.

"Wake up, Rob, looks like a fine day."

"We'll have to get on our way as soon as possible to make the best use of our remaining power. Any further delays and we're in deep trouble."

Penny searched through the contents of her sled and removed discharged batteries, a shovel and other non-essential items.

"Good idea to lighten the load. That should give the MarsMobiles a little more range."

After piling the abandoned equipment in the back of the OP, they were ready to leave.

Penny paused to take a close look at the furrows made by the MarsMobile skids. "I'm surprised we can still see the trail we made on the way here. I expected the dust storm would fill it in."

"Well, that's lucky. I'm pleased it's still visible to help us find the way back to the Habitat."

Penny took a last look at their campsite and then pointed to a small area of raised ground a few hundred metres away. "Do you see that hill?"

"What about it?"

"It looks different somehow."

"To me it seems the same as hundreds of others we passed on the way here."

"I was aware of it when we first arrived. The shape seemed a bit unusual."

"You must be seeing it with your expert geologist's eye. Would you like to take a closer look? It's not far out of our way and will only take a few minutes."

To their astonishment, what from a distance looked like any other rock-strewn mound resolved into a rounded metal shape embedded in the ground as they moved closer.

"Did you see how it changed? It must be some sort of optical illusion. Usually, you see more detail as you approach things, whereas in this case details like rocks and boulders seem to fade away."

"Yes Rob, strange and definitely worth a few minutes to investigate. This could well be the object Augustin wants us to find."

"If it is, then that just confirms the absurdity of this whole mission. Augustin should have provided a full range of instruments to examine it, things to analyse its composition, magnetic field, radiation, that sort of thing. Instead all we have is a camera. It's as though he already knows everything about it or perhaps didn't think things through this far."

They parked their MarsMobiles and moved in for a closer look. Penny pointed to the bottom of the object where it disappeared into the ground. "The whole thing seems to be surrounded by a border of fine dust."

Rob picked up a handful and threw it onto the sloping metallic surface. The dust slid down and none of it stuck. "That's amazing! Martian dust clings to everything but not this."

Penny waded through the dust surrounding the object and took a step onto its smooth surface. Her foot slipped, and she fell heavily. "Careful, Rob, it's as slippery as ice."

"Fascinating. As we can't climb it, the only thing to do is walk around the edge."

Halfway around, Penny came to a stop at what looked like a hexagonal doorway or hatch partly submerged by the accumulation of dust. "I'm guessing this is the entrance, but the crew must have been quite short. I'd have to crawl on hands and knees to get inside."

With mounting excitement, Rob and Penny shovelled the soft powder away from the bottom half of the hatch using their bare hands. Carefully, Penny brushed dust from grooves and indentations in a panel set beside the door. Parts of the pattern were quite similar to the snowflake she carried around her neck.

"This can't be a coincidence!" she said. "It must be what Augustin sent us to find."

Chapter 28

Rob stood back and surveyed the doorway set into the side of the vast black structure. "I've never seen anything like this before. Given its immense size and unusual design, I don't think it could have come from Earth."

"Yes, it's amazing. How d'you think Augustin knew it was here?"

"I've no idea, but he must have been quite certain about how to find it. Otherwise, I can't imagine him investing so much time and money searching for it."

"I'll take some photographs and pace out the length and width. Very crude, but that's all we can do with what we have available to us. It's almost as though he only wanted us to confirm it's here, but to prevent us discovering anything else about it."

Rob was in two minds about what to do next. He was anxious to start on the return journey because of the dangerously low level of their batteries. Taking into account the extra delays, he estimated their power reserves would run out well before they arrived back at the Habitat. Balanced against this was the opportunity to examine an absolutely incredible alien object. Perhaps sensing his indecision, Penny called to him. "Come on, Rob, the least we can do is complete our circuit of this thing. It's a once in a lifetime opportunity to see something this extraordinary."

The damage only became evident at close quarters.

"What do you think happened here? Is it the result of a crash landing?"

Rob waded through the fine dust to take a close look at the gaping hole. "I don't think so. Seems like the effects of extreme heat, perhaps something like a laser beam. The edges are smooth and surrounded by splashes of molten metal."

After taking more photographs, they finished their brief inspection and returned to the MarsMobiles to send a report of their discovery to the Habitat. Rob's fingers hovered over the keyboard. "If you agree, I've decided to hold back some details of what we've found. Anything we can discover, anything Augustin doesn't know about, may come in useful as a way of bargaining for our future. At present, our continued existence is totally dependent on how valuable he thinks we are. If his plans for us finish after he's sure we've located this thing, we'll need something in reserve to ensure our continued usefulness."

"Perhaps you could send something like, have located the object at the anticipated coordinates, then give an idea of its size and shape and finish off by explaining our batteries are running low, and there's no time for a more detailed examination. We can keep details of the doorway to ourselves."

After stowing the extendible aerial and preparing to continue their journey Rob was alarmed to see it was almost midday. It had taken time to break camp and a lot longer to investigate the object and make the report.

The dust storm had smoothed out the finer detail of their outward track, but it was still easy to follow, and apart from swapping over MarsMobile batteries, they had no reason to stop until it was time to set up camp close to sunset.

After many hours driving, Penny welcomed the chance to talk with Rob. "Augustin doesn't like us to speculate what the 'thing' is, but calling it 'thing' or 'object' is ridiculous, don't you think?”

“I agree. What would you like to call it?”

Penny rolled over so she could see him in the torchlight. “It looks like a huge metal whale, so we could call it Moby Dick?”

“Great idea. And that would make Augustin Captain Ahab?”

“Given his obsession with the thing, both names seem quite appropriate.”

As they settled for the night, Rob surreptitiously disconnected his umbilical cable so he was no longer drawing power to recharge his batteries. He calculated the energy saved would extend the range of one MarsMobile by about four kilometres, perhaps the difference between Penny reaching the Habitat and falling short.

~

“I can’t tell you how angry I am! How could you make this crazy decision without telling me?”

Rob had never heard Penny sound so furious.

“I knew you wouldn’t agree, but it’s the only way. There isn’t enough battery power to get both of us back to the Habitat.”

“But we could abandon one of the MarsMobiles and both ride on the other.”

“They’re not built to carry the extra weight. It might make them unstable and topple over or cause the motors to overheat. As things stand, I doubt even a single vehicle will make it to the Habitat. If you try to carry me too, I’m absolutely sure you’ll run out of power before you get there.”

She calmed a little but was still far from placated.

“You may have decided it was the only workable solution, but I would have liked to be consulted. We should have discussed who gets left behind instead of you taking matters into your own hands.”

“But there was no real choice. Your battery lasts longer.

You'd be able to walk further if your MarsMobile breaks down or runs out of power, and you're also stronger."

In aggrieved silence, Penny moved the few remaining fully charged batteries onto her sled. Without pausing to say goodbye, she set off towards the Habitat, apparently still convinced it was his fault they were parting on bad terms. As the plume of dust receded towards the horizon, regret and an increasing sense of isolation weighed on Rob's mind.

He climbed back into the tent and tried to relax, determined to make his remaining battery power last as long as possible. To pass the time, he looked at the photographs on his camera. The complicated pattern next to the hatch held his attention. He wasn't an expert on snowflakes, but the more he studied it, the more it didn't seem quite right. The only record he had of Penny's pendant was the photograph taken before they left the Habitat. After magnifying the pendant and comparing it with the pattern on the spacecraft, he realised how they were related. The pattern on the spacecraft hull wasn't a single snowflake but incorporated six copies of the pendant shape arranged in a circle, which made it look like an even bigger snowflake. Using a marker, he wrote a brief note on the tent flap. Even if he wasn't found until after his batteries were exhausted, there would still be a record of this discovery.

~

Rob's attitude had been condescending and demeaning. To avoid dwelling on these thoughts, Penny concentrated on the way ahead, conserving power by steering a smooth path around rougher patches of ground. Already she was regretting leaving behind the navigation system. Although it was impossible to get lost, the system would show the remaining distance to the Habitat.

The last of the MarsMobile batteries ran out shortly before sunset. In the current situation, sleeping was a waste of battery charge. With only a small hand torch, Penny set out to complete her journey on foot. Until the moon, Phobos, rose in the west, she had to rely on starlight to find her way, augmented intermittently by a few seconds of torchlight to confirm she was still heading in the correct direction. In a landscape of deep shadows, it was difficult to judge distances, and often she missed her footing, slipping and stumbling dangerously.

She deeply regretted leaving Rob on bad terms and could understand his decision was made with the best of intentions. As things were turning out, it had been the only sensible choice to allocate all of the available batteries to her attempt to reach the Habitat. Another consideration occupying her mind was trying to calculate the remaining distance, but eventually she concluded this was a waste of time as there were too many unknowns. Finally, with nothing satisfactory to think about, she focussed all of her energies on planning each careful step.

Towards dawn, she felt the effects Rob had described, the result of dwindling battery power. The movements of her arms and legs became slower and less coordinated. When that happened, Rob had warned her to crawl on hands and knees rather than risking a damaging fall. She didn't make much further progress before all her motors stopped working, and she collapsed. Her last thought was that she had failed.

Chapter 29

"Have the police come up with anything? It's been more than a week now." Robert was desperate for news of Anastasia. He found it hard to focus on anything else and had difficulty applying himself to any of his tasks. Augustin was adamant all interaction with the authorities must go through him and, unfortunately, he rarely disclosed information about the investigation. Again, he dismissed Robert's enquiry with an impatient shake of the head and instead asked, "When does the comms window open?" He still insisted on being present at the start of each communication session to keep informed of the latest news from Mars. Even though the information was displayed on his own screen, he liked to hear confirmation.

Ethan glanced down. "Five minutes."

It was a little past midnight. With a yawn, Augustin cradled his head in his hands. Even after a stiff cup of coffee, he was barely keeping his eyes open. "Ethan, read me the messages when they arrive."

The sound of rapid keystrokes broke the silence. "Here it is. The Habitat Computer Log #58: Elapsed time since system initialisation 9571 hours. Activities since previous log, item number 1. Via the communication link Sam and Rob report they have found the object at the anticipated coordinates and have started to establish the OP nearby. They note the object is apparently metallic, deeply embedded in the ground, smoothly rounded and, above the surface at least 120 metres long by 40 metres wide. Because of delays caused by a dust storm, their battery reserves were running dangerously low forcing them to suspend their inspection. Files containing photographs were promised when they return to the Habitat."

Augustin leapt from his chair, sending it crashing into the wall. "Yes, yes!"

With a triumphant expression, he pumped his fist. Obviously startled, Ethan appeared a little alarmed by this uninhibited behaviour. However, Robert could appreciate the release of emotion; from all the evidence, Augustin had schemed, invested, and even murdered to find something hidden on Mars. The message was unequivocal confirmation he was on the right track.

"Read me that log item again, all the way through this time."

The room was quiet for several minutes after Ethan finished speaking. As though in a trance, Augustin stared into space with unfocussed eyes. Eventually, he snapped into action. "Ethan, reply to the message. Sam must conduct a thorough survey of the outside of the target object. I want a complete photographic record and measurements. Under no circumstances should any attempt be made to open or enter it. He must complete establishing the OP to provide shelter when visiting the target object. After the object is thoroughly documented, the OP will be useful for keeping it under observation by regular visits." Once he was sure Ethan understood his task, Augustin turned to Robert. "This is an important milestone for the project. The brain scanner is now your top priority. I want you to scan one of my men and then Ethan as soon as possible."

Ethan spun around from his computer screen, a look of horror on his face. "But I thought preparing another transitioned crew was only a contingency plan in case the first mission failed."

Augustin allowed himself a slight smile. "At the time, it suited me to give that impression."

After Augustin left, Ethan cursed quietly under his breath. "Did you know about this?" He looked accusingly at Robert.

"Not at all. It's the first I've heard."

"How long before the scanner can be used?"

"In truth, it's ready now. I've been double checking everything, perhaps a delaying tactic because I can't be absolutely sure I've sorted out the morbidity problem."

"Well, thanks a lot. That's hardly reassuring."

~

Two security guards delivered Anastasia to the meeting room and then stood either side of the entrance adding their intimidating presence to the gathering. Immediately, Robert leapt to his feet and embraced her.

"Thank God! Are you okay? What did they do to you? How did you get away?"

Anastasia relaxed into his arms and closed her eyes. Augustin remained seated, showing increasing signs of impatience. "I'm sure we're all pleased Anastasia has been released safe and well and would like to hear the answers to your questions, but we have a meeting to conduct. It's essential we consider the implications of her abduction as they relate to our activities here."

"Surely that can wait till she's had time—"

Robert was silenced by Augustin's angry stare as he waved to an empty seat. With a note of suspicion in his voice, he started questioning Anastasia. "I understand from the police report that when you were found you told the police, 'humans must prevail'. What the devil does that mean?"

"I'm not sure. I was simply told to repeat it. But it's obviously something to do with Maxwell's dislike of intelligent machines."

"Then perhaps you can explain how you got yourself into this mess in the first place? Why did you leave T2 in the middle of the night? Apart from being contrary to my express instructions, that was a foolhardy thing to do and exposed you to obvious risks."

This was a question which had worried Robert as soon as he discovered she was missing.

"I received a message that my father needed to see me urgently and was sending a taxi to collect me. I didn't want to cause problems for anyone else," she glanced towards Robert, "so I kept the message to myself."

"You don't have a mobile phone or external electronic mail access, so just how did your father contact you?"

"It was very strange. I received a mail message, which looked as though it came from my own account, and somehow it was deleted as soon as I read it."

Augustin's face darkened. "That's the second time! I can't understand why our network people haven't already worked out how that was done. How did you get through the perimeter fence?"

"There's a gap. The message told me how to find it."

"A gap? Where?"

"It's quite easy to see once you know where to look. The chain-link fence isn't properly attached where it meets the base of lighting tower 3."

Although recording the interview, Augustin made a written note of this failure of security. "And the taxi took you to your father's address?"

Probably without thinking, Anastasia began tracing the outline of the scars on her left hand. "No, I was knocked out by some sort of stupefacient soon after I got into the car and can't remember much. My next clear recollection was being handcuffed and forced to read a message in front of a video camera. They took my bracelet and pocket knife and only returned them as they let me go."

"Who were these people?"

"The guy who did the talking wore a mask and didn't identify himself. He claimed to represent Limitless Boundaries. My guess is it was Maxwell."

Augustin appeared even more annoyed at the mention of the name. "This is all getting very hard to believe. In the video, there were threats of imminent harm, and yet several days later, you were released uninjured and without any concessions on my part. Why would Maxwell give up his bargaining chip without getting anything in return?"

"It does seem illogical. We talked quite a lot. He kept going on with his concerns about a world takeover by intelligent robots, and I countered with my view that such a thing is highly unlikely. Eventually the guy seemed to accept I wasn't about to change my views and moved me to a shipping container."

"What happened to you while you were locked up? Did you talk with anyone or see your surroundings?"

"I seemed to be tremendously tired all the time, so I assume I was sedated to keep me quiet. All I can remember was waking to eat and then falling asleep again. There was this music, always the same music. I'm not sure if there were little snatches of video projected onto the walls or whether I dreamt that. What I remember is all jumbled up and doesn't make any sense."

"You didn't give him the impression you sympathised with his ideas, to persuade him to let you go?"

"I'm sure I wouldn't have, but as I've said, I can't remember."

Augustin frowned and continued to glare at her. "These people must believe they'll get some advantage from releasing you. Perhaps they think you'll promote their cause in some way. Your memory problems and reports of constant music are very disturbing. It's possible they hypnotised you to extract information. Worse still, they may have implanted an unconscious compulsion to sabotage the project."

"If that happened, how would I know? I don't think so, and I would never do anything to harm Rob or undermine our work with transitioned intelligence."

"As you say, even you can't be sure, so we must be careful to limit your access to critical parts of the project. You can go now. I have a few matters to discuss with Robert."

Robert let go of her hand as she stood to leave the room. After waiting until she was well out of earshot Augustin said, "I know you're emotionally involved, but I'm relying on you to monitor her actions and report anything unusual."

"You mean spy on her?"

"No, I said monitor. Everyone's safety may depend on you keeping a close eye on her. Perhaps there isn't that much difference between persuading twenty-four Safetybots to mutiny and getting a single human to change allegiance. I'm half inclined to end her involvement with the project right now. Even though she provides a lot of useful input, she's far from indispensable."

Robert leapt to his feet to protest. "I take Anastasia at her word where loyalty to Project Transition is concerned, but if you insist, I'll keep an eye on what she does. It's extremely important to me that she's allowed to continue with the project."

As he left the meeting, Robert had to admit he wasn't sure of the limits to Maxwell's powers of persuasion. But of far greater concern was Augustin's veiled threat to Anastasia's safety. The main thing to do was to find her and to be as supportive as possible.

~

For some tasks, Augustin's need for Anastasia's continued assistance with the Mars mission seemed to outweigh his reservations. For that reason, he gave permission for her to continue attending the regular exchanges of messages. The day following Anastasia's return, Augustin re-established his usual procedure for running communications with Mars. Once contact was established, and it was clear nothing of importance would be reported, he returned to his accommodation unit and left Ethan in charge.

With Augustin out of the way, Robert had time to focus on Anastasia. "How're you feeling? You look quite stressed and anxious."

She offered Robert a distracted smile. "I'm not feeling too good, but I think we should be asking Ethan how he is."

She turned to Ethan with a look of concern, and to Robert's surprise continued, "I know we're all being forced to do things we'd prefer not to, but it must be particularly distressing for you. I wouldn't like to be ordered to have a scan."

"Yeah, you're right! But nobody else seems to think it's a big deal. What I find so annoying is that Augustin just keeps drip-feeding us bits of information as he chooses and withholds the rest. We can't refuse any of his commands, no matter how dangerous they may be, and all for what? Aren't we entitled to some answers and a bit of honesty?"

Ethan was clearly upset, and secretly, Robert had to admit he shared the same feelings.

With a pleading look, Anastasia said, "Ethan, would you be prepared to help me send a personal message to Rob? It would mean a lot to me. I'm sure Augustin wouldn't approve because all he thinks about is completing the mission. Our feelings aren't important and don't count."

Robert was instantly on alert. This seemed the sort of behaviour Augustin had cautioned him to look out for. But rather than intervening, he waited to see where the conversation was heading.

Ethan took a while to consider the request. "Does this have anything to do Maxwell?"

"No. I can reassure you one hundred percent it doesn't."

Ethan nodded. "You must feel pretty confident there aren't

any hidden microphones or cameras in this room. I'm guessing there aren't because everything that happens here is part of Augustin's big secret."

Anastasia persisted. "So, you'll do it?"

Ethan indicated his agreement. "Once sent it'll be necessary to delete the message from the communications log at this end. Your only problem would be if Sam mentions it."

Ethan appeared pleased to aid this small act of rebellion against Augustin's authoritarian rule but still wanted the shield of plausible deniability. "In a few minutes, I'm going to leave the Comms Centre for a short break. My computer will still be logged in, so you can send your message and then delete it from the communications log. When I return I don't know what you've done, right?"

As soon as Ethan left the room, Robert voiced his concern. "What are you up to, Anastasia? Are you absolutely sure this doesn't relate to Maxwell?"

"As I've said already, it doesn't. Please trust me. I've received information the object that Sam and Rob are looking for on Mars is protected by some sort of code or combination. If the code isn't entered correctly, the result could be fatal." She referred to a small sheet of paper. "Starting from 1 at the top and with positions numbered clockwise, the code sequence is 5, 3, 6, 1, 2 and 4. It would probably make more sense to someone actually looking at the lock. I know Augustin has insisted Sam and Rob don't try to open this target thing. If he changes his mind, or it becomes necessary for some other reason, they'll need this code to ensure their safety. I can't tell Augustin. He wouldn't send the code because it would look like an invitation to ignore his previous instructions. It would also raise difficult questions for me about where the code came from."

"I wish you'd tell me the whole story."

"Oh, Robert, I would if I could, but I've sworn to keep it a secret. I don't want to cause problems for anyone."

Chapter 30

Jason stood aside to allow the visitor into the scanner laboratory. "Robert, this is Joe. He recently joined ZsG and has volunteered to be transitioned into one of Augustin's new team of robots. He's come to arrange an appointment."

Robert couldn't avoid comparing him with Sam, the previous ZsG volunteer. Although of similar height, this young man appeared less athletic and, perhaps because of his glasses, more studious.

"This is still an experimental procedure. Has Jason explained what will happen and the risks involved?"

Joe drew himself to his full height and squared his shoulders. "Yes, sir, but it's a fantastic opportunity, and being allowed to participate in something so cutting-edge more than compensates for any dangers."

Robert was unnerved by the uncritical enthusiasm and attempted to give Joe a more measured view of what might be involved. "You do know that Sam, your predecessor, didn't survive the scanning process?"

"I've been told the scanner has been completely rebuilt and carefully checked. I'm confident you've done everything possible to minimise the risks."

"Okay. You realise your brain will be scanned and copied

into a robot?"

"I totally understand, sir. This is really incredible. After my scan is downloaded, there will be two versions of me, the original biological one and a robotic version."

Robert couldn't fault Joe's understanding and commitment. "Why did Augustin choose you?"

"The call for volunteers exactly matched my skills. I've technical qualifications in mechatronics and enjoy building and modifying gadgets. I was told the robot will be responsible for repairing and servicing a wide range of equipment incorporating electronics, mechanical parts, and computer programs. There was also a hint the transitioned intelligence will be sent to an exotic location. It'll be exciting for a version of me to be involved with this project."

Finding himself without any further excuses for delaying the next brain scan, Robert was forced to offer Joe an appointment for the following morning. It was only later that doubts resurfaced, and he spent the evening and well into the night reviewing his safety evaluation of the scanner yet again.

~

Anastasia had volunteered to take over responsibility for the scanner control room as replacement for one of the assistants who died in the T1 explosion. Robert waited outside her cabin and then accompanied her on the short walk to the group of connected buildings associated with the scanner. She seemed preoccupied and paused outside the building to confide in Robert. "I had the most peculiar dream last night."

"What was it about? Good or bad?"

Anastasia wrinkled her brow. "I found it disturbing, feeling my way in the dark, trying not to make any noise. In the background, someone was saying something, but I couldn't understand the words."

"And?"

"There was nothing else. I woke up."

"I think more often than not dreams and nightmares don't

make sense. I wouldn't worry about it."

"I'll try not to. It looks as though you're someone else who didn't have a restful night."

Robert realised he must look as haggard as he felt.

"That's for sure. I'm still not sure what went wrong with the equipment during the previous scans. I know the only way of gathering more information is to perform another one, but I can't help feeling apprehensive."

He appreciated her supportive smile.

As they arrived, Cheng, the new medical technician, and Jason were already preparing Joe for the procedure. His clothes were neatly folded, and on top of them a clear plastic bag contained his glasses and watch.

Robert pointed to the bag of magnetic items. "You've applied the magnetic protocol, Jason?"

"Yes, but you should double check."

Robert read through the checklist and signed at the bottom of the page.

With the preliminaries complete, Cheng administered the sedative before he and Jason wheeled Joe from the preparation area to the scanner. It was time for Robert to join Anastasia in the control room.

"I know this may be difficult for you, Robert."

"Last time I let my fears take over, but I'm confident the whole process will turn out better this time. We've had more time to prepare. Fewer things can go wrong."

~

"Wake up, Robert, the scan's over."

He'd fallen asleep in his seat, but after such a disturbed night he was grateful Anastasia had chosen to let him rest while everything proceeded smoothly. Robert knew Augustin would see this as a failure to monitor Anastasia. With some trepidation, they returned to the preparation area to check on Joe. Seeing him in good health after the apparently successful scan was a tremendous relief. It helped to balance out the many failures. Robert expressed his joy and relief to the whole room. "Finally, after all this time, we've achieved Vince's dream. We've perfected the scanning process!"

Anastasia smiled but added a note of caution. "Well done, Robert, though we won't be absolutely sure it worked until the scan is downloaded into a robot."

"Sir, how long before I meet my robotic double?" Although still affected by the sedative Joe was full of enthusiasm.

"Your scan data will be processed before loading into the silicon brain. Additional time is needed to actually transfer the data and check everything's working correctly. In all, that will take more than a day, but it should be less than two."

~

Tara Schwartz, the animatronic artist, had created the faces for all of Project Transition's robots. Robert was impressed with her design of a striking young face for the new robot. She had matched Joe's red hair and green eyes. Although the other facial features were different, there was still a strong overall resemblance. Forgetting his military discipline, Joe raced forwards and hugged his robotic double.

Robert waited until Joe regained his composure before making his announcement. "I know you'd both like to be called Joe, but that will be too confusing. Robotic Joe, we'll call you Jon. Okay?"

"That's good. I'll think of myself as a new version of Joe." Then, with a slight smile, "Perhaps an improved version?"

Although Jon and Joe looked a little different, voice and intonation were very similar. Augustin had been watching from the back of the room. After allowing the initial excitement to die down, he stepped forward to take control of the situation. "Has Jon passed all of the protocols for testing and integrating the silicon brain?"

Jason nodded his confirmation.

"Now we know the scanner's working, we need to move

forward without delay and complete my robot team. The next scan will be Ethan's. Just make sure the timing of it doesn't interfere with a communication window."

As he turned to leave, Augustin made quite sure everyone understood the need for rapid progress. "I assume there will be no problem doing the scan tomorrow?" It was more of a command than a question.

That evening, Anastasia invited Jon to join her, Robert, and Jason for a celebration. Anastasia started by saying a few words. "You're the only one here who doesn't know the history of Project Transition. It's been a long process to arrive at this point where a transitioned intelligence like you could be produced without leading to the injury or death of the human subject. It all started with Vince Conner, who had the vision to conceive and fund Project Transition. Unfortunately, Vince didn't live to see how the project developed."

Robert proposed a toast. "So, I guess the real reason we're here is to acknowledge Vince's contribution and drink to his memory."

Jon raised his empty glass as everyone else took a drink.

~

The following day, after completing further competency tests, Jon had no other allocated tasks, so he tagged along with Robert. At lunchtime, Robert became aware that several other people eating in the cafeteria were uncomfortable in Jon's presence. It was clear that after the destruction of T1 at the hands of copies of the Sam robots, they were unwilling to trust any transitioned intelligence. Aware that his companion was being viewed with some level of hostility, he found it difficult to make small talk and was relieved when Anastasia arrived.

"Hi, Robert, what do you recommend for lunch?"

"Well, I'd probably avoid the Shepherd's pie."

For Anastasia, there was something familiar about the young woman serving the hot food. She wore the usual black apron, her blonde hair pulled back tightly and trapped under a hairnet. There was no makeup to hide her pale face, or the red rings around her eyes. She looked close to tears.

"Are you okay?"

Without answering, the server used an oven glove to retrieve a plate warming under a heat lamp.

"I was thinking of ordering a salad."

"You'll change your mind when you taste the beans."

Anastasia was about to argue when the plate was deposited onto her tray with an air of finality, then the server turned and walked away. Confused about what just happened, and not wanting to cause a scene, she re-joined Robert and Jon.

"Interesting selection."

"You can say that again, but I wasn't given a choice. I'm sure I've seen that serving woman somewhere before." She swivelled in her seat as if to point her out.

Robert searched the room to find the person Anastasia was referring to. "Where is she?"

"That's strange; she's gone now. How bizarre. Probably doesn't matter."

Annoyed at having a meal she didn't want, she absentmindedly pushed the mashed potato, mince and green beans around her plate with a fork. Her mood quickly changed to curiosity when she discovered a memory chip wrapped in several layers of plastic amongst her beans. Looking around to make sure she wasn't being observed and covering her actions with her left hand, she slid the package off her plate and wrapped it in a serviette.

~

Dressed in a hospital gown, Ethan looked decidedly uncomfortable as he waited for Cheng to prepare the sedative equipment. As though Robert might have been mistaken, he asked for confirmation it was compulsory. "I've never liked needles. Is this really necessary?"

Cheng's smile held no sympathy. "If you move about too

much during the scan, the machine won't be able to track your brain, and the scan will need to be repeated. So yes, the sedative is very important."

Ethan caught sight of Robert and Jon, who had been observing preparations for the scan. "Jon, do you remember anything about your scan? Does it hurt?"

The robot frowned as though having difficulty answering the question. "Well, sir, my recollection is crystal clear until the start of the scan. After that it's confused and patchy. Certainly, there was no pain."

Apparently reassured, Ethan allowed himself to be helped onto the patient trolley, and Robert took Jon to join Anastasia in the control room. Jon had an insatiable curiosity, and for the entire duration of the scan, occupied himself with asking questions and telling anecdotes about Joe's time as a student and as a new recruit in ZsG. With this distraction, Robert didn't have time to worry and only thought to check on the elapsed time as the scan was about to finish. With a great sense of relief, he led Jon and Anastasia back to the control room and took a close look at Ethan. "How're you feeling?"

Robert almost felt a twinge of sympathy for the vulnerable figure lying on the trolley.

"A bit groggy. Was the scan okay?"

"Relax, it seemed to go fine, though we'll know for sure tomorrow evening"

~

After their evening meal, Anastasia sat with Robert on the deck outside his cabin. "Do you have access to a computer that isn't monitored?" she whispered.

"Why do you want to know?"

Instead of replying she slipped the memory chip into his hand. Without saying another word, he led her to the laboratory. Robert removed a circuit board from a drawer and connected a display screen and keyboard. Then he plugged in the chip. "This will do the job." After typing in several commands, the contents of the chip were displayed on the screen:

Dearest Anastasia,

I've asked Tracy to give you this document if anything were to happen to me. The fact that you're reading this means that my worst fears have been realised. I want you to know I've always loved you and feel proud of your achievements.

You probably thought my line of work made your mother unhappy, but actually she was quite a rebel herself and was excited by it when we first met. Unfortunately, she developed severe depression after your birth, and in spite of numerous treatments she never recovered. It was heartbreaking to see her so devoid of joy, and I coped by immersing myself more fully in my work. I deeply regret not developing a better relationship with you during this time. I've always tried to shield you from the truth about your mother, but maybe I was wrong. Shortly after you left for university she took her own life. At the time, I didn't want to burden you with this knowledge, so I took steps to conceal the truth from you. I am telling you now to give you closure.

Following your interest in the Egyptian tablets I became obsessed with finding out the full story. Augustin had been careful to use several different contractors to recover and translate each of twelve tablets. I assume he did this to ensure he was the only one who could piece together the full story. At some considerable danger to myself I gathered information about them. Recently, I've been told that Augustin found out and intends to make an example of me and ensure I cannot tell anyone else what I've learnt. I'm so glad, now, that you changed your surname. Never let him find out about our connection.

I don't want you to blame yourself. It was my own decision. I have attached a brief account of the information as inscribed on the tablets.

A goddess named Zeezee, from a place far away in the sky, was carried here on a solar barque. In her home city the selection of a dying queen's successor was decided by battles to the death amongst different groups of supporters. Zeezee did not become queen, but rather than accepting her fate she escaped in a solar barque. While fleeing, her ship was damaged and foundered on the planet we know as Mars, but she was able to use a smaller raft to make her way to Earth. Unfortunately, she was pursued by agents of the new Queen who destroyed her raft, stranding her on Earth. Even worse, it transpired that she was unable to eat any of Earth's food and was only able to survive until the supplies she brought with her ran out. Faced with this situation she decided to leave instructions for finding her damaged vessel on Mars. She hoped that as we developed more knowledge and skill it would be possible for us to recover her flying vessel and discover the secrets of travelling the universe. This would be her gift to us.

Needless to say, the technology in the flying vessel would be priceless, and I believe Augustin is intent on taking possession of Zeezee's vessel or spacecraft which must be somewhere on Mars.

I hope you can help to defeat his plans, because with this technology he would be unstoppable, and his intentions are never honourable. Take care.

Your loving father,

Savvas

Anastasia was distraught. In one evening, she'd found out she'd lost both her father and mother. Now they were both orphans, Robert was sad to realise this strengthened the bond between them.

~

Augustin sent Robert an urgent instruction. Because the scanner was now completely functional, he decided all documentation had to be immediately brought up-to-date and copied to a secure repository in case any further disasters occurred. Robert and Anastasia spent the whole day collecting together design files, records and notebook entries. When the task was completed, they rewarded themselves with a walk around the perimeter fence. This was an opportunity for Robert to try to distract her by sharing some gossip. "I heard an interesting story about Maxwell. If it's true, it gives an insight into what motivates his attitude to robots."

Anastasia's reply was curt. "Let's see. Cut off from the

outside world in this place, the only possible source of gossip would be Jason. Am I right?

Robert smiled and was forced to confirm her suspicion.

"Really, Robert? I don't know how he finds out anything these days bearing in mind the tight security around this place."

"It's about Maxwell's dislike of robots and comes indirectly via Jason's friend of a friend."

"Ah, that friend of a friend again."

Robert persisted. "Apparently, quite a few years ago, Maxwell had a brilliant career in robotics research and development. He made some fundamental advances in techniques for programming robots, and even created his own programming language specifically for the task."

At last Anastasia was finding his story interesting. "Then something turned him against robots?"

"You guessed it! One of his robots went out of control and almost took his head off."

"Was he badly injured?"

"Severely! He ended up spending a long time in hospital. Over the course of the following months, he built this incident into a deep-rooted loathing for everything to do with robotics."

"But surely the robot wouldn't have had the awareness or motivation to intentionally injure Maxwell, especially as he probably built it himself?"

"From what Jason told me, the accident was almost certainly caused by a couple of mistakes which combined to produce a disastrous result. Maxwell convinced himself the robot was to blame rather than his own errors or miscalculations."

"So, now he loathes them and gathers support for his obsession by targeting workers who fear losing their jobs to robots?"

Robert squeezed Anastasia's hand and tried to smile reassuringly. He was pleased she had joined in the conversation, but now hoped this information about Maxwell wouldn't add to her worries.

A robot with distinctive red hair stood outside the cafeteria contemplating the countryside beyond the border fence. Anastasia called to get his attention. "Hi, Jon, we haven't seen you for a day or two."

The robot turned and gave Anastasia a disdainful look. "I'm Ian, not Jon, but you can think of me as Ethan if you wish."

Anastasia's smile was replaced by a look of confusion. "But where's Jon?"

"I'm told there was a last-minute problem with the new batch of robots, so Augustin decided Jon should be erased and replaced with my scan."

"They killed Jon!"

"There's no need to be so dramatic. Joe's scan data is still available and can be loaded into another robot."

"But don't you understand? Any robot reloaded with Joe's scan won't be Jon. It'll be another version of Joe, like a twin, but definitely not Jon."

Chapter 31

"HM, I have received instructions from Earth. They note that Sam-renamed-Penny and Rob have not returned from the OP and must certainly be running low on power. You are to gather recharging equipment for them, together with two fully charged batteries. You must carry those items and follow the trail left by the MarsMobiles until you find them. Recharge their batteries and provide any other assistance they require to return to the Habitat. Remember that Sam is your first priority."

~

With a battery in each hand and cables looped over one shoulder, HM set off in the early morning. Even in the reduced Martian gravity, their combined weight exceeded its safe load and caused the robot to lurch and stagger on the uneven ground. Progress was further slowed as HM took regular breaks to allow its overheated motors to cool. By midmorning, its internal batteries were at half capacity. From that point onwards, there wouldn't be enough charge for the return trip to the Habitat, but that fact didn't register as significant.

By midday there was a major change to HM's vision. The colours blue and green were gone with everything rendered in shades of red. This was a warning that its internal batteries were almost fully depleted. HM set down its load while trying to formulate a plan of action.

In a few minutes, it would run out of power resulting in failure to deliver the cables and batteries. If it did nothing, failure was certain. It could recharge from one battery and then return to the Habitat, but that would also be a failure. To recharge from one of the batteries and deliver one could be viewed as only a partial failure. The robot decided to attempt the latter.

~

By late afternoon, fully recharged, HM continued.

"… 7,121… 7,122… 7,123 …"

Following the trails left by the MarsMobiles required little of its brain's computing power, and with nothing else to consider, HM occupied its time by counting the number of steps taken since leaving the Habitat.

Shortly before sunset, HM came upon Sam-renamed-Penny lying face down in the dust. Its first reaction was to check her temperature to see if her electronics had cooled to a damaging level. The area under her armpit was still warm, so all was well. Positioning the black rubber recharging pad across her lower back, HM connected the full battery and then spent a short while searching for Rob.

"Thanks for coming to rescue me, HM."

The robot didn't understand the implications of what Sam-renamed-Penny was saying but had been programmed to give an appropriate response. "You are very welcome, Sam-renamed-Penny. I have been unable to locate Rob."

"He isn't here. I had to leave him behind. How far are we from the Habitat?"

"I do not know. However, I took almost a full day and 10,923 paces to get here."

After fully recharging, they made their way back to the Habitat. Because HM wasn't carrying extra weight it had sufficient power to complete the return trip. As they returned

HM counted down the number of steps starting at 10,923. Penny found this repetitive but it was reassuring to have an idea of the remaining distance.

~

Recovering Rob, the two MarsMobiles, and the various items abandoned along the way occupied a couple of days of shuttling backwards and forwards. Fortunately, the backup battery in Rob's silicon brain had kept it working even after the main battery failed. Without some source of power the brain would have lost the structure coded into it resulting in Rob's death.

Once they'd both recovered, Penny and Rob set about completing the tasks they had been allocated. Top priority was a trip to the OP to increase the store of fresh batteries and gather more information about Moby Dick. They took detailed measurements of the object, including many photographs, while avoiding any speculation about its true nature or purpose. The strange message giving details of a code for safely gaining entry to the object confused both of them. More intriguing, they'd been instructed to make no further reference to the topic. The message seemed to hint at the possibility of opening the door, even though to enter the object had been specifically forbidden.

~

Rob transferred the last of the batteries into the OP tent and added radio equipment for contacting the Habitat. "We'll stay overnight and set off on our return early in the morning."

"How will we occupy the rest of our afternoon?" Penny asked the question, but they both knew what they wanted to do.

"There are still a few more measurements and photographs to take. Of course, we're not permitted to try to open the hatch, but we can take a closer look, can't we?"

Penny didn't make any comment when Rob picked up a small folding shovel. As they approached Moby Dick, Rob marvelled at the way it seemed to change from a patch of stony ground to a smooth black object. Even having seen it several times, he still couldn't imagine how the illusion worked.

They cleared away the mound of Martian dust and fully exposed the hatch and its surrounds.

"Don't!" Rob's warning was more shrill than he intended.

Penny had taken the snowflake from around her neck and was about to hold it against the panel beside the entrance. "I only wanted to see how well the pattern matches the snowflake."

"I'm thinking about that message. We don't want to do anything that might be mistaken for entering the code."

Penny turned to point at the panel. "It's pretty clear there are six identical snowflake markings here just like the message suggested. I'm prepared to try entering the code. It probably won't work considering the length of time Moby Dick seems to have been here, but perhaps you should stand well clear just in case I trigger the fatal consequences."

"I don't like the idea of you taking that risk."

Rob tried to take the snowflake, but Penny tightened her grip. "Well, Rob, consider this as payback for your decision to disconnect your charging cable."

He decided against arguing and retreated to what seemed like a safe distance.

"I'm pressing the snowflake on the number 5 position. I think I felt a slight vibration."

Penny called out the remaining positions.

"Has anything happened?"

"No … yes!"

Rob raced back in time to see a billowing plume of condensation and dust released as the hatch slowly swung open.

Chapter 32

"Are you certain the scanner is now thoroughly tested and can be relied upon to function correctly?" Augustin stared intently into Robert's eyes as though searching for the slightest hint of doubt.

"The previous two scans have worked perfectly. I have no reason to believe there will be any more problems."

"That sounds like the sort of assurance an engineer would give, but it'll have to suffice. Make arrangements to transition the third member of my team tomorrow morning."

"This will be the replacement for Sam?"

"Yes, you could say that. Also, on the subject of the scan, I don't want Anastasia allowed anywhere near the building from now and until after the scan has taken place. I still worry that Maxwell might have some sort of control over her."

Robert felt he had to support Anastasia. "But she helped out with Joe and Ethan's scans."

"That's true, but the next one is much more critical, and you'll need to cover the tasks usually allocated to her."

~

In the morning, Robert was surprised to see an ambulance and an emergency coronary care vehicle parked in front of the scanner laboratory. All entrances were guarded by ZsG personnel. He had to show a coloured badge and have his name checked against a list before being allowed to enter the building.

"Morning, Jason. Any sign of our next customer?"

"Not yet. But I was impressed by the number of medics who've turned up. We could've used them on a few previous occasions."

Their conversation was interrupted by the arrival of Augustin, accompanied by Sergeant Kirby and two fully armed ZsG military types. Augustin pointed to the patient trolley and tranquiliser equipment.

"Is everything prepared?"

Robert was confused by Augustin's question because none of the military personnel in his party looked ready to be scanned. They were all carrying too many guns and too much other equipment for that.

"It is, but who's going to be scanned?"

"I would have thought you could work that out, Robert. Obviously, I am."

In Robert's experience, having to remove your clothes makes you less sure of yourself, less assertive. Although wearing only a thin hospital gown, Augustin still managed to project his authority.

~

Jason took a deep breath. "What's your full name?"

"Don't ask me such damn stupid questions. Just hand me my clothes and tell Sergeant Kirby I want to see him."

"The sergeant isn't here. He left after the scan."

"Without waiting for me?"

"He left with Augustin Selworthy. You must realise you're not Augustin; you're the robot programed with his scan."

Quite obviously, there was increasing agitation. Jason was thankful he hadn't connected the limb motors.

"No, that's impossible. I remember who I was before the

scan, and I'm confident I'm the same person now."

Jason knew the possible difficulties of explaining the situation to a transitioned intelligence if things hadn't been thoroughly discussed before the scan. He had assumed Augustin, of all people, would understand. Modulating his voice to a calm and reassuring tone he continued. "The way Robert explains it, there are now two almost identical versions of Augustin Selworthy. They both have the same thoughts and memories. Their main difference is that one has a biological body, and the other is a robot. You're the robot."

Jason positioned a small hand mirror so that the robot could see its reflection.

"But I refuse be the robot. I have to be the human."

"You can talk about this with your biological counterpart, but if you think about it, I'm sure you can work out what he'll say."

~

The specially built second-generation robot body had been assembled with extra care. It had been given a handsome young face, perhaps how Augustin wished he had looked twenty years earlier. Augustin stepped forward and shook his transitioned self by the hand. Robert was sure he detected a brief battle of wills as each version of Augustin attempted to control the handshake.

"Magnificent. Truly impressive. We need to give you a suitable name. I've decided you'll be known as Austin."

Robert thought he detected a look of annoyance flicker across Austin's face before he relaxed to his previous neutral expression.

"Getting the scanner working correctly has taken far longer than it should have. My backers have been very patient, but now it's imperative I provide evidence they'll receive a return on their investment. Having completed my crew for the next Mars mission, we're back to our other project, of creating a marketable Safetybot and as quickly as possible."

"Will the new Safetybots be based on Joe's scan?"

Augustin took a while to consider Robert's question. "Jon has useful skills for some applications but insufficient training in weapons proficiency, riot control and counterinsurgency. Using his scan would unnecessarily limit the market for Safetybots. I'll find a suitable candidate for the next scan."

Robert followed Augustin from the room so that he could speak without being overheard. "When Anastasia and I joined Project Transition we signed up to transition human intelligence into a robot. We've worked on this project for over four years, and now that the success of the transitioning process has been demonstrated we feel we've completed what we set out to achieve and would like to move on. You have all of the information necessary to perform further scans. It's not essential that we leave right now, but we thought we should let you know about our plans."

The transformation was immediate. Blood congested Augustin's face and his nostrils flared. He took an intimidating step closer to Robert. "Don't you ever threaten me again. I'll decide who can leave and when they can do it. You won't raise this matter again if you know what's good for you and for Anastasia."

~

After finishing a barely edible canteen meal, Anastasia was only too pleased to start their evening walk.

Robert broke the silence. "Some of this is starting to make sense. I think it was Augustin's plan to send a robot containing a scan of his own brain on the first Mars mission."

"Of course, but he couldn't prepare the robot in time for the launch window because of the scanner problems. So why didn't he just cancel the mission completely?"

"That would have been a massive waste of money. I guess he would already have paid to reserve a time slot on the launchpad, and the cost of storing the rocket and its cargo would be substantial."

Anastasia indicated that she understood. "Even without being able to take his transitioned self, the first mission must be doing invaluable groundwork for the next one."

Robert thought of another result of Augustin's scan. "When the second mission arrives on Mars, I don't think Rob will thank us for helping Augustin to send his robotic doppelgänger. It'll be quite intolerable to be forced to spend a lot of time in close quarters with someone like that."

Chapter 33

Rob watched as Penny attempted to shake the dust from her hair. "What do we do now?"

She turned to him with an amused smile. "What do you usually do after opening a door?"

"Yes, but is it safe? What if we get trapped inside?"

Kneeling in front of the open hatch, Penny switched on her torch. "That's always a risk, but don't you want to know what's in here? I certainly do."

"Okay. Tell me what you see."

"Hardly anything. There's a short tunnel and then another door. Perhaps this whole thing is some kind of airlock."

"In that case, we'll probably need to close the outer hatch before the inner one will open."

Rob followed Penny, backing through the open outer hatch so he could see it from the inside. "No obvious levers or switches here. Can you see anything at your end?"

Before Penny could reply, the outer hatch swung closed, and strips of green light slowly brightened in the walls and ceiling. "What did you do?"

"Nothing, well, almost nothing. I was admiring this pattern on the wall, just tracing its outline with my finger."

"That must have triggered something. Do you feel a change

in pressure?"

They were surrounded by a rushing sound, and Rob felt his clothing flapping in currents of air.

Penny tried to twist around to speak directly to Rob. "The whole of Moby Dick must be pressurised. That's amazing."

"More than that, Penny, what's absolutely incredible is that the technology, the automatic door, the light, and whatever's maintaining the atmosphere in here is still working. Moby Dick must have been here for centuries, judging by the way dust has accumulated around it. Anything made on Earth and left unattended on the surface of Mars for that length of time would certainly have failed."

Airflow died away to a whisper, and the inner hatch swung inwards and out of the way.

Penny gave an involuntary cough. "What's that smell? It's sharp and a bit acidic."

Rob tried to place where he'd come across a similar odour. "I'd say it's similar to vinegar. Even if we come into contact with the chemical, it's unlikely to be harmful for our robotic bodies."

Penny and Rob crawled into a larger corridor with sufficient headroom to stand upright. The dim green light illuminated a long passage curving off into the distance with regular side paths branching off left and right.

"This lighting makes the place look rather spooky," Penny said. "Don't you think so?"

"It is rather gloomy. But I don't think we should allow that to prejudice our view of the whole thing."

"You may be right, but I'm starting to feel really claustrophobic, and that smell doesn't help. I'll feel safer if we don't move too far from the exit. Perhaps we could spend a few minutes looking around and then come back later?"

Rob set off down the corridor while Penny tried to find something to investigate closer to the entrance.

Penny's scream echoed around in the interconnected spaces. When Rob found her, she was pointing to a row of three tall creatures standing with heads bowed and arms relaxed by their sides. Their clothing was bright green and the attached helmets semi-transparent silver.

"Good grief. What're those things? Did they attack you?"

"I don't think they're alive, but they look so creepy. It was a real shock when I first saw them."

Rob lifted one of the arms and let it fall back into place. "Doesn't seem to be anybody inside. They could be a kind of spacesuit but made for something with four arms and two legs or perhaps four legs and two arms."

"Maybe even six legs?" Penny held up one of the arms and pointed out that each of the six appendages carried a glove for accommodating a similar pair of powerful fingers.

After discovering the spacesuits, Penny seemed even less inclined to risk exploring on her own. "I'll be much happier once we get out of here, that's for sure."

While she was speaking, Rob had been searching the room and discovered the technique of inserting two fingers into a pair of cavities and turning them to unlock small hexagonal cupboards set into the walls. After investigating a number of empty niches, he found one containing a block of black pliable material. "What do you think of this, Penny?"

She weighed it in her hand and tried flexing it. "I don't know, could be food or something like that?"

"There's something hard inside. I've found a crack." Rob dug his fingers into the split and peeled off strips of the black rubbery coating. Inside was an exact copy of Penny's snowflake. After showing it to Penny, he pocketed his find and returned the strips of packaging material to the niche.

~

On returning to the Habitat, Penny prepared a comprehensive report on the object, including the access hatch and damaged part of the hull. She omitted any mention of opening the hatch.

Her message received a swift reply, which Computer read out.

"I received your report confirming the correspondence between markings on the object and the snowflake. Now it has served its purpose of authenticating the object, you must return the token to secure storage inside Computer. Your next task is to complete and fully stock the OP."

With obvious regret, Penny detached the cord and inserted her snowflake into Computer's hatch, which whirred firmly shut.

"Sam-renamed-Penny, I will confirm the token has been returned to me for safe storage."

Chapter 34

Robert and Anastasia were enjoying an early morning coffee seated at one of the tables outside the cafeteria. They heard Jason's calls for assistance even before he sprinted into view. "Quick. I need your help, both of you. Now."

Robert had never seen Jason looking so distressed.

"What's the problem?"

Jason didn't pause to answer Anastasia's question but retraced his steps once he was sure they were following.

Austin lay on his back beside the walking track, legs and arms splayed out at crazy angles.

"I found him a few minutes ago. He's totally unresponsive."

Robert knelt beside the robot and lifted an eyelid. Control of the eyes was the last system to shut down when there was a power failure. "Not a flicker! Did you move the body before you came to find us?"

"I don't think so."

"Okay, I'll take some photographs, then we can carry him to the laboratory for a closer examination and, of course, Augustin must be told. He'll insist on answers and pretty quickly."

"Don't you think we should call the police?"

"I'm sure Augustin wouldn't agree. That would go against his demand for absolute secrecy, and what crime would we report. Excuse me, officer, I'd like to report one of our robots has stopped working? No, the police wouldn't have the expertise or willingness to get involved."

~

Jason and Anastasia positioned temporary lighting while Robert cut away Austin's clothing and plugged a diagnostic cable into the access port in his chest. Robert and Jason had barely started their examination when Augustin arrived. He appeared in a foul mood and totally devastated at the sight of his robotic-self laid out on the bench like a corpse in a mortuary. Ever since their first meeting, Robert had believed Augustin was concealing strong and even violent emotions barely held in check. Now they were more on show, and Augustin seemed about to explode. Taking a step towards Robert and pounding the table with his fist he demanded, "Well, is the battery flat?"

"No, the problem is much more serious than that. There's plenty of charge in the battery, but the main fuse has blown, and I can't run any diagnostics. It takes something catastrophic to do that."

"Well, I need answers, and I need them now! You're the engineer. Sort it out. That's what I pay you for." Turning on his heel, he stamped out of the laboratory

~

Large strips of silicone skin had been removed, and various components and circuit boards laid out beside the body. Robert pointed to some of the items. "I've stuck red labels on faulty parts and green on those that seem okay."

Anastasia stood back and studied Austin's disassembled remains.

"What could cause so much damage? It seems to have mainly affected the front of the body, everywhere from head to feet. Are there any bullet holes?"

"No, the skin seems completely unmarked, so I'm discounting gunshot, being struck by lightning or even some kind of stun gun."

"I don't suppose the silicon brain survived?"

Reverently, Robert picked up a bronze-coloured titanium cube about the size of a large grapefruit. "The local fuse blew disconnecting backup power to the brain. Even if it hasn't suffered internal damage, Austin and his memories are gone."

~

The following morning, Anastasia found Robert in the laboratory still working on some of Austin's circuits. "Morning, Robert, anything new?"

He replied with a weary shake of the head. "Augustin isn't impressed with my lack of progress in finding out what happened to Austin. However, pressure from his financial backers must be forcing his hand. I've been given a higher priority task to scan another recruit. As usual, we'll start early tomorrow morning."

"And now he's not the one being scanned he doesn't mind if I'm in charge of the control room?"

Robert gave an encouraging smile. "Apparently not."

Two of ZsG's security detail kicked open the door. "Stay where you are. We're looking for anything that may be related to the recent damage to one of the robots."

As the first guard stepped to one side to begin the search, Robert recognised his companion.

"Joe."

"Hi, Robert, Anastasia. Sergeant Kirby has launched a search of the whole compound."

Robert lowered his voice. "What exactly are you looking for?"

Joe cast a sideways glance at his partner, who was diligently pacing around the room, peering into corners, under benches and even casting an uncomprehending eye over the robot components spread over the bench top. "Obviously, things that could be linked with what happened to Austin. Other than that, I'm not sure. The sergeant just said anything that seems out of place." Joe continued speaking barely above a whisper. "Just between us, he implied the whole search was a waste of time, and we wouldn't find anything."

"I was sorry to discover Jon had been erased and overwritten with a different brain scan. I guess your scan will be loaded into a new robot when one becomes available."

Joe appeared shocked by the news that his robotic-self had been terminated, but returned to the search without comment.

~

Anastasia pointed to a screen showing a highly magnified view of one of Austin's damaged circuits. "I'm not familiar with these things, and yes, it seems very artistic. But what's this black smudge? It looks as though mould's growing on it."

Robert explained what she was seeing. "This controls one of the leg motors. The black smudge is damage probably caused by some sort of overload. All of the other non-functioning parts I've looked at suffered a similar fate."

Anastasia picked up one of the damaged components and turned it over in her hand. "Even though we don't know what caused the damage, can we replace the affected components and get Austin going again? I get the impression Augustin has a strong emotional attachment to his robotic double."

"That's not a good idea."

"Why not? We have spare parts, and it would be simple enough to do."

"We'd need to remove everything electronic even the things which seem to have survived. In all probability, they'll be 'walking wounded'."

"Walking wounded? Good grief, Robert What are you talking about."

"That means electronic parts which are damaged but still seem to work. Such things are prone to total failure sooner or later. Unfortunately, the only reusable component in Austin will be his metal skeleton. Even his silicone skin will need to go because it incorporates electronic sensors, which may be affected."

"I think Augustin would be happier if he thought Austin only needed minor refurbishment. Perhaps you could ask Jason to rebuild Austin without drawing attention to the scale of the repairs?"

~

During the following communications window, the atmosphere was tense. Ethan had reverted to his previous objectionable self. Augustin seemed withdrawn and even less communicative than normal. Robert risked asking about the investigation. "Any developments in the search for Austin's killer?"

Augustin appeared irritated and ready to shut down this uncalled-for intrusion, but after a few moments' thought he gave a surprisingly complete answer. "Well, you weren't a great deal of help with your robot autopsy. You couldn't even work out what caused the damage. Anyway, everything within the outer security fence was locked down for a thorough search, though that didn't uncover anything suspicious. Unfortunately, there's no security camera coverage of the area where you found Austin."

Further explanation was cut short by a computer alert tone. Augustin glanced at his screen. "There seems to be an unexpected situation in the scanner laboratory. You and Anastasia need to go over there and check it out."

After the outer door closed, Augustin handed Ethan a folded slip of paper. "Send this order before they get back, then delete the outgoing message log and any reply. And do not reveal its contents to anyone. We're the only people on Earth who know about this. If news of the message gets out, I'll know who's responsible."

Ethan smoothed out the paper. After an initial look of surprise, his face curled into a malevolent grin.

Chapter 35

Penny took a break from sorting items from the cargo hold and joined Rob in the spacecraft cabin. "How's the work going?"

Rob held up his hands for inspection. "Sharp edges are cutting my fingers even though I'm wearing gloves. It's fortunate we have a good supply of replacement skin."

"I know Augustin told you to help HM take apart the Mars lander, but is this really necessary? The components will still be here even if we don't dismantle it."

"I don't think it's serving any useful purpose, but he must feel I need something to keep me occupied."

"Well, you can take a break now and help me transport the next consignment of equipment to the OP. HM has loaded up the sleds with the things we'll need."

Penny pointed out headlamps attached to the front of each MarsMobile. "With these new lights, it should be safe enough to travel at night now we only need to follow the existing trail. We'll get there quicker without having to break the journey."

Rob and Penny settled into their driver's seats in preparation for the long drive and had barely started before HM waved them down. "Computer has a message for you, Sam-renamed-Penny. The message includes a direction for Rob to go on ahead, and you can catch up later."

With a shrug of her shoulders, Penny expressed her resignation. "I guess we'd better follow instructions then, Rob. See you soon." She turned her MarsMobile in a wide circle to follow HM back to the Habitat.

"What's the message, Computer?"

"Has Rob left to travel to the OP? Augustin insists it is for you alone."

"Yes, Computer, he's set off by himself."

"Here is the message:

"This communication is for Sam and must not be shared with Rob. We have discovered that Rob presents an imminent danger to the mission. The only workable solution is immediate termination. In your pre-flight briefing, you received instructions about the handguns in the gun safe and its access code. Rob should be disabled by firing a bullet into the back just below the neck. This location has been chosen to minimise the possibility of ricochets. It is recommended you use three bullets to ensure the effectiveness of this procedure. Make sure the rest of the body isn't damaged, as it will be a valuable source of spare parts."

"Am I able to tell Earth you have received the message and understand?"

"Yes, Computer, I understand." Penny's response was barely more than a whisper. She felt sick at the thought of what she'd been instructed to do, but tried to hide her emotions. Recently she'd had the impression that HM was monitoring her every move, and wondered if it was spying on her so computer could report back to Augustin.

Rob had already explained about cutting open the gun safe and had pointed out where he'd buried the handguns. Penny found a spade and retrieved them from the plastic case that had originally housed an angle grinder.

Because of their black metallic look, and even allowing for the effects of lower gravity, she expected the guns to feel heavier than they did. Acutely aware of being watched, she tried to give the impression she was as knowledgeable as Sam would have been. Fortunately, both guns appeared to be loaded and only needed the safety switch moved to off to allow them to fire.

Lining up the front and back sites with a large rock, Penny pulled the trigger. The only result was a loud click. In panic, she double checked the safety switch and then remembered something she'd seen on television. It was necessary to operate the slide to load a cartridge into the chamber. She tried again. The sound was louder and the recoil much stronger than she expected. A slight breeze carried a strong metallic smell, which brought to mind fireworks.

Although the gun fired, she couldn't tell where the bullet went. Choosing a much closer target, she aimed low, supported her wrist with her other hand, and took a firmer grip. Ten metres away, a rock splintered into a shower of fragments. After reburying the spare gun in the plastic case, she set off to follow Rob. HM could report back that she was armed and in pursuit of Rob.

~

It wasn't until well after dark that Penny arrived at the OP. Rob had rigged a small light on his MarsMobile to help her find it. Penny unzipped the cover and stepped into the tent, gun in hand. "Hello, Rob, Augustin sent me to kill you."

Alarmed, he searched Penny's face for any hint of deadly intent; instead he saw a mischievous smile.

"He directed me to terminate you with a bullet in the back, which confirms he still doesn't know I was substituted for Sam."

"I'm not surprised he's decided to get rid of me. I've had the feeling my value to the mission would sooner or later be outweighed by his doubts about my reliability."

Rob sat for a while working out the implications of Penny's news. "It will be best to give the impression you did kill me, which means I can't return to the Habitat."

"More than that, you should stay undercover. It's possible the mapping satellites could photograph you out in the open."

"If I'm to stay here, I'd prefer to move into Moby Dick. In there, I'd be out of sight and still have plenty of space to walk around."

"There's another serious problem. Where can you recharge your batteries? Computer will realise something's going on if I keep charging extra batteries and bringing them out here." Penny paused and concentrated on her pocket calculator. "Because you won't be driving back, the batteries you brought with you should last over ten days, and the spare batteries in the OP would give you another three or four days. Hopefully, we can come up with a more permanent solution in that time."

~

The following morning, Rob drove his MarsMobile close to Moby Dick's entrance and unloaded the fully charged batteries he had brought with him. Together they ferried them through the airlock and into the room containing the three spacesuits.

Rob explained to Penny how he wanted the batteries organised. "I'll keep fresh batteries at the back of the room and put discharged ones near the door. We've still got a few in the OP to use when these run out."

Penny finished checking the batteries. "We made a mistake. This one's already empty, so I'll leave it by the door."

With the batteries organised, Rob unrolled a thin sheet of plastic to sleep on. As he straightened up, he paused to look at the row of hexagonal cupboards. "That's odd. I'm sure I left this one open."

Rob inserted his fingers into the pair of cavities and turned. "It's empty."

"What've you lost?"

"The pieces of black rubbery material. I put them in here."

Penny started to dismiss his concerns. "But that was just rubbish." Then she realised, rubbish or not, they should still be there. There was no one else to move them.

Together they turned to stare at the spacesuits as though expecting them to slowly come to life. To break the spell, Rob guided Penny back into the corridor. "Rather than concentrating on a single room, I think we should follow the main passage to get some idea of the size of this thing. What do you think, Penny?"

"I'm not sure about this. The whole place is starting to give me the creeps."

"Well, I'm going to have a look. There must be so much more to discover about Moby Dick."

Reluctantly, she turned to follow Rob and had to reach out for his support. "The floor has quite a tilt; it's difficult to walk in a straight line. Obviously, this thing didn't touch down exactly level when it crash-landed."

Rob estimated they'd only walked half the length of Moby Dick before the corridor intersected with a circular open space. He pointed towards the ceiling. "We could keep going straight on or climb up."

Penny hadn't paid much attention to the rows of metal loops on either side of the corridor. Now she realised they served as a ladder for this vertical side branch. "I can see you're keen to find out what's up there, so I guess we can try out the ladder."

Rob clambered up easily. Penny had difficulty coordinating hand and footholds as she climbed. A more powerful body wasn't always an advantage. "Perhaps if I had six legs this ladder might be easier."

She accepted his assistance to clamber out of the vertical shaft. "This is absolutely fantastic. Augustin would feel his investment totally justified if he could see this." Penny circled the room trying to make sense of the alien equipment. "I guess we're in some sort of ship's bridge or control room?"

"Difficult to say, but these seats look extremely uncomfortable. I don't think I bend in the right places."

Rob sat down carefully and examined the four banks of coloured disks arranged in pairs on either side of the seat.

Penny placed a warning hand on Rob's shoulder. "Just don't touch anything. It seems likely most things here are still in working order, and I shudder to think what the result could be."

As Rob squirmed to find a comfortable position, the seat flexed in response. Soon it had accommodated to his unfamiliar shape. "That's much better. Why don't you try one of the other ones?"

"I'd rather not. Don't you find it disturbing the way it moves, almost as though it was alive?"

Reluctantly, Rob got up from the seat and followed Penny back towards the airlock.

"Tonight, I'd like you to stay with me in the tent. We can pretend I kill you tomorrow morning before I head back to the Habitat." They spent the rest of their time together chatting and sleeping in the OP.

Chapter 36

Sergeant Kirby introduced the latest candidate for the brain scanner. "You can call him Squaddie. He's been given all the relevant training for the role of Safetybot."

To Robert, he looked just like a clone of Sam, the same height and physique together with identical military posture. Leaving Jason to complete Squaddie's preparation, Robert stepped to one side to talk with the sergeant. "This guy understands what the process entails? In particular, he won't be surprised when he wakes up and finds he's a robot?"

"That's all been carefully explained."

"And he has no problems with the thought he may cease to exist at any time when his silicon brain is switched off or overwritten with a different scan?"

The sergeant looked to one side, avoiding making eye contact. "I'm sure all of those possibilities have been covered in his briefing." Checking his watch, he appeared surprised at the time. "I have to go now. Ask Squaddie if there's anything else you want to know about his preparation."

As he marched from the room, Robert caught a second glimpse of the sergeant's watch, no longer his usual rugged military style wristwatch with bold hands and rotating bezels. In its place, he was wearing a cheap plastic model.

When Robert reached the control room, he found Anastasia in an anxious mood. "Do you think I could have been involved with what happened to Austin?" she asked.

He embraced her until her breathing steadied. "I don't believe that's possible. Whatever happened to him must have required something very specialised and probably quite bulky. You don't have access to anything like that. And anyway, you were with me when it happened. Remember?"

"You're probably right, but there seems to be something going on which involves me. I had another nightmare."

"Was it the same as before?"

"Similar. Everything was dark. I was trying to unscrew the lid of some kind of container. I was becoming frustrated because it wouldn't budge. Then I worked out it unscrewed the opposite way to normal, and I woke up."

"And the meaningless words?"

"Yes, they were there again."

"Your dreams are becoming stranger each night."

"It must have something to do with Maxwell. It's still a mystery why he let me go without waiting for his demands to be met."

"Surprising indeed, and it would look bad for him to release a valuable captive without any benefit to his cause, unless—"

"Unless what?"

"Unless he's expecting it will give him some advantage."

"I'm scared about what might happen, Robert."

They were interrupted by a call from Jason. Squaddie was in position for his scan.

~

Robert, Anastasia and Jason gathered in a meeting room expecting a grilling about progress with Austin's repairs. Augustin and Sergeant Kirby were seated together, facing the other three.

Augustin started proceedings by addressing Robert. "There were no problems with performing the latest scan?"

"None at all. It's … well, it's almost becoming routine."

Augustin's grim expression relaxed a little. "The main reason I called you all here is to gather information for a report to my sponsors. I'm sure they'll be gratified to learn that we've almost finalised processing Squaddie's scan, which we'll use as the transitioned intelligence for the Safetybots.

"The destruction of T1 demonstrated the extreme level of threat Maxwell's activities represent for Project Transition and, in particular, the development of Safetybots. Moving the development effort to this more secure location was meant to guard against further interference. However, the attack on Austin, my most important transitioned intelligence, has shown we're still vulnerable, and I cannot allow this situation to continue any longer. Sergeant Kirby will outline what we intend to do about it."

"Some months ago, Robert attended a meeting of Limitless Boundaries, Maxwell's organisation, which is engaged in guerrilla warfare against all forms of intelligent robots. He did this to gather information about Maxwell's activities and went there secretly, without seeking prior approval." The sergeant cast a stern look of disapproval in Robert's direction. "But perhaps he can tell us what happened."

"Thinking back on the evening, I'm convinced they were aware of what I was doing at the meeting and engineered my subsequent car crash, perhaps to act as a warning."

Pain and distress registered on Anastasia's face at the mention of Robert's crash. Her reaction caused him to hesitate, and Sergeant Kirby picked up the story.

"My people have checked out the sports hall where the meeting was held. The same group who were there when Robert saw Maxwell have booked it again this evening. This is our opportunity to capture him. Robert's the only one we have who can recognise Maxwell, so it's essential he goes there to confirm the presence of our target before we move in."

Robert looked up in alarm. "I can't go back there. It's obvious they know who I am."

Horrified, Anastasia added her concern. "Next time they might arrange something worse than a simple car crash."

Augustin wasn't to be deflected. "We can ensure Robert won't come to any harm while he's there. As far as they know, he might be intending to join Limitless Boundaries. He'd be their ideal recruit. Absolutely too good an opportunity to miss, so I really must insist."

Robert could see that Anastasia shared his alarm at Augustin's unyielding intensity. "If I do agree to go, what am I supposed to do?"

"It will depend on you being able to talk your way past their security. All you need to do is to eyeball him and then let us know he's there."

"How will I do that?"

Sergeant Kirby held out an old-fashioned ballpoint pen. "This is a camera. The lens is at the end next to the large button. Point it at him and press the button to take a photograph when you've made a positive sighting. The pen will transmit the picture to my people outside. We'll cut power to the building and send in a snatch squad to capture him."

"And this other smaller button?"

"Press it if you get into trouble, and we'll dispatch people dressed as local police to rescue you."

~

Reluctantly, Robert stepped down from the anonymous van with blacked out widows. He was acutely aware of his disguise as he limped towards the hall. In his pocket, he held the pen and fingered its emergency call button. As he entered the building, Greta turned from talking with one of the security guards and smiled. "Hi, Richard. I was wondering if you'd decide to return. How've you been?"

Robert was expecting a confrontation and was taken aback

by the warm greeting. He mumbled a confused reply.

"There's a charge for tonight's entertainment."

Robert handed over a note and was waved through the open door, past the two security guys. Inside, the only light came from the stage, and Robert paused while his eyes adjusted to the gloom. Almost immediately, Fergus appeared at his side. "Richard, it's been a long time. Great t'see you again. You'll be having a beer?"

Robert felt unable to refuse. He was aware the layout of the room was different from his first visit. A makeshift bar had been installed, and a dozen or so high tables were scattered around the hall, each hosting groups of drinkers. Fergus led the way to a spot with a good view of the stage.

A lone figure playing an acoustic guitar was seated under the spotlights. He had an attentive audience who clapped and whistled at the end of each song. Robert was impressed by his skill with the guitar. It was only when paying attention to the words he realised every line of the songs included at least two swear words. The audience loved it.

Fergus returned with the drinks. "Great guitar playing, and great words, eh?"

Robert attempted to deflect the conversation. "Yeah, great. He's very skilled."

Fergus took a card from his wallet and handed it to Robert. "I'd better give you another business card. This one's got my new address."

As soon as he touched the card Robert knew it was different. It felt cheaper and flimsy to the touch. He turned it over in his fingers and stowed it in a pocket.

The singer doubled as master of ceremonies. Laying aside his guitar he called for quiet. "Now, I'm pleased to present the lovely girls you've all been waiting for, Roxy and Cheyenne." With an extravagant gesture, he waved two women to the stage.

As far as Robert could see, they were clothed in fishnet

stockings and feather boas, but little else.

"Gentlemen, we need a member of the audience to help out with the entertainment. Are there any volunteers?"

Ignoring several men who were pushed forward by their drinking buddies, the emcee continued, "Never mind. Roxy'll find some lucky guy."

Gingerly, Roxy stepped down from the stage on her high heels. As she weaved amongst the groups of men, she ignored offers of assistance to select a volunteer. Robert could sense that, although moving seemingly at random, she was heading towards him, and he tensed. She stopped at arm's length, unwound a loop of her boa, and raised it in the air. Robert was petrified. With a coy smile, she announced, "You'll do."

Robert was sure she was looking straight at him, but instead she circled the boa around Fergus's neck and pulled him towards the stage.

"Hell, you're only young once," he announced to those nearby.

All eyes were on the stage as Robert took the opportunity to slip away unremarked. With what seemed like a familiar nod, the two security guards on the door stood aside to allow him to leave.

~

Although it was almost midnight when Robert returned, Augustin convened a small meeting with Sergeant Kirby and Anastasia.

"My people told me nothing happened. Are you sure Maxwell wasn't there?"

"I got the strong impression they were expecting me to turn up, and they put on a special show just for me. There were definite similarities between the two meetings. I could start to doubt what I remembered from the first time. And to answer your question, I didn't see Maxwell."

Augustin frowned. "How was it similar?"

"The same people were on the door, and many of the

audience seemed familiar. On the other hand, the layout with bar and entertainment and lack of a meeting gave the whole event a different feel. I think it was an elaborate way of sending the message that Maxwell is one step ahead of us."

Robert took the business card from his pocket and laid it on the table. "Fergus even gave me another business card, just like the previous time. However, this one doesn't have a tracker built into it."

Augustin seemed deeply offended that anyone would think Maxwell had outsmarted him. "It's disappointing that Maxwell slipped through our fingers, but we cannot and will not allow his interference to deflect us from our twin missions. My team of three robots must be completed and moved to a secure location until they can be deployed on the next Mars mission."

Augustin was becoming exasperated, and as usual, started itemising the tasks on his fingers. "It's taken far too long to repair Austin. Ethan's scan is in the wrong body, and Joe's scan hasn't been loaded into a new body. This state of affairs is unacceptable. I don't care what it takes, just get those robots sorted without further delay."

He took a few slow breaths, obviously calming himself, before continuing in a more conciliatory tone. "The other project involves Safetybots. My sponsors will want to see rapid progress there. I need you to get pilot production going as soon as possible. Once we can demonstrate that they function reliably and effectively, we can put them into volume production."

Chapter 37

"Rob won't be joining us again." The words stuck in Penny's throat even though she knew they weren't true.

Computer accepted the statement without comment. "While you were away, I received further instructions from Augustin. He wants us to implement a number of measures to improve security."

"Who's going to present a security problem?"

"He was not specific but sent a list of tasks, most of which can be completed by HM. These include completely covering over all of the Habitat modules, apart from their entry ports, and building a wall in front of each entrance to give some protection from frontal assault."

"Was there anything specific for me to do?"

"Our cargo includes two short-range ground to ground missiles equipped with nuclear warheads. I am told your training did not include deployment of these munitions. You are to master the operating procedures by reading the documentation and practicing with one of the missiles. Augustin warned that during familiarisation, you must not proceed to the point of actually performing a launch."

~

Penny waited for seven Martian days before informing

Computer that she intended to visit the OP to ensure the tent was still in good condition and to add to its stock of charged batteries. HM loaded the sled with batteries, a spare tent and other items that could come in useful.

The MarsMobile had barely covered a few hundred metres before it produced a muffled explosion and came to a sudden halt. Grey smoke billowed into the Martian atmosphere. Penny peered into the mechanism where the motors were housed and quickly concluded she needed help.

HM returned cradling a large cylindrical object covered in soot. "Sam-renamed-Penny, the main drive motor has failed."

"Do we have a replacement?"

"The only similar motor is in the second MarsMobile, which Rob took to the OP."

"Well, do we have anything else that could do the same job?"

"I do not have information about any other suitable substitute. We could request suggestions from Earth."

~

The following morning, HM interrupted Penny while she was familiarising herself with one of the nuclear missiles. It was mounted on a tripod launcher, and she stood beside it leafing through a stack of instruction cards.

"If it is safe for you to come to the computer room, Computer would like to pass on a message."

Penny followed HM back inside the Habitat. "Computer, this is Sam-renamed-Penny."

"I have a reply to your question. The solution is that you walk to the OP. If HM constructs a wheelbarrow, you will be able to carry sufficient batteries to complete the outward journey. Once there the working MarsMobile and batteries can be used for the return journey."

"Yes, but…"

Penny realised this plan assumed there were plenty of

charged batteries at the OP. But, by the time she managed to walk there, Rob would have used up those he carried on his MarsMobile, leaving insufficient for the return journey. This seemed to present a stark choice: walk to the OP and spend a day or two with Rob before they both succumbed to lack of power, or stay at the Habitat and leave Rob to die alone.

~

HM loaded up his crudely constructed wheelbarrow and watched as Penny struggled to negotiate the soft ground between ruts left on previous journeys to the OP. Considering all of the technology involved in travelling to Mars, Penny considered it a ridiculous situation to be forced to use a wheelbarrow to transport essential supplies. To avoid dwelling on her and Rob's certain end when their batteries became exhausted, she concentrated on working out what she would say to him when they met. In two short days, she would need to explain how much joy he had brought to her life, and share her thoughts of their unfulfilled future. It wouldn't be easy, but she was determined to make the most of their last days together.

Chapter 38

Robert ushered the young man into the robot programming station. "What d'you think, Squaddie?"

The young man appeared overawed to see the row of seated humanoid robots sharing his light brown hair colour styled with a military crew cut. Tara Schwartz had decided his face fitted the job description of Safetybot so well she'd modelled the robots to be almost indistinguishable from their human inspiration.

"They look terrific. How many are there?"

"We've sixteen unpacked and ready to program, with another thirty-four still in their boxes."

"When can I see them in action?"

"We'll have this first group ready by tomorrow evening. You could call by then."

Robert searched through a pile of t-shirts. "Here, I've a present for you." He handed the young man a t-shirt emblazoned with a large 'S 0'. "I don't know whose idea it was to have this one made. There won't be a robot number zero, so you're welcome to take it."

"Thanks, it'll make a great keepsake."

Robert turned his attention back to unpacking more of the Safetybots.

A few minutes later, Augustin and Sergeant Kirby arrived to monitor progress. "Later today, I'll be moving Austin, Ian and Jon to a secure location. They're ready to go?"

"Yes, Jason has completed repairs to Austin. His silicon brain has been loaded with your original scan, so he'll have no memory of what happened to his previous incarnation. We've played musical chairs with the other two robots. Joe's scan data has been loaded back into Jon, the robot modelled on him, and Ethan's scan has been transitioned into a new robot body that will be called Ian. Fortunately, neither Ian nor Jon will be aware of anything that's happened since their original scans."

Augustin indicated grudging satisfaction. "Seems adequate. I'll fill in the memory gaps for Austin, but that won't be necessary for Ian and Jon. While I'm away, Sergeant Kirby will be in charge. Any problems, see him."

Turning back to the line of robots, he stepped forward to take a close look at one wearing a t-shirt marked 'S 5'. "Nice touch to have the robots designated 'S'. That could stand for Safetybot."

After a few more moments of consideration he added, "When these robots are loaded with the brain scan, how do we know Maxwell won't subvert their minds the way he did with the Sam robots?"

Robert had already discussed this at an earlier meeting with Augustin, so he wasn't sure what he could add. "It's difficult to say because we don't know what he did to the Sam robots apart from talking to them. Unfortunately, we couldn't examine one because none of them survived the destruction of T1. They all carried demolition charges, which were very effective at destroying all the evidence."

As Augustin walked away down the line of robots, Sergeant Kirby, unable to contain himself, muttered to Robert, "Another bloody disaster. Doesn't this guy ever learn?"

"You think there'll be problems with these robots like the others?"

"Like night follows day."

With an air of barely controlling his exasperation, he turned to follow Augustin out of the building.

~

The following evening, Robert and Anastasia returned to the robot programming station for their meeting with Squaddie. As they approached, Anastasia commented on the sounds of animated voices coming through the open doorway.

"Don't look now, Robert, but it sounds like your robots have drunk too much lubricating oil."

The room was thronged with excited robots laughing and gesticulating. In the centre of the commotion, Squaddie was being photographed with different groups of his doppelgängers. Robert could only distinguish him by the number on his t-shirt.

"Sorry to cause a disturbance, sir. One of the guards let me in. Probably thought I was just another robot."

At that instant, the lights flared and then died. The room was filled with a jumble of confused sounds overlayed seconds later by the rumble of a distant explosion. Now, the only illumination came from the room's glow-in-the-dark exit signs.

"What just happened, sir?"

"Some kind of power failure. Do you have a torch, Anastasia?"

"Yes, but it doesn't seem to work. Perhaps there'll be some light outside." There was the sound of collisions and a heavy fall followed by some unladylike swearing. "Careful, you two. I just fell over one of the robots."

Squaddie helped Anastasia and Robert make their way out of the building. Once in the open, Robert summed up the situation. "It's not just our building that's lost power. There are no lights to be seen anywhere. Squaddie, I suggest you go over to the guard post. They'll probably know what's going on and may be able to loan you a working torch."

"Yes, sir, right away."

There were calls for help coming from the accommodation cabins, and Robert guided Anastasia in that direction. Groups of people were gathered outdoors complaining about the power cut. A little light came from a slender crescent moon and someone holding a candle.

Jason separated from the crowd and walked over carrying a glowing green tube. "You might need these. They were left over from the last all-night rave I was at and somehow they got included in my packing." He held out two plastic tubes. "Just bend them until the inside tube breaks then give them a shake."

Anastasia gratefully accepted hers. "Thanks. Did you hear where the explosion came from?"

"Yes, and I saw it too."

Jason stood beside Anastasia and pointed so she could sight along his finger. "There's nothing to see now, but it was about there."

"That high? Was it flying?"

Before Jason could reply, three rapid gunshots echoed around the buildings. Transfixed, nobody moved. A few seconds later, a fourth shot rang out. Acting decisively, Anastasia activated her glow stick and strode off in the direction of the sound.

When Robert caught up, she was kneeling beside Squaddie in a pool of eerie green light. She had removed his t-shirt and was using it to control the bleeding from a tight grouping of three gunshot wounds to the chest. As Robert watched, uncertain how to help, Anastasia slipped off her jacket and wrapped it around a gaping head wound. Against all odds, Squaddie still clung to life, though his eyes stared unfocussed into the distance. Leaning in close she asked, "Who did this to you?"

Unable to answer, he took a final ragged breath and fell still.

~

The ambulance laboured across the grass and onto the boundary road. Flashing lights and sirens were not required. There was no need to hurry.

Anastasia's face was streaked with tears. "That was dreadful! It brought back so many terrible memories. Only last time it was you on the ground bleeding out. When is all this going to stop? Why are we still mixed up with this?"

She collapsed into Robert's arms and sobbed uncontrollably. He held her tightly as though trying to protect her from both old and new nightmares.

~

When they arrived, the police reinforcements set up portable floodlights illuminating the taped off area where Anastasia had found Squaddie. Retracing their steps with a young policeman, Robert and Anastasia described what they saw and the sequence of events leading up to the murder.

As they entered the robot programming station the young officer stopped, and with a shaking hand swept his torch over the huddled bodies.

"Why didn't you tell us there were more casualties?"

Anastasia tried to calm him down. "They're just robots. They were all disabled at about the same time as the shooting, but if it was deliberate, you'd probably classify it as property damage, not murder."

Possibly disconcerted by the sight of so many bodies tangled together in an artificial massacre, he hurried outside. "Okay, I've taken notes. I'll come back tomorrow for a full statement. You'll be here for the next few days?"

"Yes, we're always here," they both answered almost simultaneously.

~

As they walked towards their cabins, something on the ground glittered in the pool of green light from their glow sticks. Distracted by this unexpected find, Anastasia stopped. "Look at all these shreds of aluminium foil. Where d'you think they came from?"

Robert took out his camera, but it wouldn't even switch on. "That's annoying. This could be important evidence. I guess we should leave it here for the police to find." In defiance of his own suggestion, he picked up a small fragment of foil and slipped it into a fold of plastic film he found in his wallet.

~

The following morning, Robert and Anastasia attended an interview in the robot programming station. "This is a most bizarre case, but the murder is real enough." The police officer made a movement to switch off his voice recorder but then decided on a final question. "Is there anything you'd like to add to your statement?"

"More of a query. What did you make of the aluminium foil?"

The young man frowned and shook his head at Robert's question. "Where was that? We didn't find any foil."

Robert led the way past a bunch of flowers marking the spot where Squaddie died.

"It was here, quite a lot of it." Anastasia circled a patch of ground with her hand. The grass was flattened, but otherwise, there was nothing else out of place.

"You're sure about this?"

Robert handed over the fragment of foil. "I kept this small sample, but there was a lot more last night."

"Okay, thank you for that. Probably the most telling point is that someone went to the trouble of removing it."

Chapter 39

Pushing HM's wheelbarrow was physically demanding and required continuous concentration to avoid tipping over or becoming bogged. When Penny finally arrived at the OP, her batteries were almost exhausted. It was essential to sleep and recharge. The only thing preventing this was a mind full of thoughts she wanted to share with Rob, but he was nowhere to be seen. Even more worrying was the discovery that the spare batteries were still fully charged. He couldn't have survived for the time she'd been away without using at least some of them. She was desperate to find Rob, but the imperative to recharge was stronger, so she positioned the recharging pad on her lower back and allowed sleep to overtake her.

~

Penny awoke as Rob gently shook her shoulder. A smile of relief spread across her face. "Oh, Rob, I've been so worried, especially when I found out you hadn't used any of these batteries. I felt certain you'd become trapped in Moby Dick and run out of power."

"I can see how things must have looked, but really, everything here is fine. On the other hand, it looks as though you've been through a lot. Thank goodness I decided to come over each day and check if you'd returned, even though it risked showing up on a satellite image. Tell me what's happened."

"When I set out to increase the OP's stock of batteries the MarsMobile blew up. It was Augustin's bright idea that I use a wheelbarrow to carry enough batteries for the outward journey and recover the second MarsMobile for returning. I must admit, I was pretty down setting off from the Habitat; the future looked so bleak. Based on my estimate of the available battery capacity, once I arrived here there would only be enough for a couple of days, with no possibility of recharging."

Rob moved closer and put his arm around her shoulders. He could understand her feeling of hopelessness.

"As I walked, I soon gave up on HM's idea of counting my steps. Instead, I decided to think about what was important to me, the things I'd been hoping for before I became convinced we were doomed to run out of power."

"And that was?"

"My ideal future involved getting away from here and escaping Augustin's control. I know this place should be a geologist's heaven, with plenty of new and interesting rock formations to be explored and no buildings or vegetation to hide them from view. They're nice, of course, but there has to be more to my life than being confined to this little patch of Mars. Also, as well as getting away from here, I wanted to have the right to a continued existence. And freedom to decide what to do with my life and to be happy. Happy means being with you."

Rob smiled. "What you're hoping for sounds like part of the United States Declaration of Independence. You know, life, liberty and the pursuit of happiness."

He turned his head to look directly into Penny's eyes and spoke with determination. "My hopes for the future are similar to yours and, if possible, I'd like them to include all transitioned intelligences. There is a list of fundamental human rights. Perhaps the list could be extended to apply to intelligent robots?"

"You're suggesting equal rights for equal intelligence?"

"Nicely put, Penny. That could be our slogan."

"I guess it'll take time to change most human's views of robots."

"Yes, but if transitioned intelligences are able to demonstrate their value and not appear threatening, then such changes should be possible."

Seeing that Penny still had reservations, Rob tried to think of another way to express his ideas. "On the surface of any planet we can only see as far as the horizon. In a similar way, we're limited in how far into the future we can predict human attitudes to robots. I like to think of this as the intelligence horizon, the point where changes may happen, but from this distance we can't be sure how they will develop. Hopefully, beyond this horizon, intelligent robots will be accepted as having at least some rights. If all goes well and we survive beyond that point in time, we may find we have a more secure future." Rob smiled and squeezed Penny's hand.

"So, you mean even if we perish here, at least we can die hopeful of a better future?"

"Well, Penny, the way you put it is a little downbeat, but that could be our hope for the long-term. Getting back to our current situation, Augustin believes he owns and controls you, and you're dependent on his Habitat for energy. However, the situation has changed. Things I've discovered inside Moby Dick will make us less reliant on the Habitat. In fact, we could probably do without it altogether. You'll be amazed when I show you."

"I know you're trying to be encouraging, but thinking about the future, I'm starting to realise I'm not as immortal as our creators would like people to believe. They've got some improvement to do for the next generation."

"What do you mean?"

"The last time I stopped to recharge my batteries I noticed

problems with my right leg. The knee joint didn't work as smoothly as it used to do. It was a little loose, and later I became aware of a click each time I put weight on it."

She demonstrated the problem by bending and straightening the affected leg. Although she didn't complain of any pain, the grating noise set his teeth on edge.

"You should try to minimise your use of it. I guess our designers hadn't factored in walking long distances through Martian dust. I'm not sure what we can do about that problem, especially here, away from the Habitat."

"Once I was aware of it, I became obsessed with my leg. It seemed to get worse with every step. I worried it would fail completely and was so relieved when the flag and our red tent came into view.

"I propose we take shelter in Moby Dick where there's less dust and we have more room to move around without being seen. When we get inside, I want to bring you up-to-date on what's happened there."

Rob strode off eagerly. It was only upon reaching the entry hatch he realised how much Penny's leg was slowing her down. He turned to find her having difficulty keeping up. "Here, let me help." He reached out to support her and relieve some of the weight on the affected side.

Penny struggled through the airlock and into the spacesuit room. Seating herself against the wall, she brushed Martian dust from her clothes. It settled in an obvious rust-coloured patch on the floor around her. Surprisingly, the rest of the floor was perfectly clean, even though Rob had probably carried in a great deal of dust during the time he'd been living there. She took off her boots and shook out the accumulated grit and small stones. Three larger fragments of rock were made up of interesting coloured layers. "Look at this. They're obviously sedimentary, built up from layers of silt deposited under water."

Rob examined the slivers of rock in her outstretched hand

before she dropped them back on the floor. "I've something to show you too." He pointed to a row of batteries lined up against one wall. "They're all fully charged." He indicated a single battery near the door. "This one is empty. I recharged from it last night."

"That's unbelievable! How's it possible? All the way here I thought we'd both run out of power after a few days and just die."

"That must have been awful for you. But now those worries are over. I don't know how, but sometime during the day, when I'm not here, the battery is recharged, so I never need to use the others."

"Amazing! It would be great if we could rely on that. We'd be independent of the Habitat and free of Augustin." After a few moments of thought, Penny worked out the downside. Apprehension showed in her voice. "That's really creepy. If we don't know how it happens, how can we rely on it?"

Undeterred, Rob continued with his story. "That's not the only incredible thing I've discovered."

With obvious excitement, he unfolded a sheet of writing film and smoothed it on the floor. "I've started making a map. This is where we are now, and perhaps the most interesting is that room there. I won't tell you what I think it is. Wait until you see it."

Rob helped Penny to her feet and led her down the corridor past the vertical shaft leading to the bridge. They stopped at a small hexagonal door similar to the inner hatch of the airlock. "There are six of these, three on each side of the corridor."

"Do they lead outside?"

"I'm guessing we could get out through them, but they're more than that. Come inside and see."

Once through the doorway, Rob helped Penny stand.

"Wow! That's so beautiful. It must be some kind of small spaceship."

Temporarily forgetting her reservations about alien technology, she ran her hand across the smooth black hull, stopping where metal loops formed a vertical ladder.

"Climb up and take a seat, but don't touch anything. I'm going around the other side."

Penny struggled up the ladder and settled into one of two side-by-side seats, relaxing as the contours of the seat moved to conform to her body shape. "This seat has adjusted to suit me the same way yours did in the control room. And these coloured buttons look similar to those on the bridge but simpler and organised differently."

"Yes, my seat adjusted the first time I came in here, even before I sat down. It was as though someone or something recognised me and changed this seat to match the one I sat on in the control room." Rob appeared fascinated by this further example of Moby Dick's capabilities.

"Now you're making me even more worried. I have the most awful premonition of Moby Dick luring us deep inside and trapping us forever. I need to get out of here straight away."

~

When they returned from investigating the small spaceship, the room seemed exactly as it had been when they left. Rob checked the battery by the door. "Look at this, Penny."

He pressed the test button, and a full row of lights illuminated. "As usual, the battery's charged and the floor cleaned."

"Ah, not quite, Rob." She pointed to three fragments of Martian rock lying exactly where she'd dropped them. "Doesn't this worry you? Something is watching everything we do. It's even deciding the things which may be important to us and those that can be cleaned away."

Rob knelt down and examined the tiny slivers of rock. "These definitely are the pieces you showed me before."

Penny sat quietly, but it was obvious she was becoming

increasingly tense worrying about possible dangers hidden inside Moby Dick. "That's it. I'm moving to the tent. I can't stand the thought of being spied on."

~

"Thanks for coming with me. I know you'd prefer to stay inside Moby Dick. At least here in the tent I feel I can talk without being overheard."

Rob patted her arm. "And we've certainly got things to talk about. For instance, is there really any need for you to return to the Habitat. There's everything we need right here, shelter and power."

Penny pressed against Rob's shoulder and replied thoughtfully, "Although it would be great to just stay here with you, there are things which need to be sorted out. Augustin must have further plans for this place. Until we know what they are, we can't take full control of our lives. Also, you've told me a lot about Robert and Anastasia and how much you owe them. Indirectly, what happens here may also have an effect on them. We need to keep that in mind."

"You might be right. I suppose the only way to discover more about Augustin's plans is for you to return. Maybe just one more time?"

~

The following morning, Penny loaded the MarsMobile with sufficient batteries for the return journey. Squatting down to arrange them on the sled, she felt her knee joints binding and threatening to seize up all together. Although Rob had helped her walk over the rough ground in front of Moby Dick, he didn't seem to really appreciate her concern about the state of her knee joints. Mars was a hostile enough place without this added challenge. All Rob seemed truly interested in was searching Moby Dick for new alien gadgets, oblivious to the risks she was facing.

Chapter 40

Sergeant Kirby drew himself to his full height as he answered Robert's request. "What you ask is out of the question. I've been left in charge, and given the current situation, there's no way I could sanction an expedition outside the secure compound. You and Ms Anthon must be aware we're under sustained terrorist attack."

"But Augustin will demand a full report on what happened last night."

"The police are doing their investigation. I suggest we hold off until they complete their enquiries."

Robert attempted to strengthen his argument. "I doubt the police will look much beyond Squaddie's murder. Augustin will insist on finding out what destroyed his fifty Safetybots and most of our other equipment. He'll be furious if we haven't done our utmost to come up with some answers."

With obvious reluctance, Sergeant Kirby agreed. "Okay, I'll see what I can arrange."

~

The cause of the explosion, or at least what remained of it, was easy to locate. The sergeant, accompanied by a few heavily armed guards, escorted Robert and Anastasia out of the main gate and along the adjacent road.

"I'll show you what my men found earlier this morning. See if it makes any sense to you."

After a short distance, deep wheel ruts curved away from the road and headed towards the top of a small hill overlooking the compound. The group climbed in single file with the sergeant in the lead. He chose a path parallel to the wheel tracks, threading between patches of scrubby bushes.

A vehicle was lying on its side. Sergeant Kirby rested against one of its massive tyres and pointed to a logo advertising an equipment hire company. "We've established that this crane was hired a week ago using false documentation."

Anastasia took out a camera that Jason had been able to source for her and started photographing the scene. As she climbed over the vehicle, Robert found himself distracted by her poise and lithe purposeful movements. He recalled the first time they met. The same feeling of attraction was there, stronger than ever. He was determined to ensure she stayed part of his life and desperate to find a way to get them both out of Augustin's clutches.

Before they set off further up the hill, Anastasia drew level with the sergeant. "Did the explosion cause it to topple over?" She mimicked the fall of the crane with her arm.

"We assume it did."

The boom was lying on the ground, pointing directly away from the compound. They followed it, avoiding loops of wire rope, and only stopping where the end of the boom lay blackened and twisted. Robert turned to call out to Sergeant Kirby. "This thing is huge. How high could it reach?"

The sergeant caught up with Robert. "I'm no expert on mobile cranes, but I'd estimate maybe sixty metres."

"With the height of this hill plus sixty metres, there'd be a good line of sight into most of T2 from the top of the crane."

Robert turned to scan the ground close by. There was evidence of localised fires, which had scorched small patches of dry grass. "Did your men find what the crane was carrying?"

"There is something over there."

The sergeant pointed into the surrounding bushes. As they drew closer, they saw a flag marking a few deformed metal panels and a tangle of copper wire. With the hint of a challenge in his voice, he asked, "Well, what do you think it was?"

Without waiting for a reply, the sergeant and his guards spread out to keep watch. Robert and Anastasia started their search close to the flag.

"I think some of the wreckage has been removed." Robert pointed to scrape marks on the ground and trampled bushes. As he circled away from the flag, Robert tripped and fell heavily. "Oh shit!"

The sergeant and his two guards smiled and shook their heads at this obvious sign of clumsiness. For a few moments, Robert remained sprawled on the ground.

Anastasia offered her hand. "Are you okay?"

Robert moved slowly and allowed himself to be helped to his feet, in the process slipping something into Anastasia's camera bag. Behind his hand he whispered, "Don't touch it."

Sergeant Kirby called out to Robert allowing his impatience to show. "Are you done?"

"Yes, I don't think there's much more for us to see here. I'll leave it in your hands to collect the wreckage and preserve it for further examination."

~

Anastasia looked over Robert's shoulder. "What is it?"

He wiped the surface with a damp cloth and held up the shiny black object for Anastasia to see. "It's about the size and shape of a hockey puck but looks as though something attaches to the top and bottom," she noted.

He nodded and held out a magnifying glass so she could read markings on the side. Gingerly turning the puck to catch the light, Anastasia peered through the magnifying glass. "Just letters and number. Nothing that makes sense to me."

"It's a very specialised electronic component and could have killed me." He held out his left hand pointing to painful red welts on his palm and fingertips. "As I picked it up, it gave me quite an electric shock. If I'd touched it with both hands, the charge would have gone through my chest and possibly stopped my heart."

Anastasia's hand trembled as she covered her open mouth. "Is it still dangerous?"

He shook his head and pointed to a piece of wire he'd connected between the top and bottom terminals.

"Does it give us any clue about what all this means?"

"I'm not sure. This is only one small piece, and I suspect a lot more was removed before we got there."

"Okay, Robert, even if we're not sure exactly what it was, there seems little doubt it was responsible for destroying the electronics. You've got to admire Maxwell. He must have put a lot of planning into this attack."

Chapter 41

Pausing only to recover the spent batteries she discarded on the outward journey, Penny nursed her MarsMobile towards the Habitat. With no more replacement parts, she wanted its motors to last as long as possible. It was a huge relief when she topped a rise and caught her first glimpse of the crashed Mars lander. As she was parking her Marsmobile, HM appeared from the main entrance of the Habitat.

"Sam-renamed-Penny, Computer would like to talk with you. There are two issues which require your attention."

Penny sat down to take the weight off her knees. The left one was also bothering her now. It was becoming difficult to stand still because they both felt unstable.

"There has been no communication from Earth for three days, 16 hours and 23 minutes Mars time. Our radio dish can receive other signals from Earth, so it seems the problem is not with our equipment here on Mars."

"You were given contingency plans for this kind of situation. What are they?"

Although Penny had nothing better to do, Computer's long delay was annoying. Eventually, it gave the briefest of answers. "Procedure in the event of communication failure. Number 1, complete all previously allocated tasks. Number 2, maintain the functionality and integrity of the Habitat. Number 3, continue to make regular visits to monitor the OP."

"So, there's nothing that requires my immediate attention?"

"There is one other issue I must tell you about."

"Which is?"

"An unencrypted spoken message was sent to us over the radio link."

"How do you know it was sent to us? We only communicate by encrypted text and never identify ourselves."

"The sender addressed us by the Habitat coordinates on the U.S. Geological Survey Topological Map of Mars. It was obvious we were the intended recipients of the message. The sender identified himself as a member of a field survey team working for the mining company LanthanoCo. He requested permission to visit."

"Wow! I assume we weren't expecting visitors? What did you reply?"

"This situation is not covered in my contingency plans. I could not contact you or Earth, so I did not reply."

"If they decide to come anyway, do you have any idea when they'll arrive?"

"In their message, they proposed arriving about midday today."

Penny tried to work out which pieces of equipment shouldn't be on show for visitors. "HM, you know we've talked about hiding things? There are two large boxes I'd like you to bury."

~

A short length of metal pipe served as a walking stick for Penny as she joined HM on the rim of the crater sheltering the Habitat.

"I see something over there." HM pointed to a distant plume of dust approaching from the east.

"Compared with our MarsMobiles, it's moving really fast."

HM didn't respond to this unfavourable comparison with

its handiwork.

Making a series of broad detours, the vehicle avoided areas of broken ground and large boulders. As it drew closer, Penny could see that, in its own way, it was just as inelegant as HM's construction. Six wheels supported a central cylinder with many gas bottles and boxes attached along the sides. As it skidded to a halt next to them, two figures in pressure suits were visible through the windscreen. They donned goldfish bowl-shaped helmets before moving out of view. For several minutes, shimmering jets of gas and condensation were vented around the vehicle, presumably to equalise the internal pressure with the Martian atmosphere. Unsteady in their bulky pressure suits, the two visitors climbed down a rear ladder and turned to face HM and Penny.

"I'm sorry I was away from our camp and not contactable when you tried to get in touch. What can we do for you?"

There was no reply. She assumed the visitors, Victor and Gino judging by their name patches, were similarly trying to communicate over their personal radios. After a few minutes of discussion, Gino re-entered their vehicle and returned with a two-way radio.

A tinny voice carried from the radio, "Press switch to talk."

"Can you hear me?" Penny asked.

They both gave a thumbs up. Victor raised the sun visor on his helmet to provide a clearer view of his face, while Gino stepped back and didn't seem keen to get involved in a conversation.

"We do geologic survey. Base 500km that way." Victor waved his arm vaguely towards the east. "And you?"

Penny wasn't sure how to answer. She decided Augustin's first description of the Habitat would give away the least information. "We're here to set up some of the infrastructure for a permanent base that will be used to study the atmosphere and geology of Mars."

The visitors held a private conversation that didn't come

through the two-way radio. Perhaps they'd switched to a different frequency.

"How are you not wearing pressure suit?" He waved a dismissive hand in the direction of HM. "Obviously robot so no need. But you?"

Penny tried to adopt a disarming smile. "My name's Penny. I'm also a robot."

With no attempt to hide their curiosity, both visitors spent a full minute subjecting her to a close examination. She felt uncomfortable with their unabashed stares.

"Okay. We talk with person in charge?"

"Yes, Victor, you can talk with me. I'm in charge."

Victor shook his head vigorously. "No, must talk with human."

"There are no humans here. I make all the day-to-day decisions."

After more private discussion, Victor stepped forwards. "Perhaps we ask you then? We have breakdown. Other crawler vehicle kaput."

He led Penny back to his vehicle and pointed out part of the structure supporting the front pair of wheels. "Have bad collision. Bent here and here. Cannot steer."

"Don't you have any tools?"

"Some, nothing suitable."

HM moved to stand next to Penny. After a private conversation, she switched the two-way radio to 'talk'. "We think we have equipment you could use for a temporary repair. Do any of your team have experience with oxy-acetylene equipment?"

"No experience. Will work on Mars?"

He was clearly sceptical.

"HM assures me it works well providing you adjust the oxygen and acetylene pressures correctly. He'll locate the equipment and give you a demonstration. By heat-treating the damaged parts of your other crawler, you should be able to

214

bend them back into shape."

While waiting for HM to gather the equipment, and without asking for permission, Victor and Gino wandered around looking through the clear plastic doors into the Habitat, and inspecting the wreckage of the Mars lander. Their prying put Penny on edge, and she was relieved when they could be rounded up for the demonstration.

"Have no meteorological or other scientific equipment?"

Penny realised Victor had found the major flaw in Augustin's cover story for the Habitat. "That's true. Our task is to establish this base. The scientific instruments and research team will arrive later." It was an unlikely explanation but the best she could come up with. To deflect attention, she pointed to HM who had found a twisted piece of the Mars lander damaged in the crash.

"HM will show you how to use the equipment by straightening this piece of aluminium alloy."

Like a magician preparing for a conjuring trick, the robot handed around the bent strip of metal. After verifying it was well and truly bent, the visitors stood back as HM opened the valves on the oxygen and acetylene gas cylinders. With a loud 'pop' a flint lighter ignited the gas mixture.

"HM has been programmed with information about the oxy-acetylene equipment and will describe the heat-treatment process."

"I will soften the metal by annealing it at around 300° Celsius."

"How will you know temperature?"

HM picked up a sliver of wood split from a pencil and handed it to Penny. Every few seconds, HM turned the torch away from the aluminium and Penny ran the wood over the surface.

"When it reaches the correct temperature, the wood will leave a dark streak."

"What then?"

"To maintain the softness, the metal must be allowed to cool slowly. If it cools quickly, it will harden again."

HM set the strip of metal on a flat rock, adjusted the temperature of the flame, and slowly moved it away to delay cooling. Next it picked up a hammer.

With a look of astonishment Victor turned to Penny. "Why robot use hammer?"

"If used correctly, a hammer can be a very precise tool."

It was obvious both visitors didn't believe a hammer was a precision implement until HM held up the result of its handiwork. It was almost perfectly straight. Penny tried to flex the strip of aluminium with her hands. "Hammering has also rehardened the metal."

Clumsy in his pressure suit gloves, Victor tested the flexibility of the metal strip and seemed impressed.

"This is our spare set of oxy-acetylene equipment, so you can keep it. That will save you a return journey."

"Okay, we try."

As the visitors drove away with the oxy-acetylene gear, Penny realised their parting words were the closest they came to thanking her for the equipment.

"Computer would like to talk with you."

Penny followed HM to the computer room and received a report from Computer.

"While the two visitors were here, I monitored all of their conversations."

"Even when they switched frequency?"

"Yes."

"What did they say that they didn't want me to hear?"

"Once they sealed their pressure suits, it was only possible for them to communicate by radio, and this allowed me to listen in. While the cabin pressure of their crawler equalised with the Martian atmosphere they talked, mainly to complain about their boss, Ivanov. Apparently, he ordered them to change their landing zone at the very last minute."

"Did they say why the change was made?"

"Their boss wanted them to touchdown closer to the Habitat. Unfortunately for them, they are now a considerable distance from obvious rock formations, such as caves, that would provide readymade shelter from solar radiation. They also criticised the landing zone because there's only a low probability of finding valuable minerals nearby."

"It was obviously an imposition to have to visit the Habitat."

"I ascertained they were ordered to find out all they could about our mission. Their need for assistance to repair a damaged vehicle may have been of secondary importance. When reporting to their boss as they were leaving, they suspected you had not told them the real purpose of our mission. Overall, they were frustrated that, even though they did a thorough external inspection of the Habitat, they could not find out more. They worried that their boss would not be satisfied with their report."

"That's not surprising because I live here, and I'm not sure I know our true purpose."

"More worrying, they were discussing how useful the Habitat and all of our equipment would be. Victor and Gino, as well as the other members of their team, are suffering from sickness caused by solar radiation. They worked out that the Habitat's thick cover of gravel and rock would greatly reduce internal radiation levels, and discussed how good it would be to sleep and spend other downtime in the Habitat to reduce their exposure."

"Computer, I don't know a lot about radiation sickness. Do you have anything in your database?"

"There is only a brief entry, perhaps because it has little relevance to our mission. For humans, relatively brief and low levels of exposure to radiation can result in headaches, nausea and vomiting. Higher and more prolonged exposure results in hair loss, internal and external bleeding, confusion and convulsions followed by death. The exact severity and progress of the symptoms depends on the level and duration of exposure."

"That sounds absolutely horrible. I can understand their problems. Did Victor and Gino say anything else?"

"They said two robots would not be able to prevent them taking anything they wanted, and if the communications dish was disabled, nobody on Earth would find out what happened."

Penny's feelings of sympathy turned to indignation and downright fear when she discovered how her assistance was being repaid. "We'll have to arm ourselves with the guns and show we're not a pushover if they return."

Chapter 42

Robert and Anastasia joined Sergeant Kirby as they filed into the office. The call to an emergency meeting had everyone on edge even before Augustin started berating them.

"This whole situation is completely out of hand." He glowered at each of them in turn as though trying to weigh up their individual guilt. "First and foremost, I blame myself. I've been totally preoccupied with completing the crew for my next Mars mission. Now that's finalised, I can give my undivided attention to the Safetybot project." With a hint of sarcasm in his voice he turned to Sergeant Kirby. "Remind me of your progress with the investigation into the attacks on T2. You could start with what happened to Austin."

Obviously uncomfortable, the sergeant tried to deflect the questioning. "Robert has a better grasp of the technical details."

"Yes, but I put you in charge of security. Explain it from your point of view."

With no chance of escaping the spotlight, Kirby referred to his handwritten notes. "On Monday morning, Jason found the robot, Austin, lying beside the path close to the cafeteria. The robot didn't respond to any physical stimulus and was later found to have suffered extensive damage. No one saw what happened, and unfortunately, the area isn't covered by our surveillance cameras."

"In spite of my strict orders, this place is still plagued by poor security camera coverage. Unacceptable. But moving on, continue with your report."

"I had my men search the whole of T2 for anything unusual that could have been used to attack a robot and leave no marks."

"So, what exactly were your men looking for? Did you give them any sort of guidance or a description?"

"Well, no … I don't know."

Augustin allowed the sergeant's admission of ignorance to hang in the air for a long moment before swiping the surface of his tablet computer to bring up the next page. "The attack on T2 and death of Squaddie. Tell me about those events."

"Squaddie was hit by four 9mm bullets fired from the same gun." Sergeant Kirby seemed more comfortable discussing a crime he could relate to. He glanced down at a different sheet of paper. "Three shots to the torso fired from a range of ten or so metres didn't hit any vital organs and probably wouldn't have been fatal unless left untreated. The single head shot from close range certainly was."

When it was clear Sergeant Kirby had nothing more to add, Augustin turned to Anastasia. "Robert and I were close by, and that agrees with what we heard, three rapid shots, a short delay, and then a final shot."

"You were the first to arrive at the scene? What did you see?"

"I found Squaddie and tried to staunch the bleeding, but he was pretty much gone when I arrived. When I got to him there was no one else around that I could see. Other people joined me, and eventually an ambulance and then the police arrived."

Augustin snorted in exasperation and turned his attention back to the sergeant. "You've received the police report?"

The sergeant selected another sheet of paper from his

folder. "The police haven't made much progress with finding the shooter, and they seem to be giving a low priority to investigating the damage to the equipment in T2."

Augustin pointed a finger to emphasise his next question. "But you've looked into what caused so much damage to the electrical infrastructure and electronics in T2. What do you think happened?"

"There's a strong possibility it's linked to some wreckage we found on a hillside overlooking this place. Several people witnessed a flash and heard an explosion from there, which coincided with the loss of power and other damage. It's not yet clear how that localised detonation could cause such widespread damage."

"So, you've no idea exactly what happened or who was responsible?"

Slowly, the sergeant leafed through his folder of papers. Apparently failing to find any answers, he turned to Robert. "Robert and Anastasia examined the wreckage—"

Robert took over the story. "It seems obvious that a crane was used to suspend some sort of weapon high in the air. Whatever it was blew up, toppling the crane and spreading debris over quite an area. After only a brief examination, it wasn't possible to determine how the weapon worked. We asked for several items close to the source of the explosion to be collected and brought to the laboratory where we could take a closer look. That hasn't happened yet."

Augustin raised his hand. He'd obviously heard enough. "This is getting us nowhere. We need decisive action. I've called in an outside team to continue the investigation. As of now, T2 is in complete lockdown with everyone confined to their accommodation. Every square inch will be searched for clues, including the area around the wreckage on the hillside. The only exception will be people repairing the communications equipment."

When Augustin closed the meeting, Sergeant Kirby was the

first to leave.

Anastasia appeared dejected. "Looks like Augustin still doesn't trust me. He's just told me I'm not allowed to help you with the communications equipment."

"Well, I'd trust you with my life." Robert gave her a hug to emphasise his support before she left to start lockdown in her cabin.

Robert continued on to the Comms Centre and joined Ethan replacing the damaged equipment. "When he wants to, Augustin can really get things moving." Robert gestured towards the row of cardboard boxes containing replacement components.

Without looking up, Ethan connected up a piece of hardware and, after performing a quick check, attached a green label identifying it as undamaged.

"Robert Harper?"

Robert recognised the red beret of Augustin's team of investigators. "Yes."

Perhaps assuming his uniform was the only authorisation and explanation he required, the soldier continued. "We were told you could give an opinion on something we've found. Our instructions were to look for anything out of place or unusual, and this is definitely strange." The soldier led Robert outside to an area screened by a brushwood fence. Three large bins were tipped on their sides, their contents spread thinly over the ground. In the middle of the food scraps and empty containers was a large package covered in shiny aluminium foil.

"I've seen foil like that recently, close to where Squaddie was shot. I agree, it's definitely worth a closer look."

Robert watched as the package was carefully moved onto a large plastic sheet, and the remaining objects were each closely examined before being returned to the bin. The only other items of interest were a few strips of foil. He supervised the transfer of the package and pieces of foil to the main laboratory.

~

In view of the progress made by his team of investigators, Augustin relaxed the lockdown order. He was taking a keen interest in the items they'd discovered, and joined Robert and Jason as they prepared to examine the package's contents. "I can't comprehend how Kirby's search failed to find this." He peered over his spectacles to take a closer look. A few days earlier, Austin, his robotic double, had lain on the same bench as the foil-wrapped package, and this probably made him feel uncomfortable. The sight of the portable blast screens must have added to his unease. "Let me know what you find," Augustin called out from the door before leaving.

As the outside door closed, Jason and Robert donned protective body armour and pulled the portable screens into a circle. "Do you really think this thing could explode?" Jason asked.

Robert smiled through his blast visor. "I've no idea, but we can't be too careful. The X-rays show lots of things wired together, but they don't give much of a clue about what the whole thing does."

Using grabbers equipped with hand guards, Robert gently peeled away the aluminium foil. Jason recorded the process with a video camera and offered his opinion on the contents. "Looks like a military-style canvas backpack."

"Yes, but obviously it contains some kind of weapon with that corrugated pipe and hand grip with gun-like trigger. Just what I would expect of a flamethrower, though I've never seen one of those except in old movies."

Jason moved the video camera to give a better view as Robert loosened two straps and opened the top of the pack. Methodically, Robert disconnected and removed the contents.

"Okay then, Robert, what is it?"

"We've got batteries, electronics and some other weird things that look like copper pipes. I have a theory."

They both carried the items outside, well away from any

buildings. By referring back to Jason's video, Robert reconnected everything and then issued a warning.

"No electronics, no watches, no smart cards, no electronic keys?"

Jason patted his pockets and then shook his head. Robert placed a small pocket radio on a rock several metres away and tuned it to a local station. Augustin had prohibited all means of communicating with the outside world. Robert wasn't sure if the ban included pocket radios, so he kept it in the laboratory only to be used when he was alone.

"Ready, Jason?"

Jason took two backward paces as though unsure of how dangerous the device would be.

Robert directed the end of the pipe towards the radio and pulled the trigger. With a resounding click, the radio fell silent. "Do you recognise the smell?"

Tentatively, Jason stepped forward and sniffed the pipe and handgrip. "You mean something like chlorine?"

"Yes, I think it's ozone, which is produced by electrical sparks such as lightning. There's obviously some seriously high voltages in this thing."

Robert took the back off the radio and showed the insides to Jason. "See, there's no obvious signs of damage, but it's stopped working."

"This must be what happened to Austin. So, what's your theory?"

"I believe this is an EMP, otherwise known as an electromagnetic pulse weapon. It kills electronics in a similar way to cooking them in a microwave oven, only at a distance."

"Where does the aluminium foil come in?"

"I'm guessing that was used to protect it from the massive electromagnetic pulse that destroyed the Squaddie robots. Whoever had the backpack knew what was about to happen and wrapped it in a protective layer of foil. Later, they must have disposed of it, fearing it would be discovered."

"Okay, so we know how it was done. Now we need to work out why and by whom."

Together they carried the weapon back to the laboratory. Robert helped Jason organise the fragments of aluminium foil that had been recovered from the rubbish bin by trying to match the torn edges. Using a powerful magnifying glass, Robert examined each piece in turn. Some of the fragments still carried an impression of things they'd been pressed against. "Those are interesting. I know it's a longshot, but I wonder whether this piece could have been wrapped around a wristwatch. Do you remember when we scanned Squaddie?"

"Of course."

"Did you see Sergeant Kirby's watch?"

"Not particularly. I was busy getting things ready for the scan."

"Well, at the time, I noticed he was wearing a cheap plastic model rather than his usual fancy military one. And that was shortly after Austin was killed."

"So, if the sergeant used this weapon, it could have damaged his watch as well as killing Austin?"

"It's unlikely, but I wonder if there could be an imprint that could have come from the back of the watch? Often there'll be the manufacturer's name, a part number or something like that."

Jason helped darken the room and position a spotlight to highlight the indentations. "I could have something, but it's not very clear. Possibly a K and also perhaps a number seven."

~

Augustin looked up from the magnifier and slipped on his gold-rimmed glasses. Robert and Jason waited while he considered the evidence.

"You don't seriously expect me to believe Sergeant Kirby was involved on the basis of a scrap of foil with a couple of impressions that may or may not be from a letter K and a seven?"

Robert tried to make his voice as calm and reasonable as possible. "I'm just saying we should check the back of his watch. I'm sure he'd be the first to acknowledge no one should be above suspicion."

"Well, I'm sure you're barking up the wrong tree. Kirby's worked for me for years and has a strong sense of loyalty. His competence has been a bit below par recently, but I can't believe he'd do anything to harm my robots. Still, I've asked for him to be brought here straight away. The sooner we put this nonsense to bed, the sooner we can get back to trying to find the real culprits." He moved across the room to take another look at the EMP weapon.

Without knocking, Sergeant Kirby stepped into the laboratory closing the door firmly behind him. Augustin looked up in surprise. "I've just sent a couple of men to collect you."

The sergeant smiled bleakly and turned a fraction to emphasise his right hand resting on his holster. "We must have missed each other. I heard you've found something interesting, so I came to take a look. What can I do for you?"

After an uncomfortable silence, Robert decided on a question that wasn't too confrontational. "You had your watch repaired?"

"Surely you didn't summon me here to enquire about the state of my watch?"

Robert tried to be non-confrontational. With a faint smile he held out his hand. "May I?"

The sergeant glared back defiantly. After a long pause, Augustin gestured for him to comply.

Sergeant Kirby hesitated as though weighing the risks of playing along with Robert or doing something more irrevocable. Without moving his right hand far from his gun, he released the wristband and handed over his watch.

"Nice one, sergeant." Robert spent several seconds examining the face and rotating bezel. As an apparent afterthought, he flipped it over and looked at the back. "I can see your name, Kirby, and is this your service number?"

"Yes, 547993. What's this about?"

Augustin showed no signs of registering the barely hidden menace in the sergeant's voice and posture. "Robert and Jason think they've found a possible connection between your watch and a piece of foil. The same type of foil was used to protect that weapon. An EMP I think they called it." He pointed to the backpack and its contents laid out on the bench. "This is what was used to disable Austin."

In one smooth, practiced movement, the sergeant drew his gun. "Austin was just one of the latest examples of your crazy infatuation with robots." He waved the gun from side to side, alternately menacing Augustin, Jason then Robert. "Ever since you took over that ridiculous Project Transition, I've tried to prevent your obsession getting out of hand."

The gun came to a halt pointing directly at Augustin. At that moment, the door opened, and Anastasia stepped into the laboratory, balancing cups of coffee slotted into a cardboard tray. In a fraction of a second she must have sized up the situation. Sergeant Kirby was forced to raise his arms to fend off the barrage of steaming drinks she threw at him. He shook off the hot coffee and fired three shots in the general direction of Augustin, who was now crouching behind a pillar. Without waiting to find out if any of the shots hit their target, he threw Anastasia to one side and fled from the room.

Augustin pulled himself to his feet, and spoke into a two-way radio. "Dr Selworthy here, Sergeant Kirby has gone rogue, terminate with extreme prejudice."

In the distance, they heard raised voices followed by a volley of shots and then silence.

~

A soldier opened the door wide to allow Augustin to leave. "We think it's safe now, sir." Robert, Anastasia and Jason followed on behind. "Kirby exchanged fire with one of my men, and both were hit. Unfortunately, the sergeant was able to escape. We tracked him to the outer fence. I'll organise a couple of search parties to take it from there."

The soldier led them to a point where the chain-link fence had been cut in an area hidden from the security cameras by a water storage tank. "It looks as though he went this way, but the ground outside is too dry to show footprints."

Augustin examined the gap in the fence. He pointed to several drops of blood and then gazed out over the surrounding scrubland. Turning to the soldier, he made sure there was no doubt about his orders. "There hasn't been time for him to get far. He's too dangerous to be on the loose, so I'm relying on you to neutralise this problem."

~

There were many things Robert wanted to discuss with Anastasia as they walked back to her cabin so she could change out of her coffee-drenched clothes. Only after closing the door did they see the seated figure doubled over in pain. "Sit down and don't do anything foolish." Sergeant Kirby waved his handgun to indicate two kitchen chairs.

"You're bleeding; you need a doctor."

Ignoring Anastasia, he used his free hand to increase pressure on an abdominal wound. "Whatever happens, things don't look good for me. I want to set the record straight. Bear in mind, everything I did was with the best intentions."

"At least let me see if there's anything I can do to help."

The sergeant waved Anastasia away with the barrel of his gun. "You'd be wasting your time. I know enough about tactical trauma assessment to work out how this is going to go." He twisted in his seat and rested the handgun on his knee. "You know, Robert, I didn't plan on you being hit by shrapnel when I told my men to take out Robot 3. I'm really sorry about that."

"Did Maxwell persuade you to do that?"

"No, it was only afterwards that Maxwell got to hear how

much I hate robots and would be agreeable to helping his cause."

Anastasia looked at him accusingly. "So, you had something to do with the destruction of T1?"

"Only indirectly. I turned a blind eye, but Maxwell assured me no one would be injured, and the robots would evacuate everyone before setting off the explosives. The needless loss of life was devastating."

She persisted. "And yet you continued to work against Augustin's robotic projects."

Kirby managed a grim smile. His voice sounded a bit weaker as he gritted his teeth. "Austin was just a robot infected with Augustin's hideous personality, a double reason to destroy it. The Safetybots would have displaced real soldiers. But I deeply regret what happened to Squaddie."

"Did you shoot him?"

"It was unintentional and his own fault really. I was hiding, waiting to mop up any of the robots that escaped the main EMP attack. Squaddie was wearing the same kind of t-shirt as the robots and, at night, I couldn't tell the difference. My EMP weapon had no effect, so I hit him with three shots at fifteen metres. When I got closer, I realised he was bleeding and not a robot. He was in a bad way, so I finished him off with a shot to the head to end his suffering."

"And so he couldn't identify you?"

The sergeant looked away and didn't answer Robert's accusation. He groaned as he started to stand up, distress lining his face.

"Nothing turned out the way I wanted, but now at least, you know the truth. To make amends for some of the things I shouldn't have done, I'd like to give you a warning. I overheard Augustin and Austin discussing your future. They agreed you both knew too much to be allowed to leave. Originally, there was going to be a fatal 'accident' when the scanner was shown to be working correctly. That accident has now been postponed until you are no longer needed for communicating with Mars."

Doubled over in pain he shuffled out of the door. Before Robert or Anastasia could react, there was the sound of a single gunshot.

Chapter 43

"Sam-renamed-Penny, I have received a message from Earth. They report having had technical issues with their communications equipment. All is now back in working order, and they request a status report."

"Thank goodness it's all working again. Okay, Computer. Obviously, yesterday's visitors were unexpected, and that's why you hadn't been given an appropriate plan. Pass on to Earth everything we discovered about them. We need to know more about LanthanoCo and what we should do if they return."

"I will send the report and ask those questions."

"To ensure we receive useful answers, I've thought of some scenarios which would need a response. Least threatening could be, they return and ask for help with another problem that can be easily solved without using any of our resources."

"And the most threatening?"

"They could threaten to take over the Habitat by force if we didn't cooperate."

"Is there anything in between?"

"I can imagine them asking for unreasonable amounts of equipment or even insisting on taking shelter in the Habitat."

"I will put all of those questions into a reply. The current communication window lasts for another two Earth hours, so we should receive an answer very soon."

Before the arrival of Victor and Gino, Penny already had a number of problems to contend with, including her deteriorating body and being wary of Augustin's remote influence. The visitors provided a new and very immediate threat. She took the opportunity to sit and exercise her knee joints. Range and smoothness of movement were both getting worse. It may have been her imagination, but she was certain her arm and hip joints weren't moving as smoothly and accurately as they should, either.

~

"Sam-renamed-Penny, I have a reply. Augustin only recently found out about the LanthanoCo mission to Mars. They arrived in Mars orbit shortly after we touched down. Because they had the whole of Mars to choose from, he assumed it highly unlikely they'd land anywhere near the Habitat and so didn't think it necessary to warn us. The latest images from the mapping satellites show activity about 500 kilometres east of here centred around a group of four landers. A fifth craft remains in Mars orbit."

"Who are they really?"

"They seem to be an exploration and mining company, as they said. On Earth their main interest is in rare earth minerals, but on Mars they may extend that to any useful and easily exploitable resource such as water ice."

"From what Victor and Gino said they changed their plans specifically to take a look at the Habitat. That's very worrying. Any change to their landing site represents a big commitment of their resources. They must believe we're onto something valuable."

"The message also sets out responses to different levels of threat from our visitors. Future requests for assistance should be denied, citing a lack of supplies, equipment or expertise. Attempts to take anything from us without permission must be resisted by force if necessary. In the event of an overwhelming takeover, the attacking force must be eliminated using one of the short-range missiles."

"The missiles with the nuclear warheads?"

"That is correct."

"And if the attackers have already reached the Habitat?"

"The warhead must be set off here to deny the attackers access to the base and minimise what they can discover about our mission. In that event, the bomb must be detonated at ground level, maximising residual radiation but also minimising the size of the affected area. Care must be exercised to ensure fallout from the bomb does not contaminate the area around the OP."

Penny was alarmed by the thought of being sacrificed on Augustin's whim. "You have no problems with destroying yourself?"

"I will always follow instructions, even if they result in my own termination."

~

Penny unearthed the second handgun and carried it to the computer room. "HM, do you know how to use this?"

"Yes, Sam-renamed-Penny. I have full instructions on the use of that type of weapon."

"As we have been instructed, any attempt to steal our equipment or take over the Habitat must be resisted by force. Do you understand?"

"I understand."

Computer gave a low musical chime which it used to get attention. "Sam-renamed-Penny, I am receiving a transmission on one of the frequencies used by our two visitors. They appear to be talking amongst themselves and not trying to contact us."

"Can you work out what they're doing?"

"Their conversation is difficult to follow. It appears to be comments from one complaining about the driving skills of the other. One thing seems certain; the strength of the transmission is increasing. They are coming closer.”

~

With HM’s assistance, Penny started the timer on one of the nuclear warheads. If the visitors overpowered them and the timer wasn’t reset within half an hour, the Habitat and its surrounding would be vaporised. Augustin’s secrets would be safe.

Penny and HM squatted on the ground and tried to give the impression they were repairing the damaged MarsMobile. This gave them a plausible reason to be out in the open where they could intercept their visitors before they got too close to the Habitat. To be seen to be expecting them would reveal that Computer could monitor their personal communications.

For the second time, Penny loosened the bolts holding the burnt-out motor and prepared to disconnect it.

“The visitors have arrived.” HM pointed to a crawler following the wheel-ruts left from the first visit. The vehicle pulled to a halt close to the two robots. There was only a short delay before Victor and Gino negotiated the rear stairs and walked towards Penny and HM. She reasoned the cabin of the crawler hadn’t been pressurised, therefore they’d only made a short trip.

“Was your repair successful?” she asked.

Victor operated the two-way radio. “A little. Not skilled like your robot.”

He gave the impression Gino was the one lacking the skills.

“We’re pleased the repair was at least an improvement.”

There was an awkward silence. Penny deliberately avoided asking if they needed any further help. Finally, Victor spoke again. “Like your rocket, we have crash landing, destroyed things. Urgent need solar panels. You have spare?”

At last, the question she feared but expected. She pointed towards the wreckage of their Mars lander. “As you can see, we had problems with our landing, and this led to the loss of some of its cargo. I regret we now have a shortage of many delicate pieces of equipment, including solar panels. Therefore, we are unable to help you."

"But you have many."

"Solar is our only power source for transport, communications, heating and to supply the energy requirements of us robots. We need a reserve in case of dust storms or more panel failures."

"We borrow reserve panels, return if needed?"

"I am responsible for the operation of this research station. I'm sure you would return the panels if we required them, but not having them actually on site would pose a critical risk to our mission that I am unable to consider."

Rapid hand gestures hinted at an animated conversation otherwise hidden from Penny. Eventually, Victor and Gino turned to include her in the conversation. "We trade for panels?"

"Unfortunately, there is nothing we need which would balance the increased risk to our power security."

As she said this, Penny remembered the burnt-out MarsMobile motor, but decided it was unwise to encourage further interaction. She didn't want to give the visitors any further opportunity to evaluate their security and decide what would be worth stealing.

For a long moment, the visitors stood as though deciding their next move. Almost imperceptivity, Penny signalled to HM. With little attempt to disguise its intentions, HM reached into the toolbox and its fingers closed around the handgun.

"We regret you unable to help. Another time?"

Without waiting for a reply, they returned to their crawler. After watching the vehicle recede into the distance, Penny left HM to keep watch and re-entered the Habitat. On the way, she disabled the timer on the missile.

"Computer, what did our visitors talk about that they didn't want us to hear?"

"They were disappointed you could not be persuaded to

give them some solar panels. When it became obvious you would not change your mind, they discussed if they should overpower you and HM using the guns they had in their crawler or return when better prepared. They saw HM reach for the handgun and decided they needed to return with more effective weapons."

"That amounts to a declaration of war. We must be on our guard."

~

Later that afternoon, HM notified Penny that Computer had received another message for her.

"Sam-renamed-Penny, Earth have sent further instructions. The second missile is to be transported to the OP and buried beneath the flag. There it can be used to discourage any attempt to take possession of the object."

"I guess I must do what I'm told. But I think it's very risky to leave the Habitat guarded only by HM."

"Yes, Sam-renamed-Penny. Perhaps they feel that the threat of the nuclear bomb can give sufficient protection."

Penny couldn't see how a bomb could act as a deterrent if the attackers didn't know about it, but decided not to argue. "Can a MarsMobile carry that much weight?"

"It can if you only take sufficient batteries for the outward journey. It will be necessary for you to use some of the charged batteries stored at the OP for your return."

~

At first light, HM helped Penny load one of the missiles onto the sled and added as many batteries as it judged safe.

"You have the other nuclear missile ready for deployment, HM?"

"I have set up the built-in timer as instructed. Once it is activated, the bomb will go off twenty minutes later unless I deactivate it. At the first sign of trouble, I will start the timer and will switch it off in the event of a false alarm."

Penny entered the computer room to tell Computer she

was leaving for the OP even though she was certain HM would pass on the information. "Computer, I'm taking the second missile to the OP. I do worry about the threat from yesterday's visitors. If they return, you and HM must do your best to deal with any problems."

"I will transmit that information to Earth during the current communications window, Sam-renamed-Penny."

With nothing further to add, she returned to her MarsMobile. HM was shielding the early morning sun from its visor as it looked to the east. Penny leaned on her improvised walking stick and gazed in the same direction

"Sam-renamed-Penny, I think I can see a vehicle. I will start the timer."

"How far must I travel to be safe in the event that the nuclear bomb goes off?"

"The blast radius for ground burst deployment is half a kilometre. It would be wise to be well beyond that distance. Fortunately, there is a gentle wind from the north, so radiation will be blown away from you and the OP."

Penny set off directly away from the rising sun. After travelling for close to fifteen minutes she estimated she'd covered about one kilometre. Parking the MarsMobile sheltered at the base of a low hill she climbed to a higher vantage point.

The vehicle had already arrived at the Habitat. Penny thought she heard gunfire, but it was difficult to be sure. Sound didn't travel very far in the cold, thin Martian atmosphere. A few minutes later, the crawler circled and headed in her direction. Her dust plume must have been obvious to the visitors. With its significant speed advantage, there was no point in trying to outrun the crawler. Instead, Penny returned to the MarsMobile and crouched down beside it, head pointing away from the Habitat.

For a long moment, the flash easily outshone the early morning sun touching the peaks of taller rocks. The accompanying flash of radiation had a severe effect on Penny's silicon brain. Her mind was overloaded with kaleidoscopic patterns, all sensory information swamped by random noise. A fraction of a second later, the ground heaved with the arrival of the first shock. The following seconds of calm seemed to draw out for an age. When it arrived, the atmospheric shockwave knocked Penny to the ground in a cloud of billowing dust.

Gradually, she pieced together the situation, who she was, where she was and what had just happened. As the atmosphere cleared, she brushed off her clothes and climbed to look back at the Habitat. A vertical column of dust and debris marked where the base had been. Closer than the crater carved out by the explosion, a six-wheeled vehicle lay flipped onto its side and crushed out of shape. There were no signs anyone had survived the blast and flash of radiation. HM and Computer had always interacted in a very mechanical way, completely lacking in personality. In spite of this, Penny was sad she'd never be able to talk with them again.

Surveying the devastation, Penny knew a fundamental change had happened. Now, life on Mars would be even more isolated and problematic. With the communication link and Habitat destroyed, Augustin would have no more control, but they had also lost contact with Rob's friends on Earth, and there were an unknown number of hostile humans remaining on Mars. With a bittersweet feeling, Penny started the MarsMobile and chose a heading calculated to meet up with the route to the OP while keeping clear of the contaminated area.

Chapter 44

Icy fingers of apprehension squeezed Robert's chest, making it difficult to breath. In vain, he had searched the satellite images looking for familiar outlines of the Habitat or lander wreckage. Shuffling between sheets of electronic film, he traced the MarsMobile tracks returning from the OP and discovered that they ended in a large area of unfamiliar and unnaturally smooth ground. After minute examination and comparison with earlier images, he was forced to conclude that the Habitat had been wiped off the face of Mars. This could only be the result of a powerful explosion. After so much effort to help build Rob and then watch over his development this was a devastating turn of events. Gathering the images, he headed for Augustin's office.

After negotiating with the sentries, Robert was allowed to enter the small, nondescript office. As he shared his news, Robert was surprised by the unusually calm way Augustin accepted the setback. He gave the satellite images quite minimal attention. There seemed to be something else on his mind.

"Tell me what's been happening, and this time start from the beginning."

Robert referred to his tablet computer. "The last message

from Computer described a second visit by those guys from LanthanoCo, Victor and Gino. In a private conversation, which the visitors didn't realise was being overheard, they discussed receiving orders from someone called Ivanov. These seemed to concern plans for taking over the Habitat by force, if necessary."

Augustin held up his hand to stop Robert and his face darkened. "Ivanov? Did the reports mention a first name? It wasn't Pavel, was it?"

"In Computer's report, there's no mention of Ivanov's full name. But that name is familiar. Anastasia told me about someone called Pavel that she came across on Aeaea. I think he was one of the Safetybot investors."

In an instant, Augustin's attitude changed from relaxed to fiery and intense. "At that meeting all names were supposed to be confidential. How did she find out about Pavel?"

"I think someone else in the group called out to him while he was photographing your collection of stone tablets. But that guy couldn't have any connection with the Mars mission, could he?"

Augustin took a few moments to regain his composure, then set his jaw firmly and changed the subject. "You were telling me what else you found out."

Robert slid one of the satellite images to the centre of the table and traced a circle. "The Habitat has been wiped out. The scale of the destruction shows it must be the result of a nuclear explosion. There would be no way to transport sufficient conventional explosive all the way from Earth. Some distance from ground zero, there's wreckage, which could be the remains of the Mars lander and also some unknown vehicle. The force of the explosion has smoothed the surface for some distance. In a hopeful sign, there are fresh tracks almost certainly made after the explosion, which start from west of where the Habitat used to be and head north towards the OP." With sadness in his voice Robert concluded, "If the tracks were made by either Sam, Rob or HMM23 and they manage to get to the OP, they'll soon run out of power now that the Habitat's solar panels have been destroyed."

"I can confirm it was almost certainly a nuclear explosion. I sent an instruction to destroy the Habitat if a takeover became unavoidable. That was necessary to maintain the project's secrecy. The level of radioactive contamination will deter anyone else from investigating the area around the Habitat for quite some time. The last update sent by Computer indicated a steady wind from the north, which would carry radiation away from the OP. Given the obvious interest shown by these LanthanoCo people, things couldn't have worked out better. I imagine the threat of further nuclear bombs will give any survivors pause for thought."

Robert was deeply shocked by the news. "You sent an atom bomb up there? And ordered its use?" he continued angrily. "Rob was probably closer to me than a brother. It's devastating to think he's been destroyed or doomed to expire through lack of power."

Robert started to leave, then realised he still needed to report on the EMP. Shaken by what he'd just discovered about events on Mars, he mechanically unpacked a number of blackened and twisted items and arranged them in the centre of the table. He tried to keep his voice neutral to avoid antagonizing Augustin. "We know Sergeant Kirby's backpack was a short-range EMP weapon. I believe a much larger version of the same type of device destroyed most of the electronics in T2."

Augustin prodded a blackened and twisted lump of copper with his pen. "But why the explosion? Kirby's backpack thing didn't explode."

"This one used explosives to release the huge amount of energy necessary to send a burst of microwave radiation over a wide area. The pulse fried most electronics in line-of-sight of the explosion. To reduce any shadowing effects of nearer buildings, it was raised as high as possible, hence the crane. All in all, this was a very well-planned and sophisticated attack."

"Obviously, Kirby was only ever a bit player in this whole affair. The planning and resources involved point to Maxwell. The main question is, who else is working for him? We're alone here. Tell me who you suspect."

"Anastasia saved your life, so we can exclude her."

Augustin polished his glasses in a contemplative manner. "Taken at face value, it does seem as though she intended to foil the attempt on my life. Another interpretation would be that in the split second after entering the room, she believed you were under threat and acted to save your life."

There was no use arguing. Augustin seemed determined to doubt Anastasia. Robert resolved to keep quiet and let him do the talking, anything to get the meeting over and done with as soon as possible.

"Events have shown, in spite of my best efforts, this place is too difficult to protect. I've decided to relocate to a more remote and easily defended location. If these attacks are really directed at me, then this will take pressure off T2."

For a fleeting moment, Robert saw the prospect of getting away from Augustin's direct control. "Will both the Safetybot project and Mars mission remain based here?"

"I have a deep commitment to Mars exploration. I'll be relocating the communications dish and associated equipment together with my new Mars crew in preparation for the next mission. It'll be essential that you, Anastasia and Jason come along. I'll need your assistance with the equipment and probably the crew as well."

"But who'll be in charge of Safetybot production?"

"I don't really need Ethan for the Mars mission now we have his brain scan. It may be a little out of left field for him, but I'm sure he can use his organisational skills to manage it."

Chapter 45

Guided by the Sun, Penny chose a heading which would cross the well-marked path to the OP. Before long, new problems became evident, demonstrating she'd not completely avoided injury from the nuclear blast. Covering her left eye highlighted large patches of lost vision on the right side. Several finger joints were frozen, which made it difficult to control the MarsMobile. Coupled with the existing knee joint problems, it wasn't clear she would be capable of completing the journey to the OP. She hoped there wasn't even more hidden damage that would cause trouble in the future.

With the monotony of following the established track, Penny's mind was free to range over many topics but always returned to Rob. Would she end up being a burden to him? She felt such a wreck, barely functioning. Wouldn't it be better to avoid recharging her batteries and gently slide into oblivion? Fortunately, the overpowering desire to see him again displaced those morbid thoughts.

~

At the next stop to replace the MarsMobile battery, Penny asked herself why she was still following Augustin's order and taking the second missile to the OP. With the communication link cut, surely, she could stop pretending to be Sam? But in her present state of mind, it was too complicated to think about other possibilities and much simpler to stick with the original plan.

~

She almost drove past the observation post. It was only the lack of tracks which alerted her. Pulling to a halt by the tent, she was overjoyed to see Rob again. Dismounting from the MarsMobile proved almost impossible, and he rushed forward to help.

"Oh, Rob, I'm so pleased to see you. The Habitat's gone."

"Gone?"

"Completely wiped out by one of Augustin's nukes. I was ordered to bring the other one with me." She collapsed unto his arms.

When she regained some composure, Rob stepped back to examine her tattered clothes and lacerated skin. "You look in a bad way. How close were you to the explosion?"

"Probably too close to avoid some serious effects."

Rob helped support her weight as she limped towards Moby Dick's airlock. As they drew near, Penny started to resist. "You know I don't want to stay here. This place makes me nervous."

Rob wouldn't allow Penny to back away and talked to her gently until she was persuaded to continue. Once inside, Rob unrolled a second thin bedding roll for Penny to lie on and selected a fully charged battery. "You probably haven't had any sleep for nearly two days. You need to rest and recharge. I promise, nothing bad will happen."

~

Rob lowered himself carefully to the floor. Penny was still sleeping soundly, and the clean clothes made her look in a much better state than when she'd arrived. The numerous stains, cuts and tears on her face and hands were gone. He gently touched her shoulder.

"How long have I been asleep?"

244

"Well over a day."

Penny sat up, examined her pristine clothing, and flexed the fingers of each hand. "Who did this?"

"I don't know, but I assume the 'something' which recharges our batteries and sweeps the floor also does repairs."

"That's what I find so frightening about this place, the unknown. If I could see who or what was doing this and perhaps communicate with it, I think I'd have fewer doubts."

"I understand, but I've come to accept the hidden way it works."

Penny seemed calmer after they returned to the OP. Rob was pleased to see she was now walking without any difficulty. After burying the missile, they took shelter in the tent. Penny still couldn't think beyond the mysterious events that happened while they were asleep.

"I was right about Moby Dick. You must agree there's something inside, something watching us?"

"I'll admit that, but I've decided it's probably just an automated maintenance system and not something malevolent that will cause us any problems."

"Have you seen it or tried communicating with it?"

"Whatever it is, it seems obsessed with keeping out of sight. However, my big success was asking for another snowflake key. Before I went to sleep, I put my key next to the empty battery and said out loud I'd like another one. I felt like a child leaving a tooth under my pillow for the tooth fairy. When I woke up, there it was."

"That's a very hopeful sign. Obviously, it understood. Did you ask anything else?"

"How long have you been here? Where did you come from? What happened to the crew? I spoke the questions and wrote them down, but no response."

"How frustrating. There are so many things we need to find out. It must know the function of all those coloured buttons and switches around the place, but without that knowledge, I don't think we should risk touching any of them."

For a while, Penny experimented curling and extending her fingers. "To repair my damage, this maintenance system must have discovered a lot about how we work and also be capable of reproducing the technology. You could ask it to build a copy of one of us, but with a version of its mind in it. I assume it has what we would call a mind."

Rob looked doubtful. "That would be a huge task to analyse and reproduce each of our components. On Earth, the best-equipped laboratory could take years to do that job. What's more, even if this mind is copied into a robot body, how can we be sure it'll talk to us?"

"We can at least try."

~

Moby Dick's guardians worked in their usual hidden manner and in two Martian days there was a result. The copy looked similar to Rob, apart from physical size, lack of hair and its alarmingly green skin. Penny squatted down and examined its face. "In a way, it looks quite like a five-year-old version of you. Perhaps it was made smaller to save on materials, but I don't know about the green skin. How d'you think we switch it on?"

The eyes blinked open and swivelled between the two of them. "Unnecessary, I am already enabled."

Taken aback, Penny leapt to her feet and grabbed Rob's arm.

"The colour of our epidermis was selected to match every entity we have ever encountered, apart from you. Do you find it objectionable?"

"Not at all, but it was a surprise because it's so different from our skin."

The green robot turned its attention to Rob. "We are not barred from answering questions, so can respond to those you asked. We have been on this planet for over two thousand of its orbits around the sun. The solar system where this craft started its journey is visible in the night sky, and we would be able to identify it for you if you wish. Soon after arriving, Zeezee, the only crew member on this trip, used a short-range ferry craft to journey to the next adjacent planet you call Earth. She has not returned, and because of the passage of time, is unlikely to do so now."

The answers were spoken in a flat, even tone, which matched the expressionless face. Recovering from her surprise, Penny stepped forward. "How do you know our language?"

"We have monitored wireless communications since your planet first developed that capability. Even after extensive analysis, it has been difficult to discover the structure and meaning of some of the transmissions coming from Earth. We were able to identify several different language groups, but on occasions their meaning was unclear. Being able to monitor the way your speech relates to your actions has been of great assistance in improving our understanding of this language."

The green figure attempted to struggle to its feet and then gave up. "Standing up and walking will need practice. This would be so much easier if we could have equipped ourselves with four legs instead of just two."

Clumsy as a newborn child, the miniature version of Rob seemed to captivate Penny. "I'm Penny, and this is Rob. What's your name?"

"We do not have a name. Our purpose is to protect, repair and maintain this vessel. By design, we always remain out of sight and previously never communicated directly with passengers or crew."

"We're grateful those restrictions don't apply to us."

"We think our designers did not anticipate the current situation, and so there are no applicable rules. And, in that case, we would like to have a name."

"Do you have any preference?"

"We understand that Greek mythology is often used as a

source of ideas in some of Earth's cultures. For that reason, Cerberus, the three-headed dog of Greek mythology, would be appropriate."

"I don't know about Rob, but I think of the creature behind that name as rather intimidating."

"There are three of us, a triple redundancy, we think you would call it. If one of us fails or operates incorrectly, there are always two others who can work to detect and correct the problem."

As though that was decided, Cerberus moved to its next question. "We have always wondered what happened to Zeezee, the pilot who brought this ship here. She left in one of the ferry craft shortly after we arrived. We expected she would return for additional equipment and supplies, but that did not happen."

"When it became obvious Zeezee wasn't coming back, why didn't you return to your home planet?"

"Our purpose is limited to protection, repair and maintenance. We were not designed to be involved with planning or executing the ship's mission."

"Do you have any idea what happened to Zeezee?"

"Because you originally came from Earth, we were hoping you could inform us. The extent of our knowledge is that Zeezee took two keys on her trip to the surface of the planet Earth. For a great length of time, both keys were located very close to each other. It is not possible she could still be alive, but if there were children her decedents might live there now. We were extremely interested when one of the keys commenced the return journey, but were surprised it travelled so slowly. Eventually, you used it to enter this ship."

"The three suits hung up in the room where we sleep. Would they fit Zeezee?"

"Yes, they're about her size."

"And her skin?"

"Like us and the suits. Her skin colour was green."

248

"I'm sure Rob will agree there's no one currently living on Earth who looks like that."

Cerberus' body language spoke of its disappointment.

Rob pointed to the key hanging round his neck. "There's another key like this one still on Earth?"

"That is correct. Recently, it has moved and is currently somewhere in the middle of a body of water. We are too far from Earth to determine an accurate location. The one that travelled here from Earth ceased functioning before Penny returned."

Penny squatted down beside Cerberus and felt the texture of its skin. "Using your new body allows you to communicate with us directly. Are you able to move outside?"

Cerberus flinched. "That is what you would classify as a terrifying idea, exposed and unconstrained. Would we be safe? How would we decide what to do and where to go?"

Penny adopted a comforting tone of voice. "When outside, I usually have something to do. If not, I choose somewhere interesting or a random destination just to enjoy walking."

"We would find that unsettling as it would require us to function well outside our design parameters and previous operating conditions."

Rob stepped forwards and offered his hand. "Those are problems for a later time. Right now, I think we must teach you to walk."

~

Penny slowly transferred her weight from one leg to the other. It was such a pleasure and a relief to have knee joints that worked smoothly and silently. After another sleep in Moby Dick, one or two other minor problems had also been resolved by the ship's hidden guardians. She watched Cerberus struggle to master the challenges of walking upright with both arms raised high above its head to help balance. "You're progressing well. In the future, I'm sure there will be many useful things for you to do if you were able to move around outside."

Even with a blank, inexpressive face, Cerberus managed to convey discomfort through its posture. "Is that necessary? We do not think we are fully prepared."

"It'll be okay. To start with, we'll take you to see the damage to the outside of the hull. I'm sure you'll find that interesting, and it isn't far to walk."

~

Holding one hand each, Rob and Penny guided Cerberus through the drifts of loose dust. Upon seeing the ragged fissures in Moby Dick's outside hull, the guardian's avatar seemed to forget its fear of open spaces. Penny helped push dust and gravel to one side, exposing more of the torn metal, and Cerberus lay full length on the ground to take a closer look.

"From what we can see from the outside, we believe our internal repairs will prove effective. The scout-ship should be able to take off and manoeuvre safely. We did not repair the outer hull because that would require us to leave the ship, which we were not designed to do."

Rob pulled Cerberus to its feet and helped brush off its clothes. "Perhaps now would be a good time for you to show us some interesting things inside the ship?"

"We are unsure about what you would find interesting. Although you have used it before, the word 'interesting' is unfamiliar to us."

Penny took hold of Cerberus' hand to guide it back to the airlock. "I'd like to find out about the beings who built and used this scout-ship, and I know Rob can't wait to find out how it travels the vast distances between stars."

~

"This is the door to the crew quarters. When surveying a new planet, this scout-ship would carry a crew of six, and this is where they would eat and sleep."

Cerberus slid the door open and led the way into an extensive room. The pervasive sharp acid smell became stronger. Clustered in the centre of the area were six low tables, but nothing resembling a bench or chair. Rob investigated a number of cavities and doors set into each wall. Doors were secured with the same catch as the cupboards in the spacesuit room. He opened a few and peered inside.

"The larger ones are sleeping capsules." Cerberus demonstrated how to use strategically placed handles to slide in feet-first.

Rob continued his inspection finding various containers and utensils.

"If you were capable of ingesting biological food, we wouldn't recommend eating anything from those canisters because it probably won't be good after so much time."

Rob continued his search and came to a halt in front of a picture. "This must be a previous crew?" he said to Penny. "They look exactly as I would imagine after seeing the pressure suits in the room where we sleep. Something like rather muscular ants with huge compound eyes. Their skin colour matches Cerberus and the suits."

Penny pointed to one of the crew who was standing on two legs rather than four.

"Standing on two legs is a sign of authority, although more difficult and tiring than using four," Cerberus explained. "When this photograph was taken, she was in charge of the mission. We think you might call her the captain. Lower caste workers are only permitted to walk on two legs when they need four limbs to complete a task such as fetching and carrying."

"This room has been fascinating. Now, I think it's Rob's turn to see something more technical."

~

"The mechanism that carries us between solar systems is in here at the exact centre of the scout-ship."

Cerberus slid open a door and stood to one side, allowing Rob and Penny to duck through the low entrance. Inside, they lined up along a parapet overlooking an immense chamber.

Rob gazed at four vast, slowly rotating metallic spheres caged in a massive framework. They were arranged in a triangular pyramid. He felt as though his whole body was being gently flexed and buffeted by irresistible waves of alternating attraction and repulsion created by the spheres. "Impressive! "How does it work?" Immediately, he regretted asking.

"We are not sure you would understand."

"You could try explaining."

"Of course, but we were not designed to provide instruction. We were never taught anything of significance so have never seen how that would be done. Most of our knowledge was built-in when we were constructed."

Cerberus pinched together its right thumb and forefinger to indicate something very small. "You know a mathematical point, or zero-dimensional object, is a location in space with no size?"

"I'm sure one of my maths teachers told me that," Rob conceded.

"Very well. Did your teacher introduce you to the minus one dimension?"

"I don't think so. That's hard for me to imagine."

"Without the minus one dimension and minus two dimension there would be no space or time. We will be unable to describe how this machine works if you are not familiar with these elementary ideas."

Penny stepped in with a simpler question, saving Rob from further embarrassment. "Why're they rotating? Surely this scout-ship hasn't moved for a long while?"

"If they stop moving, their own weight will distort them out of shape. Of course, in use, they'll be spinning considerably faster."

Cerberus stopped and held up its right hand. "A radio transmission has been received. We should deal with this straight away."

It gained a little extra speed by pulling itself along by the metal loops set into the walls and ceiling. There was a near disaster when the alien mechanism almost lost its footing climbing the vertical shaft to the bridge. Rob and Penny followed.

"The transmission occupies the same frequency range as other communications intercepted between your Habitat and Earth. We've displayed the message in several forms, one of which you may be able to understand."

Rob leant forwards and searched among a myriad of coloured patterns floating in mid-air. "This must be the message. It reads, 'Robert to Mars. Do you read me?'"

Penny pulled gently on his shoulder to get his attention. "That can't be right. Someone must be trying to trick us. Cerberus, was this message encrypted?"

"No, this is exactly as we received it. All we have done is convert it to various optical patterns we hoped you could understand."

"Augustin always gives maximum attention to security. He wouldn't authorise sending unencrypted messages," Penny insisted.

"The lack of encryption is concerning. But in a way, it's fortunate because we don't have Computer to handle coding and decoding messages. There is still the question of what to do about it. Perhaps it really was sent by Robert."

"If you agree, Rob, we could reply by repeating 536124, the door code. It'll show our connection with the Habitat. I'm very keen to keep in contact with Robert and Anastasia. They're our only real allies back on Earth. With their help, we may be able to counter Augustin's plans."

Chapter 46

With an unsteady hand, Jason tipped a double dose of sugar into his coffee and stirred vigorously. "Thank God that's over!"

"What's the problem? You don't look happy." Robert moved his jacket so Jason had room to sit down.

"I spent the morning preparing Augustin's robot crew for their move to his secure hideout. It was quite a performance. Following his orders, Ian and Jon were shut down for storage."

"Shut down?"

"I had to disconnect their main batteries. In order to avoid alarming them, I pretended to be making a small adjustment to their motor circuits. By the time they realised what was happening they were paralysed and couldn't do anything about it. A few seconds later and they'd lost consciousness."

"That's horrible. They'll both die when their backup batteries run out, but at least they won't be aware of anything for those five days."

"What I was told to do to them, almost equivalent to murder in my book, didn't seem to bother Augustin. For him, the robots are easier to deal with if they're confined to packing cases. They don't need to learn anything more than Ethan and Joe knew at the time they were scanned, so their silicon brains can be reloaded just before take-off.”

“Did Austin receive the same treatment?”

“Not at all. Augustin wants him to remember everything that happens in the period leading up to the launch, so he hasn’t been switched off. He was confined to a packing case, but with his battery still connected. There are arrangements to keep it charged.”

“So, he’s conscious and trapped in a box for several days. I’m sure he wasn’t pleased.” Robert allowed himself a slight smile.

“Quite right. He became extremely belligerent. It took three of us to force him into the crate and nail it closed.”

“If Austin wasn’t to be switched off, why did he need to be stored in a crate?”

“I think it was Augustin’s way of showing who’s in control. Maybe he feels threatened by this younger looking version of himself. One with a potentially much longer life expectancy as well.”

While Jason sipped his coffee, Robert turned the conversation towards what was uppermost in his mind. “In some ways, I’m going to miss this place. Do you have any idea where we’re going, any rumours?”

“I’m almost certain it’s that island where Augustin took Anastasia at the time T1 was destroyed. From what she told me, it sounds quite idyllic for a short vacation but a bit claustrophobic for any longer. I can appreciate it from Augustin’s point of view, small, isolated, easy to defend and difficult to approach without being seen.”

Jason looked at his watch and sighed. “Unfortunately, duty calls. Our last task before we ship out to this holiday destination is to dismantle the communications equipment.”

~

Robert joined Jason in the Comms Centre. “Ethan has spat the dummy. Because he’s no longer in charge of communicating with Mars, he’s being extremely unhelpful. If I have to call for his help, I'll have to pass my request for assistance through Augustin."

Jason looked at the banks of complicated equipment. "I can see why you wouldn't want to give Ethan that satisfaction. But are you sure you'll be able to reconnect all of this stuff correctly?"

"I have a plan. First, we'll check it's still working, then photograph everything before disconnecting it."

After switching on the communications equipment, Robert thumped the desk and pointed to the computer screen. "Great, looks like it's still working. At least Ethan didn't sabotage anything. I'm sure I've seen these signals before. They come from the satellites orbiting Mars."

"They demonstrate we can still receive okay. Shall we try sending something?"

Robert was doubtful that would achieve anything. "With the Habitat destroyed, there's nobody on Mars we'd want to exchange messages with. Ethan hasn't given me his password for sending coded messages either."

"Just send an uncoded message. It can't do any harm. There's a very outside chance we can communicate with whoever escaped the explosion."

Robert's fingers hovered over the keyboard. "This can't possibly work, but just to please you I'll send, 'Robert to Mars. Do you read me?'"

"Not very imaginative."

~

Robert and Jason spent time photographing and labelling plugs and their matching sockets. Eventually, they couldn't wait any longer before starting to disconnect the equipment. Jason looked over Robert's shoulder. "Any reply yet?"

"I know it's almost impossible, but I think there might be. What I'm getting is 536124 repeated over and over again. That's the secret code Anastasia insisted we send to Mars. It's a long story, Jason, so please don't ask me to explain now.

Another time maybe. However, it could only have originated from Rob, Sam, Computer, or perhaps the HMM23 robot."

Jason looked at him quizzically. "We know from the satellite images there was at least one survivor when the Habitat was destroyed, but how is recharging and communication possible? Perhaps, whoever it is collected sufficient spare equipment to put something together."

"Whatever's happened, please don't pass this on to Augustin. He doesn't know about the code and would definitely react badly if he found out, and it'd certainly raise some awkward questions. I'm not sure how to respond, but there's no more time now."

Chapter 47

Robert, Anastasia and Jason gazed through the salt-crusted window as the hydrofoil lined up to dock at the pier.

"This is definitely Aeaea," Anastasia confirmed.

The cloudless blue sky and comfortable temperature were a welcome change and would have put Robert in a relaxed mood, but for the realisation that the island would provide no chance of escaping Augustin's control. After docking, Jason supervised unloading the passengers' luggage and three coffin-sized crates labelled Austin, Ian and Jon.

Always pleased to greet visitors, Tony shook hands at the bottom of the gangplank.

Anastasia introduced Robert and Jason and then pointed to the crates. "You have three more visitors in those boxes." Lowering her voice and pointing towards Austin's crate she added, "You may have some trouble with that one. He's Augustin's robotic double."

Like a funeral cortege, the new arrivals followed the three crates as white-uniformed stewards carried them to the accommodation wing. Boxes containing Ian and Jon were stacked by the door to Augustin's treasure gallery.

Austin's crate was delivered to one of the smaller bedrooms at the far end of the corridor. Having watched as he was confined to his crate, Jason probably wasn't looking forward to seeing it opened again. Two of the stewards prised the lid open with crowbars. Inside, Austin was already struggling to free himself from the close-fitting plastic packing. "Well, don't just stand there, help me up."

After removing many wedges of plastic and disconnecting his power cable, the men pulled him to a sitting position.

Austin looked around with a malevolent glare for each person in the room. "Where's Augustin? We need to get something straight."

With a welcoming smile, Tony, ever the diplomat, stepped forwards to help Austin step out of the crate. "It's great to see you again, Augustin, though to avoid confusion I'll need to call you Austin."

Tony obviously had a good understanding of how Austin would view his place in the world.

"Don't try to put me off. I demand to see Augustin, immediately!"

"He flies in this morning. In fact, I was expecting he would get here before you docked."

"When he arrives, tell him I insist on seeing him straight away."

Brushing fragments of packing foam from his clothing, Austin marched from the room. As soon as he was gone, everyone else let out a deep breath and smiled. Tony turned to Robert, Anastasia and Jason. "The components of the communications system have already arrived. You could check that everything is in order while we sort out your luggage."

~

"I don't care if you do feel you're entitled to it, you're not having my suite."

The argument could be heard down the full length of the corridor. Austin's luggage had been unpacked in the room next to Jason's. Augustin always reserved the spacious corner suite for himself, but before he arrived, Austin had insisted on moving in with his luggage and recharging equipment.

"If necessary, I'll call security, and they'll return you to your allocated room by force."

"We're both equal, and I was here first."

"Don't be ridiculous! There is no equality between us. I'm the original, and I'm human. You're just a robot, and you'll do as I say!"

At the height of the argument, two young men strode down the corridor. They were dressed in the usual cool white uniforms, but this was the first time Robert had seen any weapons since arriving on Aeaea. Shortly afterwards, they returned Austin to his original room. After the battle of wills, Augustin took a few minutes to regain his self-control. Seeing Anastasia through her open doorway, he called to her. "You may be interested to see this. I remember you commented on an item that was missing on your previous visit." Augustin had opened up his gallery so the crates containing Ian and Jon could be moved inside for safekeeping. He led Anastasia to the display cabinet containing the row of stone tablets. Pulling her by the elbow, he positioned her in front of what had been the empty plastic frame beside the corroded metal disk. Only now the frame wasn't empty.

"That's absolutely beautiful. The snowflake shape is so different to your other treasures."

As she moved to leave, Augustin was still holding her arm. To distract his attention, she pointed to a row of steel cabinets, another recent addition, and asked about them.

"They contain the only complete set of documentation for Project Transition held here for safekeeping. There are disks holding every brain scan performed for Project Transition, except for Robert's, of course." He relaxed his grip as he spoke and she made her escape.

~

Over the following days, Robert and Jason assembled the communications dish while Anastasia organised the electronic equipment and reconnected it using Robert's photographs. Perhaps realising preparation of the comms equipment was almost complete, Austin came to check on progress. "In my position as mission leader, it's important I keep up to date with everything to do with the second Mars expedition. This equipment will be essential for maintaining contact, just as it was for the first mission."

While he was speaking, he made for the seat in front of the largest display screen but was blocked by Augustin who had also just arrived. "This is my place. You're welcome to use any of the other seats." With obvious satisfaction, Augustin sat and scanned the screen. "You've got it working?"

Robert pointed out a graphic that showed a planet currently above the horizon. "We're tracking Mars. The slopes of Aeaea block some of the sky, but at the moment this hasn't reduced the communications window by much."

Augustin turned to another part of the screen. "These are the signals you're receiving at the moment?"

"Yes, these two peaks correspond to two known satellites orbiting Mars."

"And this one?" Augustin asked.

Robert had hoped he could hide information about the additional peak until there was time to examine it in more detail. "Ah … that's a transmission on the same frequency as the one we used to communicate with the Habitat."

Augustin sat bolt upright in his seat. "How's that possible? The Habitat was destroyed."

"I don't know, but the transmission is just six meaningless numbers sent unencrypted and repeated over and over again. Perhaps Rob or Sam was able to put together some sort of jury-rigged communication equipment to send out a distress call. What would you like me to do?"

Augustin scratched his chin and looked at the column of repeated numbers. "I'm quite certain this wasn't sent by Rob. That would mean Sam is more competent than I would normally give him credit for."

"But how can you be so sure? I'd think Rob was the most capable, technically speaking."

Ignoring Robert, Augustin turned to Austin. "It's highly unlikely Sam will still be functioning by the time you get there, but if he is, it looks as though he would be a most useful resource."

Robert looked up from his screen. "The communication window is now closed, but next time it's open I could reply. What would you like me to send?"

"You could ask about the state of the battery reserves. That's obviously of critical concern without having access to the Habitat's solar panels."

After Augustin and Austin left, Jason confided in Robert. "I don't know who we're communicating with on Mars, but I know for certain it isn't Sam."

"How can you be so sure?"

"Sorry, can't really say. Seems like we've both got secrets. Augustin would go ballistic if he ever found out."

~

Anastasia's dreams were becoming more frequent and troubling. The need for reassurance seemed to outweigh her desire for periods of time alone, and she now spent every night with Robert. Even though he realised her change in behaviour was probably caused by her anxiety, he hoped it also indicated increased trust.

"Are you awake?" Anastasia whispered.

For a moment, Robert lay still, slowly adjusting to the unfamiliar surroundings. Cool silver light from a full moon sliced across the bedroom floor and walls. He turned to face Anastasia. "Another nightmare?"

"Very similar, almost like a continuation. I opened the container and tipped out three strips of hard white plastic. They each had tiny gold contacts down one side. I remember that in amazing detail. Then, somehow, I was in another room and pushing one of the strips into a slot. That was repeated another twice."

"And the words?"

"Yes, they were there again. I could almost make them out, but not quite."

Robert had no idea what the dream meant, but his mind turned to the puzzle he'd been grappling with as he fell asleep. "There's something else you could think about to take your mind off your dream. Jason told me he was sure Sam didn't send the message from Mars. If that's correct, who did?"

Anastasia rolled over to face Robert. "I'm not sure we're sufficiently alert to solve a whodunit. Still, your puzzle shouldn't be difficult to work out with the limited number of suspects."

"There's Sam, Rob, HMM23 and Computer. Tell me if I left out any other possibility."

In the moonlight, he could see her head move side to side.

"Jason told me it couldn't be Sam, Augustin ruled out Rob, but neither will tell me why. The explosion must have destroyed Computer because I doubt it could have been moved from the Habitat. Finally, I assume HMM23 wasn't programmed to work out what to do in this kind of unlikely situation."

"So, you've eliminated every suspect."

"That's not possible, so I've overlooked something," Robert replied.

"In the morning, you could ask Jason why he's so sure Sam couldn't have sent the message. That's unless you think Augustin would be willing to explain why he ruled out Rob. Right now, we should try and just empty our minds or we'll never get any sleep."

Robert gently stroked Anastasia's hair until her breathing became slow and regular.

~

Anastasia poured three coffees from a vacuum flask. Robert

and Jason accepted their drinks and made themselves comfortable on the coarse black beach sand.

"Jason, it's important we understand the situation on Mars. Robert told me you're sure the messages aren't coming from Sam. It would help if you could explain why you're so sure."

Jason looked up and down the beach as though reluctant to speak or worried about being overheard. "Okay, but just between us, it all relates to what happened after ZsG forced us to scan Rob's friend Penny. I was absolutely gutted when she died, but we did end up with a disk containing her scan even though no one seemed interested in doing anything with it. They'd only used her to test the scanner, and that had been a failure. Sometime later, I was preparing the third crewmember for the Mars mission. Augustin had decided this robot containing the scan of Sam's brain would be kept in hibernation until the mission was about to touch down on Mars. I'm assuming before the landing there'd be nothing useful for Sam to do."

Robert finished his coffee and held out his cup for a refill. "I guess once Sam's scan was loaded into the robot, it would need to be trained for the mission before putting it into hibernation?"

"Yes. That was my job. I'd just finishing it when I was also told to erase the disk containing Penny's scan because they wanted to reuse it. I couldn't just delete the data. I felt it was like a memorial for the young woman, and I'd promised her the scan would be transferred into a robot. Not only that, I'd told her I'd do my utmost to reunite her with Rob. It was my one and only chance to keep my word, so before parting with the disk, I erased Sam's scan and loaded Penny's scan into the robot. The documentation had already been signed off on, and everyone was so preoccupied with other parts of the mission that there were few checks on what I was doing. And Augustin's never had any occasion to doubt me."

Robert was incredulous and delighted by the news, and he

could tell Anastasia also appreciated the risk Jason had taken.

"That would set up an interesting situation. What had you decided to do when Penny popped up on Mars instead of Sam?"

Jason took a minute to consider Robert's question. "It was all done on the spur of the moment without thinking it through in any detail. I just seized the opportunity. I guess I was going to blame a most unfortunate mistake on someone's part, but all of the reports from Mars have mentioned Sam and not Penny. Did I actually load the robot with Sam's scan after all? I don't really think so."

"So, things are still unclear," Anastasia said. "I suggest Robert sends a message simply asking who we're talking to. We must hope one of you can delete the reply before Augustin or Austin see it."

~

Everyone was converging on the pier to await the arrival of the weekly hydrofoil. Even Austin leaned up against the railing to watch the activity.

On his way to the steps, Tony paused to say a few words to Anastasia. "Hi, are you enjoying…" Stopping in mid-sentence he glanced from Austin to Anastasia and then fixed her with a steady stare. "The wind is from the north." Slowly and deliberately he repeated the same phrase.

Robert was alarmed by the strange behaviour. "What did you say?"

Tony blinked and appeared confused as though he'd blacked out for a few seconds.

"Are you feeling okay? I'm sure you said something about the wind coming from the north."

"No, no, Robert, that can't be right. Here the wind always blows from either the east or west."

Still appearing disorientated, Tony descended the steps to the pier.

"That was weird, don't you think?" When Anastasia didn't

reply he looked at her more closely. "What's happening? Is there something wrong with you as well?"

"I'm not sure. I had a sudden flashback to those dreams, but it's gone now."

~

The communication window with Mars opened late in the evening. Austin leaned over Jason's shoulder and saw the blip as soon as it appeared on his screen. "Looks like we have answers to our questions."

Jason read from his screen, "My battery levels are adequate."

"Is that everything?" Austin queried.

Jason swivelled his screen around as an unspoken offer for him to read the message for himself if he wished.

"This reply doesn't seem worth bothering Augustin with. You know he's being totally negligent in managing the situation on Mars. He doesn't have a clue about what's going on. Jason, send a message asking Sam how many fully charged batteries he has left. Do you think he's worked out a way to recharge them?"

This question was directed at Robert.

"Perhaps if he'd taken a few spare solar panels to the OP it would be possible, but I don't think he has the skills to make that work."

"We'll ask about that anyway. In the same message, we need to ask what equipment he's using to transmit and receive radio communications. I suppose you'll tell me Sam wouldn't be capable of setting up the communication link either?"

"After observing a number of robots incorporating the scan of Sam's brain, I believe Jason and Anastasia would both agree that Sam lacks the necessary technical skills."

"You're starting to make me doubt we're communicating with Sam, but that's easily sorted out. Jason, add a request for confirmation of who's sending us messages from Mars."

Chapter 48

"This ferry has sufficient range to travel between planets in any medium sized solar system," Cerberus said with a hint of pride in its voice.

Rob slid his hand over the cool frictionless surface. "Does it still work?"

For an automated maintenance system with no feelings or opinions, Cerberus seemed almost offended by the question. Later, Penny suggested grafting Cerberus onto a humanoid body had somehow infected it with some emotions.

"Everything on this scout-ship is kept in full working condition, including this ferry."

"Could it carry us to Earth?"

"Even a return trip would be well within range. Zeezee used an identical craft to transport a significant quantity of cargo to your planet. There would have been plenty of fuel for the return trip if she had chosen to use it."

Penny's excitement was obvious. "Do you know how to fly this thing?"

"We have complete knowledge of the results of operating each of the controls and how that is achieved in technical terms."

"Okay, perhaps I should have asked are you able to fly it?"

she added.

"No, that would involve leaving the scout-ship, which we are not designed to do. As I have told you before, what you are suggesting is very worrying and distressing."

Robert lowered his voice to avoid putting extra pressure on Cerberus. "Could you show us which controls we should use to fly to Earth?"

"Would it be necessary for us to go with you?"

"It would be better if you did."

Penny thought Cerberus had taken fright and would never answer, but eventually it did. "This particular ferry cannot leave the scout-ship." Waving a hand towards the doors in front of the ferry it explained. "This side of the ship is deeply embedded in the ground as a result of the crash landing."

It looked as though Cerberus was about to add more detail but then froze for a few seconds. "You have received another message from Earth."

Once they'd returned to the bridge, Rob searched the projected symbols until he found the ones he could read. "It seems Augustin isn't too sure about who he's communicating with. There's a list of questions, including where we're getting power from and how is communication possible. He finishes with a blunt question asking us to identify ourselves."

"We need to keep this communication channel open, so it'll be necessary to tell him something," Penny said. "It must be plausible, but it doesn't have to be the truth. I think you'd be good at making up a believable story."

Rob was captivated by the way Penny formed Sam's face into a mischievous smile even though uncertain her last comment was a compliment.

"How about this? You are communicating with HMM23. I have salvaged sufficient solar panels to supply my energy needs. Communication is via the mobile short-range radio, which I have modified to work on a different frequency and at increased power."

"They'll never believe any of that."

"Why not? It's all vaguely possible, and it really doesn't matter so long as they keep in touch."

~

On the bridge, Cerberus explained to Rob the purpose of the controls on each side of the pilot's seat. Penny was more interested in experimenting with a display that could call-up magnified images of the surroundings.

The room was flooded with a high-pitched chime. Cerberus moved beside Penny and took control of the display. "Several objects are flying towards us."

Rob joined them. "What are they?"

"I do not know, but they are almost certainly Earth technology."

After examining the images for a few moments, Rob offered his opinion. "They look like some kind of helicopter drone, too small to carry a person."

Penny moved to the windows and pointed out a triangular formation of three aircraft closing in on Moby Dick. "Augustin's plan of discouraging attention by nuking visitors doesn't seem to have worked. All it's done is demonstrate there's something worth defending close by."

One of the helicopters separated from the formation and flew tight circles around the scout-ship.

"Can they see us through the window?"

"No, Penny, they will see nothing because for these windows light only passes from outside to inside and not the other way."

Their visit lasted less than a minute and then the helicopters turned to go. After watching them disappear from view, Rob turned to speak with Cerberus. "Can this scout-ship defend itself?"

"This ship has a strong outer carapace, though as you have seen, powerful weapons can still damage it. Other than that, it has nothing you would consider to be a weapon."

"The atom bomb we buried at the OP might be a problem. I'm sure it would be sufficiently powerful to destroy this ship."

"Oh no! You're right, Rob! There's no time to lose. I'm guessing those helicopters have a short range and must have been launched from nearby. To prevent the nuke being used against us, we must move it inside Moby Dick."

"It's okay, Cerberus, you don't need to come with us. You can watch what we're doing through the window."

Penny drove the MarsMobile while Rob walked behind. Now, more than ever, the slow speed of the vehicle caused serious frustration.

"Where did we bury it?" Rob asked.

Penny paced out the distance and started to dig, With Rob's help, it didn't take long to unearth the crate and load it onto the sled. They were so intent on working quickly they didn't notice the six-wheeled vehicle approaching slowly and quietly. The tent shielded it from view.

"Step away from the vehicle and don't make any sudden movements."

Two pressure-suited figures pointed guns obviously modified for use by heavily gloved hands. The taller person had a two-way radio clipped to his belt.

"What is this?" He pointed at the crate and switched the radio to transmit so that he could hear the answer.

Penny probably decided there was nothing to be gained by avoiding the question. The answer would be obvious when they opened the crate. "It's a low-yield atom-bomb."

The figure with the radio addressed Penny. "Is this the same type as the one you used to blow up Victor and Gino?"

"Obviously neither of us were there or we'd have been incinerated."

There was a long conversation, which wasn't audible because the radio was muted.

"Hands behind your back."

Penny gave Rob a despairing look as she complied.

Their hands and legs were restrained. Rob was pushed to the ground and an opaque bag pulled over his head. From Penny's complaints, it appeared she was receiving the same treatment. Fingers wrestled with the access hatch in his chest, and in spite of his struggles, he felt it spring open. After the distinct click of wire cutters, Rob's body went limp, and his whole world faded to black.

Chapter 49

Waking at all times of the day and night was playing havoc with Robert's sleep patterns. After another late-night session trying to follow the situation on Mars, he was exhausted and soon in a deep sleep. On the other hand, Anastasia lay in bed staring at the ceiling, waiting until his breathing became slow and regular. She sat up with no conscious plan or motivation. The moon had set, so it was necessary to use a carefully shielded torch to find the bracelet. The large blue stone was difficult to turn, but gripping it with a damp piece of cloth gave her enough purchase to unscrew it. Following the instruction in her dream, the left-hand thread didn't cause a problem, and soon three white plastic strips nestled in her hand.

Leaving two strips with the bracelet, she held the third tightly in her left hand and quietly slipped down the corridor and into Austin's bedroom. His recharging system comprised a small box plugged into a wall socket. A cable ran from the box to the rubber pad positioned in the small of his back. There in the recharger box was a slot familiar from her dream. By touch, she manipulated the white plastic strip and lined up its gold contacts with the slot.

Robert's hand closed on the plastic strip and pulled it from her grasp. She offered no resistance as he guided her out into the corridor and back to his bedroom.

"What were you doing in Austin's room?"

By the light of a bedside lamp he searched her face for answers.

"I'm not sure. The first thing I remember was you holding my hand next to Austin's bed."

"Yes, but why did you go there?"

"I don't know. I was having that dream again. It was dark. I unscrewed something by turning it the wrong way. I was pushing something into a slot, and then you woke me up by grabbing my hand."

"And the voices in your mind?"

"Clearer than before. This time I could make out the words. The wind is from the north."

"That's what Tony said to you down by the pier."

Robert looked at the white strip he'd taken from her hand and matched it with two others lying beside her bracelet.

"They were in my dream. Do you know what they are?"

He turned them over with his fingertips. "I'm guessing they're intended to inject some malevolent code into Austin to damage or even destroy his silicon brain. I'm tempted to take a closer look, but I think they're extremely dangerous and should be destroyed immediately. Ever since you told me about your strange dreams, I've wondered if they were the result of hypnosis. Now that I've seen how they could be related to an attempt to destroy Austin that seems even more likely."

Robert opened the bottom drawer of a small side table where he'd previously discovered a mosquito coil and box of matches. He removed the coil from its metal support.

"I thought they were banned years ago over health concerns."

"That's true, but we're not trying to frighten off mosquitos."

He bent the frame so it would support the three plastic strips and carried them into the bathroom. After switching on the exhaust fan, he lit a match. The acrid smell of burning plastic confirmed the strips had been destroyed.

Anastasia cradled her head in her hands. "That's great. As soon as I saw those things destroyed my mind became so much clearer. Hopefully the effects of the hypnosis may have gone now."

She flung her arms around Robert in a tight embrace. After a couple of minutes, she straightened up, smiling. "Oh, Robert, I can't thank you enough. I'm so pleased you stopped me completing Maxwell's plan. I hope that's the end of it now."

"It's not that I have any objections to destroying Austin, but we don't want to give Augustin another reason to kill us."

~

After breakfast, Robert found Tony, who was supervising removal of the final few boxes of supplies delivered on the previous day's hydrofoil. "Yesterday you said something strange to Anastasia."

Tony turned to look at Robert. "I don't recall saying anything."

"Something about the wind blowing from the north."

"Now you mention it, I remember you asking me a similar question yesterday."

Tony gazed out towards the horizon. "Some time ago, I had a long discussion with one of our other guests, and I'm sure the topic of the prevailing wind direction was mentioned. It's strange though because I can't remember who it was or even picture the face."

~

Austin arrived early for the communications window and lowered himself slowly into Augustin's seat with a challenging look for anyone who might think this wasn't permitted. "What's the reply to my questions?"

Jason busied himself typing on his keyboard. "We've just established contact. The sender is identified as HMM23."

"But that's a really dumb robot. It couldn't possibly be

running things on Mars without assistance."

Silently, Robert had to agree with that opinion.

"So, what did HMM23, or whoever it is, have to say?"

"It claims to have established communications by modifying one of the mobile short-range radios to work on a different frequency and with increased power. By salvaging some solar panels, it's also been able to cover its energy needs."

"That sounds like total rubbish. Is it even vaguely possible?"

"It's not impossible," Robert conceded.

"Jason, I want you to collect together recent satellite images of the OP. I believe there's something very strange going on."

Augustin must have eavesdropped on the conversation. He slammed the door behind him as he entered the room and marched over to menace Austin where he sat in the forbidden seat. "Austin, you don't have permission to allocate tasks. Jason won't be taken off his current duties to suit your whim."

"Can't you see? You're blind to possible problems. I don't want to be sent to Mars only to find the situation there is out of control."

Augustin raised his fist as though intending to hit Austin. "If you don't stop this, I'll have you reprogrammed and put into hibernation until close to launch. That way you won't be around to cause me any more problems. Now get out of my seat."

Chapter 50

Even though Rob and Penny were outside the scout-ship and therefore no longer the responsibility of the maintenance system, Cerberus was concerned. It was obvious the visitors had maintained radio silence before attacking and disabling Rob and Penny, but now they talked over their radios.

"Snuffin' Victor and Gino was a real kick in the guts, but trashin' these robots won't help. The boss was clear he wants 'em in good nick because he might be able to find a use for 'em. That's why he told us to cut the battery wires without doin' too much damage."

"Yes, but all of this chasing after robo's is wasting time. What we need to find is some sort of cave to shelter from the radiation. That should be our top priority. We're all sick, and no matter how valuable this thing is, it'll be no use to us if we all die."

"I know, but the boss won't be pleased if we leave with the job half done. He wants us to take a close look at this thing and see if we can work out what it is and why it's so valuable. It's strange we can't see it from here."

The shorter figure turned away from the robots and squatted down to look at something on the ground. "Hey, look at this shiny badge, looks kinda like a snowflake. Okay with you if I take it. It'll make a great souvenir."

"Sure, but don't let the boss see it. I doubt he'd let you keep it." The taller figure swept a hand in the direction of Rob and Penny. "We can load the robo's and bomb after we've checked on this thing."

Cerberus watched them follow the well-marked path between the OP and scout-ship.

"Close up, this is even more impressive than it looked in the drone photos. I think most of the footprints are heading for that hatch or doorway over there." The taller one stopped to gaze up at the immense scale of the structure while his companion hurried forwards to take a look at the hatch.

"Definitely must be the way into this thing. All the footprints end here. There are some marks here that seem to match this badge. I'll see if they fit together. Perhaps it's some sorta key."

"I don't think you should do that, buddy."

"It's okay. They do fit together, but nothin's happened. I'll try it in the next one."

High-pressure jets of bubbling white froth sprayed from several points around the hatch.

"What the hell? I can't see."

"Looks like you've been covered in white goo. Hold still, I'm coming to give you a hand."

"Okay, but hurry. This stuff's sticky. I can hardly move."

Cerberus watched as the taller figure bent to touch the white foam.

"This goo seems to have set solid."

"I know that! I can't bend my arms or legs. You've gotta do somethin' and fast. It's startin' to get hot in here. This stuff must've blocked my suit's climate control."

"Calm down. You're panicking, and that's why you think you're overheating. Hang in there while I fetch the crawler."

With careful strokes, the taller figure used an emergency axe to chop away the patch of Martian dust solidified around his companion's feet. Once freed, he dragged the rigid figure up the back steps and into the crawler.

"Forget the other stuff; it'll keep till later. Just take me back to base. If I get any hotter, you'll havta cut me outa this pressure suit. This heat's gettin' unbearable."

~

After the crawler passed out of sight, Cerberus wondered what to do. By design, its responsibility ended at the hatch leading to the outside world. Everything inside was in good order with nothing needing attention. But in the distance, Rob and Penny lay on the ground, obviously requiring help, and in between was a long stretch of open space. Cerberus computed what would be required to improve the situation. Leaving the scoutship without assistance and crossing unbounded terrain full of chaotic rocks and gravel was an overwhelming prospect. This action would contravene all operating procedures, but those restrictions seemed to hold less meaning for a maintenance system now equipped with a body and limbs.

Cerberus opened the outer hatch and looked out, then, holding onto the hull with both hands, stepped into the dust. The snowflake was still firmly embedded in the solidified foam where it had been dropped by the shorter figure. Using a few drops of liquid from a metal flask it softened the foam, releasing the key.

Cerberus chose the lighter load, Rob, as the first to be rescued. The MarsMobile was a crude and inelegant machine, but it did the job. After much trial and error, Cerberus managed to master the operation of the strange mechanism and used the sled to ferry Rob back to the entrance hatch.

The person who'd disabled Rob had cut a number of other wires in addition to those connected to his battery. It took many valuable minutes to repair the damage.

Rob sat up and looked around the spacesuit room. "Where's Penny?"

"I left her outside while I repaired you. We need to return

to the OP and bring her back here so I can repair her as well."

They stepped out of the hatch and were just in time to see a crawler disappearing into the distance.

"Is that the same crawler that was here a short while ago?"

Cerberus looked in the direction Rob was pointing. "I do not think it is. The markings on the side are different."

It didn't take long to work out what the crew of the second crawler had been doing. The MarsMobile lay crumpled and twisted as though it had been run over. They walked to the OP, but there was no sign of Penny or the missile, just more crawler tracks coming and going in an easterly direction.

"What will we do now?" Cerberus' voice, if not facial expression, registered concern.

"I don't know. How far away do you think they've gone?"

"Not far. I overheard radio transmissions calling for assistance when the crew of the first crawler got into difficulties. The second crawler must have been able to get here and pick up Penny plus the bomb while I was repairing you, so perhaps half an hour of your Earth time."

"How far can you walk?"

"I do not know for sure, but in many ways, our body is a copy of yours, so perhaps we can all walk a similar distance."

"Okay, we should recharge our batteries and collect together the things needed to repair Penny."

~

Cerberus carried a satchel over one shoulder and seemed reluctant to start walking away from Moby Dick until Rob offered a comforting hand. The sun had already set, and with his free hand, Rob adjusted a torch to cast a narrow band of light at their feet as they followed the crawler tracks.

"Does the darkness and open space not worry you, Rob?"

From the question, he gathered they were a problem for Cerberus. He gripped the small hand even tighter and tried to turn the conversation in a different direction. "Where did you come from originally? What I mean is, where were you made?"

"In our society, all spaceships are produced by the same community based on the planet Outpost 1. We were built into our scout-ship there. When complete, the ship was traded to Outpost 31 in exchange for a supply of food, minerals and young workers."

Cerberus paused and with its free hand pointed to the centre of one of the bright bands of stars making up the Milky Way. "From here the two outposts seem very close together."

"What are scout-ships used for?"

"One of their principal applications is to search other solar systems, looking for places to establish new colonies. In each colony, the queen is mother to most individuals except for those old enough to carry over from the previous queen. Once in every epoch, there is a ritual to find a replacement for the aging queen when she no longer produces sufficient offspring. During the ceremony, young fertile sisters are inseminated by drones. Sometimes two or more sisters become impregnated and survive to the end of the ritual. If a new planet has been found which is suitable for establishing another colony, one of these queens would be transported there together with a supply of materials and workers."

"And if a satisfactory planet hasn't been found?"

"Then the queens fight until only one survives. Usually they recruit a group of followers who do the actual fighting to avoid injury to the eventual winner."

"You've investigated planets suitable for colonisation?"

"In the past, our scout-ship has been used to confirm four other acceptable planets."

Rob was fascinated by the story, and it seemed to be keeping Cerberus' mind off its fear of open spaces.

"That explains a lot, but how did you end up here? Surely this wouldn't be considered a habitable planet?"

"A fugitive queen, Zeezee, took control of our scout-ship while trying to avoid being killed. As you have seen, the ship was damaged, and this caused it to crash here. She took one of the ferry craft to investigate your Earth, the closest neighbouring planet, which also appeared habitable. The ferry never returned."

Rob tried to turn the conversation to a lighter topic. "Could you find those other habitable planets again?"

"Yes, we can calculate their current locations."

"What are they like?"

"At the time of our visit, we heard the crew discussing each planet. Because the conversation concerned places outside the ship, we had no interest in such details. With our new curiosity about things beyond our scout-ship, we realise those planets were probably fascinating and beautiful. You understand we are not sure what those words mean, but they seem positive. They are the translation of comments made by the crew."

"That's sounds fantastic. Penny and I would be extremely interested to visit them. Does the scout-ship have sufficient fuel to travel that far?"

"For moving between solar systems, fuel is not an important consideration. Provided the ship's potential energy is compensated, trips of any distance consume the same quantity of fuel. All that is required is a small amount to start and end the journey. We have enough for many of those trips."

As Phobos appeared above the horizon, Rob switched off his torch and tried to navigate by moonlight. Cerberus rarely stumbled and must have been built with better night vision.

"Out here we have no way of recharging our batteries. Are you sure we are not going to run out of power before we get back to the ship?"

This was one of many things worrying Rob. He wasn't sure, but he gave the answer many parents use to reassure their children. "Not far to go now. Just around the next corner."

Without realising it, Rob had spoken the truth. Compared to the surrounding hills picked out in grey moonlight, the camp was a blaze of light and colour. There was no obvious attempt to hide it from view. On a relatively level stretch of ground, three crawlers were lined up beside four pressure domes. The dome-shaped accommodation modules were lit up from the inside through their semi-transparent walls, making them impossible to miss.

Cerberus pulled Rob to a halt. "Is this where they took Penny?"

"I'm sure it is. We need to move closer to find out how the camp's organised and if anyone's on sentry duty."

"This place could have so many hidden dangers. We feel uncomfortable approaching any closer."

Rob released Cerberus' hand and tried to reassure his companion with a pat on the back. "You've done very well to come this far. Wait here while I take a closer look."

Rob counted four figures sitting around a table in one of the domes. None wore helmets, and only one seemed to be dressed in a pressure suit. The other domes appeared empty. If there was an original crew of two for each crawler, there were still two unaccounted for. He assumed the person who'd triggered the scout-ship's protection system had survived. Cerberus had described what had happened and the effects of the jets of white goo. It explained that in many situations the goo could be lethal if it interfered with a creature's breathing tubes.

Circling around in the shadows, Rob made for the crawlers. He assumed there would be no reason to unload Penny and the missile. They would just take up valuable space in the domes.

An ungainly figure stumbled from the shadow of one of the crawlers and raised its right arm. There was a blinding flash, a bang, and Rob felt his left leg give way. Seconds later, a pressure-suited figure towered over him and switched on a hand torch.

"I knew you'd come, you murdering bastard. Easier for us to lure you here rather than searching half of Mars to find you. All I need to know now is where's the other robot, the one that repaired you? Or are there more than one?"

Rob struggled to sit upright but was forced down by pressure from a boot.

"If you don't tell me, I'll start dismembering you, one limb at a time. The only tool I have is this pistol, so it won't be very neat."

The torchlight caught a shiny sphere as it arced through space and then shattered on impact with the pressure suit. Splashes of white foam bubbled as it spread over the arms and chest, dripping down onto Rob. He touched the foam and instantly regretted the experiment when his fingers stuck together.

Cerberus reached up to grasp the torch frozen in the pressure suited hand and used a few drops of liquid to melt the foam, freeing the torch. Next it shook a second sphere and then lobbed it at another figure emerging from one of the domes.

"It'll take the other three a while to get into their pressure suits. We should find Penny and get out of here. Could you deal with this foam?"

More liquid released Rob from the foot planted on his chest and the splashes of foam gluing him to the ground. Cerberus carried its satchel and supported Rob's weight as he attempted to hobble on his shattered left leg.

"I am detecting high levels of radiation from this first crawler. The bomb and probably also Penny may be inside." Cerberus climbed up the rear ladder of the crawler and peered through the hatch. "They are here."

As Rob dragged himself up the ladder and into the cabin, there was the sound of distant gunfire. Easing into one of the two driving seats, he had a clear view of the camp through the curved windscreen. A handgun muzzle flash gave away the location of a figure firing from behind a pile of crates. "That guy doesn't seem keen to get too close. Can you throw that far?"

Without answering directly, Cerberus climbed down the back-access ladder. The first sphere fell well short of its target. Perhaps having compensated for the distance, Cerberus' second sphere shattered at the feet of the emerging figure covering it with the contents. The pursuer managed a few paces, each one slower and shorter than the previous one. Finally, with feet firmly anchored in place, all that was possible was to wave both arms in a frantic call for assistance. Rob watched in the large side mirrors as Cerberus disabled the other two crawlers by coating their wheels and steering mechanisms with white foam.

Over his shoulder Rob called out, "Cerberus, can you see any switch or lever to retract the stairs?"

While he waited, Rob peered into the darkness between the brightly lit domes, searching for signs of pursuit. Two space-suited figures emerged from one of the domes and moved towards their companion beside the pile of crates. Sorting out the stair was taking too long, and Rob tried to pull himself onto his good leg before he heard the whine of a motor followed by a thump as the stair lifted clear of the ground.

"Are you able to control this machine with your damaged leg?"

Because he hadn't driven a crawler before, Rob wasn't sure it was possible, but he discovered that the controls were designed to be easy to operate with gloved hands. The only foot control was a brake pedal, and he could work it using his good leg. With a tremendous feeling of relief, Rob executed a wide turn and headed back towards Moby Dick.

When the camp was out of sight and there were no signs of pursuit, Cerberus asked Rob to stop the crawler. It picked up its satchel and moved to the back of the cabin. "This is a good place to repair Penny. We'll need her help to carry you and the bomb into the scout-ship. Unfortunately, we didn't realise this body would be required to do heavy lifting when we constructed it."

Chapter 51

Austin wasn't prepared to allow anyone to treat him with such blatant disrespect. What Augustin needed was a little lesson, nothing major, but something to put him off balance. Austin made some minor adjustments to Augustin's bedside lamp, creating a fault that would look like it had been there for years.

While Austin worked on his minor act of defiance, human guests ate a buffet dinner served in the conference room. The luxurious surroundings were already losing their attraction for Robert, but having Anastasia return to her normal self was more than adequate compensation. He stole a look at her face in profile, highlighted by the candlelight. Her air of composure and mystery continued to captivated him.

~

Later, as people returned to their bedrooms for the night, Austin lay awake watching the glow of his night-light, waiting. The light flickered out. An overload caused by the faulty lamp had cut power to all of the guest rooms. Shortly afterwards, Augustin emerged from his room yelling for assistance. Austin allowed plenty of time for others to go to his aid before joining the crowd in the corridor. Eventually, Tony arrived to sort out the fuse box and replace the faulty lamp. It appeared Augustin hadn't fully recovered from the mild electric shock, and his hands shook as he complained to Tony. The whole episode had played out perfectly.

~

Jason called up the most recent satellite images from Mars. "I think there may be another problem." He circled vehicles and fresh tracks converging on the OP.

Austin leaned over his shoulder.

"These must be more people from LanthanoCo, the same outfit that attacked the Habitat," Robert speculated. "Obviously setting off the atom bomb hasn't dissuaded them. It probably only piqued their interest."

Ignoring Robert, and in an apparent attempt to show he was across the situation, Augustin explained what was known. "Recently, a number of spacecraft landed about 500km east of our site. As far as we can tell, that mission is run and financed by LanthanoCo. The vehicles that threatened the Habitat came from there." He squinted over the top of his gold-rimmed spectacles. "Judging by their tracks, these new ones come from the same place. In a worrying coincidence, the managing director of LanthanoCo is named Ivanov. Someone with the same surname, Pavel Ivanov, is an investor in the Safetybot project, and as such, he could have found out a great deal about our activities. If it is the same person, that would indicate he's trying to muscle in on my project. That won't be happening, believe me."

"Sounds a bit like our mission, similarly shrouded in secrecy." Augustin's look should have told Jason he'd said enough. Apparently, he wasn't going to allow a stern look to silence him. "A friend of mine mentioned a new exploration company focussing on outer space. Could be the same people. They're proposing to stake claims to mineral-rich areas of Mars."

Austin cut across Jason's description. "Send a message to HMM23, or whoever we're communicating with, asking if any other group has tried to make contact. By drawing attention to ourselves, we've jeopardised the whole Mars mission. If these people take control of the object, there's no point in even considering our next launch."

Jason turned to Augustin with a questioning look. "What's the object?"

"Just get on with typing the message, Jason."

As he continued to type, Jason returned to his original theme. "Surely there's no internationally agreed way of staking a claim to chunks of Mars or anything abandoned there?"

Anastasia offered her opinion. "International agreement or not, there are companies who've been selling title deeds to blocks of land on most planets, moons and asteroids in the solar system. I'm sure no thinking person would expect they were worth more than the paper they're printed on. But if the blocks of land were actually explored for minerals, pegged out like claims on Earth, perhaps even registered in some flag of convenience country, then who knows how enforceable they might be."

Austin continued his criticism of Augustin, emphasised by contemptuous looks in his direction. "Of course, where the law's unclear, having possession and being able to police it would give anybody a strong claim. That's why it's essential we maintain control over our discovery on Mars."

Seemingly unwilling to take any more criticism, Augustin stormed out, banging the door behind him.

~

With no communication window and no other commitments, Anastasia and Robert relaxed on the beach in the shadow of the sea wall.

"Are those more of Augustin's rich friends?" He waved his hand out to sea.

Anastasia shaded her eyes and looked in the direction Robert had indicated. "Looks a lot smaller than the yacht that brought his backers. As far as I can see, this one doesn't even have a helipad."

"Unidentified ship approaching, alert level one." The announcement echoed off the buildings and surrounding slopes of the volcano. Instantly, Robert recognised that the ship could pose a serious threat. While trying to appear calm, he scrambled to help Anastasia move to somewhere less exposed. Once she appreciated the urgent need to take cover, she made a suggestion. "Perhaps the chapel."

As they hurried past the dock area, a number of Tony's men were unpacking guns and portable missile systems.

Like Anastasia, Austin must have decided the ancient stone building was the most solid structure on the island. Sheltered behind its thick walls, he was talking with Tony, who clearly wanted to get away.

"No, the ship hasn't responded to our calls. I'm sure they don't intend to appear belligerent, but if that changes, we can defend ourselves."

As Tony hurried away, Augustin's alter ego turned his attention to Robert. "You've heard all the communications with Mars. What do you think of the situation there?"

Robert was surprised that Austin was worried about Mars with another threat much closer to hand. He tried to pick his words carefully to avoid antagonising Austin or passing judgement on any of Augustin's decisions. "It's difficult for me to say because I'm not privy to all of the details. However, the attention of this other group, LanthanoCo, must be worrying. They don't seem to be easily put off even when they sacrifice some of their people."

"But you've seen the photographs and know what's happening close to the OP?"

"Yes, but you and Augustin must know much more than I've been told, otherwise you wouldn't have invested such fabulous amounts of money and effort to put together this mission. Surely, if you expected to find something valuable, you must have made plans for protecting and exploiting it?"

Austin made a dismissive grunt and left, just as Jason

turned the corner of the building. He was on top of the latest rumours. "It's very suspicious. They claim to be suffering from all manner of technical problems and need to drop anchor while they repair their main engines. Because the seabed shelves so steeply, they're anchored very close to shore. There's no obvious signs of weapon systems, but the ship does seem to have more communication equipment and radar scanners than would be usual for a pleasure craft. Augustin's denied them permission to come ashore."

Robert had a feeling of helplessness as he thought about the possibility of some sort of attack. "I don't know about you, Jason, but I feel pretty exposed here. If we're attacked, there's no way to escape, except out to sea. There's nowhere else on the island to go to, and hardly any buildings to give shelter. We could try following the goat tracks up the side of the volcano, but the ground isn't very stable, and we'd be totally exposed."

"Yes, you're right. The lack of any means of escape is a definite weakness. All we can do is watch the ship and look out for any suspicious move."

Jason left to find out how things were developing. After a quarter of an hour, he returned. "Looks like they're leaving. I heard sounds as though they were trying to start their main engines. They made a tremendous racket and eventually it kicked into life with a huge plume of sooty smoke. Now they're raising the anchors and heading away from the island."

"So perhaps all they really wanted was a safe place to anchor while they repaired their engines," Anastasia said.

"Possibly, but they did hang around long enough to have a really close look at the island and could even have mapped the ocean depth close to shore. I'm sure they were also interested to see what sort of response there would be to a threat from the sea. Now they know how many people would defend Aeaea and what sort of weapons they have."

Anastasia said what they were all thinking. "You think they may be intending to pay us another visit?"

Chapter 52

On the scout-ship bridge, Penny watched as a small drone circled the OP and then weaved backwards and forwards across the track leading to the entry hatch. "They're back. This time they haven't returned in person. Possibly the white goo has made them more careful."

Cerberus finished its repairs to Rob's leg by smoothing the surface of the silicone skin. "You should be able to walk without difficulty now."

Tentatively, Rob got to his feet and joined Penny by the window. Having located the crawler and surveyed the ground around the OP and Moby Dick, the helicopter turned to head back the way it had arrived. Penny turned from the window, worry lining her face. "What d'you think they'll do now?"

Rob had no idea, and could only manage a non-committal reply. "That depends on how interested they are in this ship and what they're capable of."

"I'd say they're still very interested and probably motived by thoughts of revenge as well." She turned to Cerberus. "I suggest we don't hang around to discover the answers to those questions. You said this ship's in full working order. How do we take off?" She moved to sit in one of the seats with its banks of coloured buttons. Her fingers hovered over them, threatening disaster if she touched the wrong one.

Cerberus placed a small dumbbell-shaped object into her open hand. "This controls the ship's manoeuvring thrusters. We believe you must squeeze it to change the scout-ship position. When you apply sufficient pressure, it turns blue, and then moving or twisting your hand makes the ship mirror the command."

"How do I stop if something goes wrong?"

"We have never been required to operate this control. That is beyond our remit. To the best of our knowledge, if you stop squeezing, the ship maintains the same speed and direction."

"Okay, why don't I give it a try?"

A three-dimensional image floated in front of Penny showing a side-view of the scout-ship and surrounding ground level.

"Are you absolutely sure you want to try this?" Rob queried.

She ignored his question and instead concentrated on following Cerberus' instructions. Several of the buttons on the control panel were protected by sliding covers. She uncovered and pressed a large blue button. There was vibration and an increasing roar. A vast cloud of dust billowed up, obscuring the view through the windows. Fortunately, the three-dimensional display wasn't affected.

Rob watched it closely. "I think we're stuck. We haven't moved."

Penny lifted her hand, sensing the ship's resistance through the hand control. The roar of the engines increased in pitch. First the back of the ship rose from the ground, and she felt the dumbbell rotate in her grasp, mimicking the movement of the spacecraft. She twisted the control to compensate, and the whole ship rose evenly. With more confidence, she moved the ship sideways to a level stretch of ground and set it down. When the whine of the motors faded and dust settled, Cerberus uncovered its eyes and made sure Penny had correctly switched off the manoeuvring thrusters.

Rob relaxed his grip on the handles set into the wall. "Excellent job, Penny. You've proved this thing works, but we can't stay here. If anything, we're more exposed than before."

Justifying Rob's concern, a crawler appeared in the distance and zig-zagged towards the ship using areas of higher ground as cover. He dragged his eyes from the distant dust plume and turned to address Cerberus. "I wonder what they think they can do against this ship. Have these visitors talked on their radios?"

"There was nothing until Penny moved the ship. Then, when they described what had happened, the reply was to stop us leaving at all costs."

Penny joined Rob at the window. "They're obviously taking precautions in case we have some kind of weapon. They've hidden their crawler behind a low ridge."

The head and shoulders of someone wearing a spacesuit barely showed above the crest of the hill. After a few seconds, a plume of white smoke shrouded the figure. Something, at first almost too small to see, rapidly grew in size as it sped towards its target.

"They're attacking us!" was all Rob had time to call out.

The grenade glanced off the side of the hull and exploded in a brief orange flare.

When the reverberation died down Penny grasped Cerberus' arm. "Did that damage the ship?"

"It will take us a little time to be sure." Cerberus became still and stared into the distance.

"The visitors have broken radio silence again. They believe the grenade had little effect. Having done their best to follow instructions, they are leaving fearing retaliation."

There was another long silence as they all watched the crawler disappear into the distance.

"We have concluded that the explosion caused very little damage and did not compromise the safety of the ship."

Now that the danger seemed to have passed, Penny relaxed her hold on Cerberus' arm. "If we could boost this scout-ship into orbit around Mars, we'd be totally safe from ground attack. How could I do that?"

"Launching to a stable orbit is partly automatic." Cerberus rapidly ran its hands over the banks of coloured buttons. "Select the orbit you want with these controls, then when you have taken off, press this one."

Penny stared in bewilderment at the control panel. "Can you help me with the orbit, Cerberus?"

"This is another aspect of running the ship that is outside our allocated responsibility, but we have records of the settings used for other planets, some similar to Mars. We'll choose one for you."

Rob and Cerberus selected two of the self-adjusting seats. Appearing fearful of what might happen, Cerberus braced itself, head on knees, and covered its eyes.

~

Rob relaxed and looked out of the windows. Below the scout-ship, the surface of Mars slid past in differing shades of red and brown. It soon became clear that their orbit was taking them over the planet's icy poles.

During take-off, several arms had extended and restrained the passengers to prevent them floating about the cabin in zero gravity. Penny peeled hers back and gently pushed herself towards the windows. "There's a fabulous view. I could spend hours just watching the surface of the planet scrolling past."

Rob joined her at the window. "There's no big hurry, but we should decide what to do next. It's been a long time since I felt I had the freedom to make any sort of choice about my future. Cerberus, what would you like to do now?"

It uncovered its eyes and stared at Rob. "We are still unsure how 'like' applies to us. If there are repairs or maintenance tasks to be undertaken inside the scout-ship, we must complete them. Anything beyond that does not affect us. Except…"

Penny smiled encouragingly. "Except what, Cerberus?"

"Except having heard reports of other planets, we would like to visit some of them. Not just orbit in this ship, but go down in a ferry and explore their surface. Before, when a landing party returned to the scout-ship, they would talk of all the things they had seen. At the time, such details were of no interest. Now, we realise what we have been missing. For instance, this is our second visit to your solar system. Perhaps this time we can see more than we were able to on the first occasion."

Cerberus's answer prompted more questions from Rob. "Why did the scout-ship come here the first time?"

"That was an exploratory mission to survey your home planet for possible colonisation. Long range analysis had indicated its surface temperature, atmosphere and gravity might be suitable for establishing a new outpost."

"But Earth wasn't colonised, was it?"

"The landing party produced a negative report. Although the air was indeed breathable, temperature tolerable and gravity acceptable, there was one negative factor which proved decisive. The unusual biochemistry of all living matter on Earth meant there was nothing edible growing there."

"Couldn't they just grow their own food?

"That wouldn't be easy. It was judged that, taking into account local conditions, our crops would be outcompeted by the local biome. They could only survive in protected enclosures. In order to feed an entire colony, that would be impractical. The survey team proposed another solution, which was to completely sterilize the surface of the planet to a considerable depth to ensure complete eradication of all pre-existing life. Once decontaminated, there would be no competition for our crops. For some reason, that solution was not pursued."

With a degree of understatement, Penny replied, "What an awful idea. Rob and I are pleased that didn't happen. Earth should certainly be our first port of call, but perhaps we'll keep our first visit as short as possible. We'll have to be very careful. Augustin, the man who sent us to Mars, would stop at nothing to get his hands on this ship."

Rob offered a suggestion. "If we only stay for a short while, we should contact Penny, the biological Penny, and make sure she's okay."

Penny seemed excited at the prospect of meeting her human twin. "My parents are probably our best bet for finding out where she is now. You know we weren't on speaking terms, but just before my scan I'd decided to try and repair our relationship, so hopefully they'll help us. But we have a problem. Now being transitioned into this body," she indicated her robotic frame, "I'm not sure they'd be inclined to talk to me. In fact, they probably wouldn't believe I have any real connection with their daughter. But perhaps they'd talk with you, Rob."

"In that case, I'll go and see them and we could include a visit to Robert and Anastasia. I'm sure they'd be pleased to see us. They could fill us in on how Project Transition is progressing and what Augustin is up to. Now, let's get more practice controlling this ship and sorting out how the ferries work."

~

Leaving the scout-ship orbiting Mars they used a ferry to head to Earth. The camouflage capability of the ferry appeared every bit as good as that used by the scout-ship. Even though flying close to the ground, they were not challenged. From above, it was difficult to recognise T1. Rob was alarmed to discover the building had been completely reduced to rubble. The second destination was the home of Penny's parents. They arrived in the early morning. Flying slowly and as quietly as possible, Rob guided the ferry to land in a small clearing in dense bushland close to the canal, a location convenient for both Robert's flat and Penny's family home. The spacecraft was almost ten metres long, but Cerberus assured Rob that its camouflaging system would hide it from everything but very close inspection.

"Are you sure you want to come with us, Cerberus?"

"Yes, this is the start of our new existence. We must use every opportunity to experience new things."

Cerberus walked between Rob and Penny holding their hands. Before leaving the scout ship they had requested the ship's guardians to make additional clothing for Cerberus. A scarf, hoody and gloves covered most of the bright green skin, and dark glasses hid the rest. The sight of plants, flowing water and animals seemed almost too much for Cerberus to take in.

A short distance from the house, Penny ran her fingers through Rob's hair and tried to arrange his clothing to make him more presentable. Leaving Penny and Cerberus hidden in the bushes, Rob approached the front door. In response to the bell, a conservatively dressed woman opened the door. She appeared old enough to be Penny's mother. After looking Rob up and down, it became obvious by her expression the woman wasn't impressed by what she saw.

"Good morning. My name's Rob, I'm a friend of Penny's from Wivenhoe College. Can you tell me how to contact her?"

The colour drained from the woman's face, and she staggered backwards holding onto the door for support. "How dare you come here asking that."

"I'm sorry to upset you. I've been out of the country for over a year, and I'd really like to get in touch with her again."

Barely controlling the tremor in her voice, she replied, "Penny's dead."

"Oh my God! How? When?"

Regaining some of her composure Penny's mother replied, "We were told she was electrocuted in some underground tunnel at that college. She chose to live there in squalor to spite her family. This whole affair has been most distressing. Please go now, and don't cause us any more trouble."

Before Rob could reply, the door was firmly closed in his

face. Memories of biological Penny with her rebellious, psychedelic hairstyle haunted Rob as he walked the long driveway back to the road.

Taking Penny into his arms, and with a breaking voice, Rob shared the devastating news. "I'm so sorry. Your mother told me that she's dead. She was reported to have been electrocuted in the tunnels."

Pulling away, Penny buried her face in her hands and sank to her knees. "Oh no! That's horrible. Did she tell you where my body's buried?"

"No, she wasn't prepared to say any more."

"My grandparents have a family plot in the local cemetery. We should try there. I'd really like to see it. I guess that when this robotic body of mine wears out it won't receive any kind of burial."

~

They stood beside the modest granite headstone inscribed with Penny's name and dates of birth and death. It was a short distance from the other family graves as though, even in death, she hadn't been forgiven for not conforming. With Rob's help, Penny searched surrounding hedgerows for wild flowers to lay on the grave.

"This has cured me of any wish to return here. There's nothing left for me now. I'll leave it up to you two to decide where we go next."

~

Rob was keen to make contact with Robert, and led his friends along the canal towards his flat. "Before I became Rob, I lived near here and used to enjoy visiting this place. I guess I still do."

They walked on in silence, allowing Cerberus plenty of time to absorb every sensation.

Rob rang Robert's doorbell. He was disappointed when there was no reply. He had hoped Robert might be home on a Saturday afternoon.

"I think I'll leave a message with one of the neighbours. I don't want to abandon you, but it might be better if I do this on my own. That way there'll be fewer tricky questions."

Rob arranged to meet Penny and Cerberus by the canal and then returned to knock on the neighbour's door. "Helen? Hi I'm Rob, a friend of Robert's. I've rung his doorbell, but he doesn't seem to be home. Could you possibly help me out?"

After an initial look of bewilderment, the neighbour gave a welcoming smile. "Well! Robert always did lead an interesting life and seems to be having a rather disjointed one lately. He's rarely home, and I haven't seen him for quite some time. Come inside."

Rob recognised the layout of the rooms as the mirror image of Robert's flat.

"I've a small present for Robert. Do you have a pen and some paper so I can leave a message?"

Rob wrote half a page and added it to the small rectangular package covered in plastic film. "Please keep this in a safe place, and tell Robert the note explains everything."

After thanking Helen for the offer of a drink, and not accepting even a glass of water, he took his leave and walked to the bench beside the canal. Penny couldn't contain her curiosity any longer. "What was in the package?"

"There's a snowflake key. I thought it would make a nice memento, and, provided Robert keeps it close by, we can use it to find him. I also wrote a very brief description of some of the things that have happened to me since we last met at this very place. I wasn't too specific so that it wouldn't mean very much if someone else read it, but enough to reassure him I was okay."

"That doesn't seem like a very great gift. Couldn't we give him something better, like one of the ferry craft? We could park it in a high Earth orbit where it would be totally undetectable from the ground. After all, it'd be completely camouflaged. Robert could then call it down using the key."

Rob tried to justify his choice. "That would be a fabulous present, probably what Augustin has spent most of his working life and fortune trying to acquire. But, at the present time, giving Robert a ferry would put him at serious risk. Augustin would go to any lengths to gain possession, and nowhere on Earth would be totally secure. On the other hand, we can keep out of harm's way and move on to the next galaxy if necessary. After enough time, when things settle down and the situation becomes clearer, we could contact Robert and make plans for the future. Who knows, by then we may be close enough to the intelligence horizon to be reasonably sure about the future of intelligent robots on Earth."

The three of them sitting on a bench beside the canal had the feeling of an intimate family group. Rob appreciated their contrasting and complementary personalities. Cerberus became totally absorbed watching a butterfly, which had landed on its gloved hand. Rob turned to look at their small companion. "Just like you, we'd like to experience different worlds, perhaps one of the places your scout-ship visited in the past. Which one do you suggest?"

Chapter 53

Jason's exclamation alerted everyone in the Comms Centre, "Looks like it's gone!"

Augustin's head jerked up. "What are you talking about? Speak up, man."

Jason stood and moved behind Augustin so he could indicate where to find the image he was talking about. "I've just been looking at the latest satellite photographs of the area around the OP, and there's nothing there."

"But the object's camouflaged. We don't expect to see anything."

Jason took control of the screen and magnified the image. "Now there is something to see. Look at that. A big hole in the ground."

Augustin's knuckles turned white as he gripped the edge of the table. "That's impossible. It's been there for thousands of years. It couldn't just vanish."

Austin pushed Jason to one side and stared at the screen. "All we can say for certain is this bit of Mars looks different. The object may have changed the way it disguises itself, or it may have moved. Jason, send a message asking HMM23 for an update, particularly to confirm the location of the object."

Augustin turned in his seat and glowered at Austin. "I'm

the one who gives the orders around here. Don't send that message, Jason. HMM23 will contact us if there's anything to report. Sending unencrypted communications is just giving away information to our rivals, particularly LanthanoCo."

In obvious frustration, Austin pounded his fist on the desk and stormed from the room.

~

After a quiet dinner, Robert and Anastasia sat on the balcony watching the full moon reflect off the ocean. The temperature, buzz of cicadas and smell of the ocean all combined to create a feeling of intense calm and relaxation. Unfortunately, Jason arrived and spoiled the quiet intimacy of the moment. "Hey, Robert, you know the latest satellite images showed that something strange had happened near the OP?"

"Yes, but it wasn't clear if the object had moved or just changed the way it hides itself."

"Well, a little bird told me the object's definitely gone … totally disappeared."

"Does Augustin know?"

"He will shortly. Austin has just found out, and to say he's angry would be an understatement."

In the stillness of the evening, sounds from the pool terrace were clearly audible on the balcony. The voices of Augustin and Austin were so similar it was difficult to tell them apart. "Jason has intercepted a message from the LanthanoCo cowboys who've been taking an interest in the object. They've sent a report which, if true, is an absolute disaster for our project," one of them said.

"I haven't heard. I've been too busy preparing for the next mission."

"They claim they saw the object take off, and if that's happened, it's all because of your total mismanagement."

"That's impossible. It couldn't just take off. As you well know, it's been there for centuries, thousands of years, in fact. If it's gone, and we can't find it again, everything we've worked for will be wasted. Losing the object would be a failure too terrible to contemplate." There was the sound of the scraping of a chair. "I'm going to find out who's responsible and make them pay!"

"Well, you won't need to look far; it's your failure. I knew we needed a better cover story for the mission, some scientific instruments and a program of experiments and exploration, to deflect attention from our true purpose."

"Coming from you, that's totally ridiculous. Up until my brain scan a few weeks ago, we were the same person. We're jointly responsible for every decision."

"I've had reservations about the project for years. It's your pigheadedness that's got us here. I could run things much better without you."

"No, you couldn't. You're nothing, just a machine. On your own, no one would take you seriously."

Robert had no way of knowing who produced the gun, but there were sounds of a struggle and of tables and chairs being upended and pushed to one side. A single shot rang out, then silence. Cautiously, Robert descended the stairs to the pool terrace, closely followed by Jason and Anastasia.

Even with the poor lighting, the widening pool of blood gave away the fact it was Augustin lying between the chairs.

Anastasia picked up a towel and knelt beside Augustin's head. "This wound looks serious. Don't just stand there, Jason! Run and find Tony."

Augustin struggled to clear blood from his mouth. "If I don't survive, it's essential nothing happens to Austin. He's my future."

Anastasia's look hardened and she bent down to whisper in his ear. "How about I give both of you the same chance of life you gave to my father?"

"But I've never met your father."

"Savvas Dimas was my father."

Augustin's eyes widened with shock and then fear as he

seemed to realise how his future was about to play out. Anastasia dropped the towel beside him. "If you can manage it, use this to staunch your bleeding, but you don't deserve my help." Without looking back, she turned away to sit beside Robert.

He could imagine the mental turmoil she was going through, balancing aid for an injured person against revenge for her father's death. If she had decided to avoid further involvement, then that was quite understandable, and he had no wish to persuade her otherwise.

The sounds of Augustin's ragged breathing became steadily weaker and had stopped altogether shortly before an explosion caused the lights to flicker and dim. Then a second detonation cut power completely. A vast mushroom of burning gas erupted from the buildings adjacent to the pier. For a few seconds, the heat was unbearable. Robert helped Anastasia to her feet. "There goes the gas supply for the fuel cells. We'd better round up some torches. Who knows what's going to happen next."

They followed the wall, searching for stairs leading to the balcony.

"Stop where you are and show your hands."

A red torch beam shone into their faces. A second person made a rapid pat-down search.

"Where're the robots? There'll be less chance of unfortunate mistakes if you tell us now."

Robert decided their best chance of survival lay in cooperating. "There are three robots, two stored in the gallery, still in their shipping crates."

"And the third?"

"I don't know. I assume it was that robot, Austin, who shot Augustin a few minutes before the explosion." Robert motioned towards the crumpled figure lying on the terrace.

One of the masked assailants shone a torch into Augustin's face and checked the carotid artery. "Selworthy, dead."

Robert and Anastasia were forced to sit on the steps with their right hands tied to the railing. After ensuring the plastic handcuffs were secure the two figures climbed the stairs.

"What do we do now, Robert?"

Without answering, he reached down with his free hand and untied his left shoe. After partially unthreading the lace to make one of the loose ends longer, he slipped it through the plastic loop securing his right hand. Alternately pulling down on the lace with his left hand and foot, the lace sawed through the restraint. In only a few minutes, Robert had freed them both.

"Wow, impressive. Where'd you learn to do that?"

The roaring fire down by the dock provided a steady background noise and flickering light. While sitting on the steps taking stock of the situation they became aware of sounds of a pursuit interwoven with cries for help and curt commands. On the far side of the pool, a shadowy figure appeared, hurriedly pushing aside chairs and tables, trying to create a clear path. Not far behind two pursuers edged closer. The figure in the shadows turned and raised its right arm. "This is my island, and you're trespassing."

Seemingly undeterred, the pursuers edged forward crouching low.

Four shots rang out, a loud click, and then, with a curse, the gun was thrown to bounce along the tiled pool surround. "Don't touch me!"

After a brief struggle, there was a large splash. Expanding ripples marked the entry point. Two torch beams combed the pool, settling on a motionless figure lying on the bottom. A thin stream of bubbles broke the surface. The pursuers watched for a full minute and then, apparently satisfied there were no further signs of movement, they turned and walked away.

"That must have been Austin," Anastasia whispered.

"Yes, and he sank like a lump of concrete. We never

actually tried immersing one of our robots, but I'm sure the salt water in the pool will have completely destroyed his electronics."

The inky blackness of the pool surface reflected a myriad of stars. This mirror was disturbed by occasional bubbles. Anastasia seemed fascinated as she watched them, but caught her breath as the source of bubbles started to move closer. She clutched Robert's arm and pointed as a hand broke the surface and gripped the pool ladder. Very slowly, another hand appeared, followed by a head. Pool water streamed from hair and clothing. Every movement was slow and unsteady. Incredibly, Austin managed to kneel at the top of the ladder and then rise to his feet. Standing on the edge of the pool, he seemed to recognise Robert, and holding out a beseeching left hand, took a faltering step in his direction. "For pity's sake, help me! I'll pay you anything you ask."

From a technical point-of-view, Robert was impressed. "This latest batch of robots must be more waterproof than I imagined." He stepped forwards as though about to offer some assistance. Perhaps misunderstanding what was happening, Austin watched passively as Robert lifted his t-shirt and opened the access hatch in his chest. It took all of the strength of Robert's two hands to bend the hatch cover out of shape so that it couldn't close to keep out water. Taking a step back he shoulder-barged Austin into the pool. Entangled together, they both sank to the bottom. Austin clung on tightly, obviously sure he could outlast the air in Robert's lungs. The strength of the second-generation robot limbs was too much for Robert. He couldn't break free and felt himself starting to pass out. The last thing he remembered was a tremendous concussion forcing the remaining air from his lungs.

~

Anastasia turned Robert onto his side to allow water to drain from his mouth. After a few minutes, he felt strong enough to sit up. She finished drying herself on a pool towel and moved to sit beside him. "Are you feeling better now? I'm guessing that'll be the last we hear from Austin. The salt water must have worked its way through the open hatch and into his battery. There was quite an explosion. As I pulled you out of the pool, I worried that it had injured you as well."

Robert rested his head on Anastasia's shoulder, and she stroked his wet hair away from his eyes. "Do you think it could really be all over?" she asked. "There were so many things tying us to Project Transition. Now, with those two gone, we'll be free at last."

Robert gestured towards Austin and Augustin. "Well, we can forget about all those contracts, pressure to fall in with their plans, and threats of unspoken consequences."

"And now Rob has probably been destroyed on Mars, there's nothing we can do to help him."

Robert turned to watch flames still burning over by the jetty. "I felt committed to completing the development of Vince's vision, but I did worry about how the technology for transitioning intelligence would be used. Now it looks as though Maxwell is hell-bent on making sure that doesn't continue to be a problem.

"Don't take this personally, Robert, but I for one intend to have nothing further to do with intelligent robots."

Before Anastasia could continue, Jason appeared and sank to his knees beside Augustin.

Anastasia moved over to stand next to Jason. "He's dead and Austin's at the bottom of the pool. D'you have any idea what's just been happening over by the harbour?"

"While I was looking for help I was bailed up by some military-looking guys. When Tony freed me from their ties I had a quick look round. It seems those guys arrived on the beach in several inflatable boats. It's probable they were dropped off from that motor yacht we saw earlier in the day. They were well organised and overpowered Tony's men before blowing up the power plant. The batteries and stocks of natural gas burnt really well."

Robert joined Anastasia and Jason. "This attack has all the signs of being organised by Maxwell. Obviously, they really wanted to get rid of Austin, but what else are they here for?"

As though in answer to that question, there was a sequence of explosions from the guest wing, which blew out windows, raining shards of glass onto the pool area. Flames poured from several of the rooms.

Anastasia pointed to the burning building. "The gallery. That's where Augustin has hidden all the documentation from Project Transition, the brain scans, everything. I'll bet that was one of the targets of the attack."

Jason sprang to his feet. "There's a fortune in Egyptian artefacts there as well."

"Forget it, Jason, it's not worth risking your life to save them."

Ignoring Robert, Jason raced up the stairs.

~

The whole of the accommodation wing was on fire. Jason guessed a number of incendiary devices had been planted at strategic locations. The door to the gallery stood open with flames and smoke billowing across the ceiling and out into the corridor. He draped a damp towel over his head and dropped to his hands and knees. The roaring flames added a savage beauty to Augustin's display of gold artefacts. Heat had already shattered the toughened glass protecting some of the treasures, but Jason ignored the temptation. At the far end of the gallery, next to Ian and Jon's crates, a row of steel cabinets contained the Project Transition archive. This was the treasure that interested him! Jason read the labels and used a corner of his towel to open a drawer. The radiant heat was melting the clothes on his back. He turned over several tie-on tags until he found the one that read 'Austin'. Removing the damp towel from his head, Jason carefully wrapped it around the disk.

Acknowledgements

I am deeply indebted to all those who have helped me complete this sequel to Intelligent Consent. One again, the input of my editor, Kathryn Moore, has proved essential and I hope I am learning from her many corrections and suggestions. Monash Writer's Group continue to provide an inspiration for my writing. I am indebted to Robert New who is the motivating force behind Tale Publishing, the publisher of this novel. Catherine Larsen's artwork for the cover is outstanding and nicely complements the cover she created for Intelligent Consent. As always, the biggest thankyou goes to my wife, Glenyce, for her encouragement, patience and inspiration.

About the Author

In retrospect, the first book I can remember has probably exerted a strong influence on the course of my life. Time has faded many of the details, but certainly it was an illustrated story featuring a mechanical alarm clock. The dial incorporated a beaming smile and, making it even more appealing, the clock could speak. The idea of a talking clock was totally fascinating and I had to have one. Using cardboard and coloured pencils I attempted to recreate this mechanical friend, but my version fell far short of matching the one from the story. In spite of this setback, my passion for developing animate mechanisms continued, leading to a career in robotics research. My research robots had many capabilities such as communicating using puffs of air, licking the floor to follow chemical trails or burrowing through the ground searching for chemical leaks. However, none looked remotely like an alarm clock or could hold a conversation. Having moved away from research my fascination with robotics has turned a full circle. Now I enjoy imagining and writing stories about all manner of intelligent robots.